All's Fair in Love and Law

All's Fair in
Love and Law

ALAN HAMMOND

© Alan Hammond 2011

The right of Alan Hammond to be identified as the author of
this work has been asserted in accordance with the
Copyright, Designs and Patents Act 1988.

First published in Great Britain in 2011 by Orion Books
An imprint of the Orion Publishing Group Ltd
Orion House, 5 Upper St Martin's Lane,
London, WC2H 9EA
An Hachette Livre Company

A CIP catalogue record for this book
is available from the British Library.

Typeset at the Spartan Press Ltd,
Lymington, Hants

Printed in Great Britain by CPI Mackays,
Chatham, Kent

The Orion Publishing Group's policy is to use papers
that are natural, renewable and recyclable products and
made from wood grown in sustainable forests. The logging
and manufacturing processes are expected to conform to
the environmental regulations of the country of origin.

www.orionbooks.co.uk

To Eileen, who brings love to my life and life to my love.

Contents

A Very Specific Legacy

Henry Middleton frowned at his watch and sipped thoughtfully at his gin and tonic. This was the first time in fifteen years that Charles Dufty had been late for their Friday evening chess game in the lounge bar of the Dog and Tadpole – over ten minutes late, in fact. The board was set up in their customary secluded corner, Charles's whisky and water was placed ready for him but . . . 'Ah! There you are!' Henry rose, stiffly, to greet his old friend. 'Thought perhaps you'd bottled out after last week's crushing defeat.'

Charles was apologetic: 'Busy week at the office,' he explained, easing himself into his chair and taking a welcome pull at his whisky.

Henry sat up straight and assumed an expression of outraged amusement. 'Busy week at the office! You haven't had a busy week anywhere for twenty years or more. I thought you only popped in for a couple of afternoons a week just to do the crossword and make a nuisance of yourself.'

Charles chuckled, his shaggy white eyebrows ruffling as his features crinkled in pleasure. 'Reasonable summing up of the situation,' he wheezed. 'Just so happens there's been a bit of reorganisation to attend to; one or two decisions to be made. I am still with the old firm on a consultancy basis, you know. Occasionally they listen to the rubbish I spout.'

'That son of yours, Hugo, has his head screwed on. He's supposed to be running the place now, isn't he? I think you should let him get on with it.'

'I do let him get on with it,' Charles responded, somewhat peevishly. 'Hugo's in sole charge of all matters relating to the work of the firm. If he wants my advice on a particular case or a difficult client, he asks for it and I give it. My only concern is to ensure that the firm I founded almost fifty years ago continues to fill the role for which it was intended.'

'And what role is that?' asked Henry.

Charles Dufty scratched his cheek reflectively. 'Dufty Dufty Popple & Dunn was set up as and continues to be a small provincial firm of solicitors, catering for the needs of the people of Hockam and the surrounding villages. No more, no less. That's what I envisaged when I founded the firm and I like to think of it as my legacy to Hockam. It's a role we've filled very successfully for half a century – that's who we are. But if we try to be something we're not, we'll lose our identity.'

Henry regarded him quizzically, the dome of his bald head reflecting the wall light above him. 'Hugo been talking about expanding again, has he?' he asked after a few moments.

Charles sipped his whisky and looked back at him through narrowed eyes. 'Don't miss much do you, old friend?'

~

A blustery wind was rattling the shop blinds in Hockam's little High Street and periodically ruffling the feathers of a solitary, disgruntled looking pigeon attempting to take an afternoon nap on the gable end of the half-timbered building which housed the offices of Dufty Dufty Popple & Dunn, solicitors and commissioners for oaths.

Inside, in the little reception area, a tall, slim woman, perhaps in her late forties, her fair, shoulder-length hair neatly tied back, was peering through Christian Dior glasses at Conchita, the recently employed Spanish receptionist. 'Is he in?' she asked, inclining her head towards one of the two panelled doors in the wall to her left.

Conchita raised large, dark eyes from the copy of OK

2

Magazine on her lap. 'Mister Hugo is on his desk where he will have a client in five minutes.'

The woman took off her glasses, raised her eyebrows and regarded the receptionist with every appearance of being a headmistress, which, indeed, she was. 'I think you mean *at* his desk, Conchita.' She suppressed a smile, seeing the girl's puzzled frown, and walked to the door indicated, where she paused and looked over her shoulder. 'Oh, and Mr Hugo will be *seeing* a client, not *having* a client . . . Well, I assume that's the case, anyway.' She opened the door and went in.

Hugo Dufty looked up from the papers littering his desk, pushed a lock of floppy black hair from his forehead and greeted his wife. 'Hello, Helen. You're a bit early, I'm interviewing a possible new trainee any minute and I'll be with him for half an hour at least.'

'I haven't come to give you a lift home,' said Helen. 'You came in your car today, remember? No, I just popped in to ask whether you've done anything yet about the empty premises next door. The place is still empty I see and the "To Let" sign is still up. The agents are Rookham and Selby in Walchester.'

Hugo leant back in his chair and sighed, massaging his jaw where a troublesome tooth had been plaguing him for over a week. 'No, I'm still not sure it's the right thing to do – or the right time to do it. Conveyancing's a bit down at the moment and . . .'

'Oh, Hugo!' Helen flopped down in a chair in front of the desk. 'It was only last night we were talking about the need to expand the firm and you agreed that the extra couple of rooms would enable you to take on at least one more fee earner and another secretary – both of which are much needed if the firm's to increase its client base and achieve some sort of growth.'

'Yes, yes, I know, Helen. But the property market won't pick up until next spring and, with the extra rent and salaries, we'd have a pretty lean few months. It might be better to wait until next year and then look for larger and more suitable premises to move the whole firm into.'

Helen drew a deep breath and exhaled slowly. When she spoke, her voice was rigidly under control, as though she was addressing a recalcitrant pupil who had been sent to her study for the second time that week for the same offence. 'Hugo, I was under the impression that we had discussed this at some length last night and that we were in agreement. However, let's remind ourselves of the main points: firstly, how often do office premises come on the rental market in Hockam? And secondly, where would you find a better arrangement than taking over the premises next door to this? Dufty Dufty Popple & Dunn have been here in this building for almost fifty years. Why move the firm when you could just expand into next door? And you agreed that expansion would be a good move – space is at a premium here. Even this new trainee you're thinking of taking on will have to be jammed into the secretaries' office with Trish and Miss Metcalfe. It was you who said last night that these days standing still is not an option. And, looking to the future, if James does decide to take up the law – and he's already showing an interest in what you do even though he's only eleven – shouldn't you be making sure there's room for him in the firm?'

Hugo leant his elbows on the desk and rubbed his eyes. 'Yes, I know. It's just that this might not be the best time. But I will look into it.'

'When?' asked his wife.

'Well, it's too late today, the agents will be closed when I've seen this potential trainee. And I'm in Malverley Magistrates Court tomorrow morning. I'll try and fit in a call to the agents tomorrow afternoon – after my two-thirty client, that is. Client work must come first, Helen.'

She sighed again and walked to the door. 'Well, it's your firm, Hugo.'

'Not entirely, Helen,' he pointed out, picking up the internal phone to enquire whether the applicant for the post of trainee had arrived.

She paused, her handle on the doorknob. 'Ah!' she said. 'Your father's been talking to you about it, hasn't he?'

Hugo put down the phone and faced her. 'As a matter of fact, Father and I haven't even mentioned the empty premises next door. In any case, he knows that, as the senior resident partner, all decisions affecting the firm are mine to take. I know you think he's a meddler, but . . .'

'I don't think he's a meddler, Hugo. You know perfectly well that I think the world of your father. He's the dearest, most loveable man I know. But he's also the cleverest. If he wants the firm to stay as it is, it will, whether or not you decide otherwise.'

The door closed firmly behind Helen, and Hugo slumped into his chair, staring bleakly at the papers on his desk and trying to ignore his aching tooth until his secretary Trish came in to remind her employer that a Mr Bernard Summers was waiting in reception.

The aforesaid Bernard Summers, uncomfortable in his interview suit, had been nervously leafing through last January's edition of *Homes & Gardens* for the past fifteen minutes, his gaze flicking between an article headed 'Modern Colour Schemes in Vintage Settings' and the surprisingly lustrous eyes of the receptionist as she spoke on the telephone in a fascinating Spanish accent. Inadvertently catching her eye as she put the receiver down, he coloured slightly and lowered his tousled head quickly to resume his intent study of a glossy picture showing a *chaise-longue* on which reclined a rather haughty looking woman, stroking a small, pug-faced dog and staring at a bunch of yellow flowers in an orange vase.

He was considering whether it would be appropriate to initiate a conversation with the receptionist when one of the two doors leading off the reception area opened suddenly and a tall, slender woman wearing spectacles came out. She closed the door very firmly behind her and swept past the reception desk. At the same time, a young secretary appeared from the passageway to the side of the reception desk, drew back to allow the woman to pass and watched as the street door banged shut behind her. The girl turned her friendly, freckled face to Bernard, made a wry expression and disappeared into the room from which the woman had emerged.

Bernard was about to make an almost certainly lame remark to the receptionist when he was saved from doing so by the door again opening and the young, freckle-faced secretary reappearing to say: 'Mr Dufty Junior will see you now.' She stood back to allow him to enter, murmuring 'Good luck' as he passed.

The office he entered was lit by the afternoon sun peering through the leaded light window and casting diamond-shaped patterns on the piles of files and papers littering the antique desk behind which sat his potential employer, who appeared to be massaging his jaw and frowning. Seeing Bernard, however, he smiled and stood up, extending a pale, long-fingered hand in welcome. 'Mr . . . er . . . Summers?' he said, his voice well modulated and enquiring.

Bernard nodded and shook the offered hand. 'Mr Dufty, how do you do,' he replied. Surprised and a little embarrassed by his own, unaccustomed old-world courtesy, he went on: 'It's Bernard, by the way.'

'Bernard! Of course,' Hugo smiled. 'Do have a seat, Bernard. Now then . . .' He leafed through the notes on his desk. 'I see that you live in Walchester.'

'I do at present,' Bernard confirmed. 'After I finished my law degree at Birmingham University, I went back to stay with my mother. But, obviously, if I . . . well, that is, if you were kind enough to offer me a position here, I'd move to Hockam – I understand there's a small flat vacant in the High Street only a few doors away.'

6

The solicitor regarded him thoughtfully. 'You don't feel that, after university in Birmingham and then the comparatively bright lights of Walchester, Hockam might be a little . . . shall we say . . . quiet?'

Bernard shook his head. 'I want to gain all-round experience and I feel I'm more likely to get that with a smaller, general practice than with one of the larger firms which tend to slot their trainees into specialist departments. In fact, I've already been for an interview with a large firm in Walchester who offered me a two-year training contract but I found the atmosphere there very . . . impersonal. Whereas I'm inclined to think that legal practice should be about people and their problems.'

'Which firm was that?' asked Hugo.

'Pollock's,' replied Bernard.

Hugo was silent for some moments before saying: 'Dufty Dufty Popple & Dunn was founded by my father some fifty years ago as a small provincial firm, catering for the needs of the people of Hockam and the surrounding villages. That remains our aim and, to that extent, I agree with you that those needs are best served by a more general and . . . personal approach than that offered by firms such as Pollock's. However . . .' He stood and walked to the window where he looked out at the activity in the High Street, which, at that moment, consisted of an elderly man in a trilby hat walking a dog. 'In these modern times,' he continued, 'standing still is not an option. To survive, we must look to the future. We must change with the times and we must grow. Plans are already afoot to expand and to . . . modernise.'

The solicitor was silent for some minutes, during which Bernard opened his mouth but, unsure what to say, closed it again.

Hugo returned to his desk. 'And our desire to take on an articled clerk is, of course, part of those plans.'

Bernard looked up from his shoes, which he had been studying during Hugo's reverie. 'Actually, the term "articled clerk" is no longer used,' he ventured. 'We're now known as "trainee solicitors".'

But Hugo was again lost in thought, his hands clasped before him, his forehead resting on his extended forefingers, his eyes closed. At length, he looked up and placed his hands on his desk. 'When could you start?'

The tousle-haired young man's eyes widened. 'Well, I . . . I suppose . . . Well, I'm free to start at any time, though, of course . . .'

'Tomorrow?'

'Well . . . yes. But, of course we have to . . .'

Hugo stood up. 'Yes, naturally, we'll have to agree terms and draw up a contract – articles and so on, but I'm sure we can arrive at a mutually, er . . . Suppose you come in tomorrow morning and I'll get Miss Metcalfe to introduce you to everyone and we can talk about arrangements and so forth.'

Bernard nodded, slightly bewildered, shook hands, made his goodbyes and left.

Hugo Dufty's morning at Malverley Magistrates Court proved more successful than he had anticipated. His client, Jason Pullman, was exonerated of all blame in the incident involving his motorcycle and David Barstow's prize dairy cow, the wind had dropped, the sun was shining, yesterday's toothache was much abated and he arrived back at the office at around twelve noon, feeling more positive than he had for some time.

Slightly perturbed at finding the reception desk deserted, he popped his head round the door of the secretaries' room. 'No one on reception?' he enquired.

Miss Metcalfe, Charles Dufty's secretary, looked up from her computer screen, her friendly, motherly features smiling beneath greying hair. 'Oh, Mr Hugo. We didn't expect you back just yet. Conchita's just popped out to buy some tea bags – the ones Mr Dufty Senior likes – we're completely out of them. But I'm keeping an ear open for anyone coming into reception. She'll be back at any moment.'

Hugo nodded. 'That's fine, Miss Metcalfe. When Conchita's back, I wouldn't mind a cup of tea before my one o'clock client, if that could be arranged. Trish, could you pop in with the file on Mr and Mrs Draper, please?'

Trish jumped up to do as bidden and Hugo withdrew his head and closed the door, only to open it again almost immediately. 'Good morning, Bernard. We'll have a talk in a few minutes and thrash out a contract – terms and so forth. I see Miss Metcalfe's already sorted you out a desk . . . or should I say *work station?*' Pleased with his attempt at modern parlance, he smiled brightly at everyone and again went out.

Bernard murmured 'Good morning' to the closed door and turned his attention back to his newly acquired 'work station' which consisted of a small, chipped desk which Miss Metcalfe and Trish had extracted with difficulty from the basement where it had reposed, undisturbed, for many years. This was wedged into a corner, leaving just enough room for a hard wooden chair, access to which was achieved by adopting a crab-like approach around the corner of the desk, a procedure which required care to avoid serous injury to the tenderest parts of the male anatomy.

Taking his training file out of his briefcase, he attempted, unsuccessfully, to open the top drawer of the desk. 'Try the third drawer,' suggested Miss Metcalfe. 'The other two seem to be jammed. I think the runners need replacing.'

She turned to Trish. 'Mr Hugo seems in a better mood this morning,' she remarked. 'Perhaps his toothache's better.'

'Just as well,' said Trish, pulling the Draper file out of the filing cabinet. 'I've got to tell him Mrs Biggs is coming in at three thirty about the sale of her cottage and we've lost the deeds.'

'We haven't *lost* the deeds, Trish.' Miss Metcalfe's tone was admonitory. 'We're just unable to locate them at present. It may be that they're deposited with Mrs Biggs's bank.'

'Well, Mr Hugo's still going to be in a bit of a spot when she comes in.' Trish's freckled features were unusually flustered. 'And it's me that's got to tell him.'

And tell him she did, as she placed the Draper file on his desk.

To her surprise, he shrugged. 'The deeds are probably either at her bank or with Pollock's in Walchester who acted for her when she bought the place. It's not a problem, Trish, I'm sure we'll sort it out. I think I heard Conchita coming into reception – any chance of that cup of tea, do you think?'

Charles Dufty's portly frame appeared in the open doorway, his shock of white hair even more ruffled than usual. 'Did I catch a passing reference to tea?'

'Hello, Mr Dufty,' said Trish. 'I was just going to make some for Mr Hugo so I'll bring you one as well. I think we've got some chocolate biscuits, too.'

'Trish, you have an instinctive ability to make an old man very happy. I'll take it in my office. 'Morning, Hugo. How d'you get on with the beaks this morning?'

'Very well, actually. In fact we got what could be termed a result. Young Jason Pullman was delighted.'

'Splendid!' beamed Charles. 'Onwards and upwards, eh?' He headed for his own room next to Hugo's.

'Actually, Father, I wanted a word, if you've got a moment,' called Hugo.

The old man turned back. 'Yes, of course, old boy. Problem?'

'No, not a problem exactly.' Hugo hesitated, his positive frame of mind faltering momentarily. 'It's, er . . . it's just something I think we should discuss.'

Charles closed the door and sat down. 'Fire away, I'm all ears!'

Hugo thought for a moment and then made up his mind.

This was no time for procrastination. This was a time for taking charge of the situation. 'Father, I think you know that I have, for some time, been considering the possibility of expanding the firm.' He studied his father's impassive face, watching for any sign of dissent or hostility. Finding none, he continued: 'Obviously, we would wish to preserve the ethos and . . . special characteristics of the firm which have been built up over the fifty years since you founded it – indeed, that objective is as close to my heart as I know it is to yours. But, that said, I am convinced that, in today's world, one must move forward in order to survive. With that in mind, I have been considering ways in which we could expand our operations and increase our client base whilst still retai—'

'How about the empty premises next door?' said Charles.

Hugo stopped talking, his mouth still forming the word 'retaining'. Trish entered bearing a tray.

'Ah, the lovely Trish!' boomed Charles. 'Bearing refreshment for weary souls and choccy biccies to fortify us in our deliberations. Pop it down on the table over here, my dear, and I'll do the necessary.'

When the door had closed, Charles busied himself pouring the tea. 'Good girl, that,' he remarked. 'Knows just how to slot into the firm so as to keep the wheels turning smoothly. There we are, m'boy. One cup of Ceylon Orange Pekoe and two biscuits each. Now, what were you saying about the empty premises next door?'

Not for the first time in discussions with his father, Hugo felt the initiative slipping inexplicably from him and passing, almost imperceptibly, to the other. Surprised as he was at the old man's willingness to discuss the premises next door, he was determined to retain the lead role in the proceedings. Expansion had been his own idea and he must continue to manage its implementation. He took a bite out of a chocolate biscuit which broke into two pieces, one of which fell into his teacup, splashing the Draper file on his desk. Dabbing at the droplets with his handkerchief, he said: 'Well, actually, Father, it was you who mentioned it but, since you brought it up, I *am* proposing to look into the possibility of taking on the lease. Obviously, much will depend upon the terms offered – the amount of the rent and so on – but, assuming that the premises prove suitable and reasonable arrangements can be made to . . .'

'Well, you'd better get a move on, old chap,' said Charles. 'I rather gather that some interest has already been shown in the place. If I were you, I'd pop in and see the agents straight away – Rookham and Selby in Walchester, I believe. No point in dithering, you know.'

Again surprised and encouraged by his father's lack of opposition, Hugo replaced his handkerchief in his pocket and nodded. 'Absolutely, I agree. I intend to visit their offices at the very first opportunity.'

'When will that be?' asked Charles.

Hugo studied his desk diary. 'Well, I was planning to go this afternoon but I've just been told that Mrs Biggs is coming in unexpectedly so . . . Ah, tomorrow is out because I'm seeing Jonathan Bradshaw in chambers all morning, then there's a Law Society lunch and then, of course, there's that blasted meeting with the Dyson family at the Manor House. Let me see, I may be able to fit in a couple of hours on Thursday, that is if . . .'

'Why don't I go?' suggested Charles.

'You go?' said Hugo.

'Yes, me go, Hugo. Seems to me we need to do something about it straight away before someone gets in first – if they haven't already. I'm free this afternoon, I could drive over to Walchester and see the agents for you. Find out what the score is and report back to you. That is, if you're serious about this?'

'Yes, of course, I'm serious. It's just . . . well, yes, I suppose that would make sense. If you're sure you don't mind?'

'Not at all, m'boy. Happy to be of some use. Let's see this young fellow you've got lined up as an articled clerk and then I'll pop over and see the estate agents and let you know how I get on when I get back – or, more likely tomorrow morning, there's a meeting of the Gilbert & Sullivan Society Committee this evening so I'll probably eat in Walchester after seeing the agents. How's that?'

'Perfect,' said Hugo, draining his teacup and pressing a button on the intercom. 'Trish, could you show Bernard in now, please?'

Bernard was again shown into the dusty office, straightening his best tie as he went. As before, Hugo Dufty stood to greet him, as did a short, rather portly elderly man with a shock of unruly white hair and the bushiest, whitest pair of eyebrows Bernard had ever seen. The old man, whom Hugo introduced as his father, Charles Dufty, shook Bernard's nervous hand firmly, the corners of his surprisingly bright blue eyes creasing into deep crow's feet as he smiled reassuringly at the young man. 'Don't know about you, young fella, but I can't stand interviews. Difficult to be yourself when you're expected to be someone else, eh?'

Bernard, feeling a relief of the tension he had been experiencing all morning, grinned back. 'Well . . . I suppose there is always a bit of that. But I'll try and be as honest as I can – this is definitely me.'

'I can see that,' chuckled Charles, waving him to a chair and settling himself back into his own. 'I gather from Hugo that if you take a position with the firm, you'll be moving here to Hockam from Walchester?'

'That's right,' Bernard confirmed. 'I think it's important to be a part of the community in which you work. I've always believed that legal practice is about people rather than . . .'

'Do you have any friends in Hockam?' asked Charles.

Caught slightly off-balance, Bernard paused with his mouth

slightly ajar. 'Er, well, yes, there is someone I know here, though I . . .'

The old man leant forward in his chair, smiled conspiratorially and lowered his voice: 'Pretty is she?'

Mentally cursing his unmanly tendency to blush, Bernard smiled back. 'Well, *I* think so, but I . . .'

'So, you want to serve as an articled clerk and qualify as a solicitor, eh?' Charles continued, seamlessly.

Hugo cut in: 'Actually, Father, the term *articled clerk* is no longer used. These days, they're referred to as *trainee solicitors*.'

'Same thing,' pointed out Charles. 'Tell me, Bernard, in not more than three words, why do you want to be a solicitor?'

Passing a hand through his dark, curly hair, Bernard Summers stared at the desktop in front of him, thought for a few seconds and then looked squarely at Charles Dufty. 'To practise law,' he said, almost defiantly.

The old man nodded. 'That'll do,' he said, rising stiffly from his chair. 'Now, I'm afraid I must leave you – spot of business with an estate agent in your home town. I'll leave Hugo here to sort out the paperwork and so forth. If you do decide to throw in your lot with our little undertaking here, I shall look forward to working with you.'

Harold Selby, a short, spare-framed man who habitually sported a well-trimmed moustache and a bow tie, ushered Charles to a chair in his tiny room behind the spacious general office of Rookham and Selby, estate agents.

'Charles, come in, take a pew. Haven't seen you since that joint Rotary do the year before last in Hockam – sorry, "*Hokum*" – as in "poke 'em",' he added, remembering the pronunciation favoured by local residents. 'How're you keeping?'

'Pretty well, thanks, Harold, aside from the inevitable ravages of *Anno Domini*. How's business?'

The estate agent grimaced. 'Bit slow at the moment, actually.

Bit of a flat patch in the market. Still, should pick up in time. Usual ups and downs, you know. Things haven't been easy since Ed Rookham retired. How are things in the legal racket?'

'Well, I don't play much part in it these days. I'm still with the old firm on a consultancy basis but my son, Hugo, runs the show now. Good job he makes of it, too – though he says conveyancing's down at the moment. The property market affects us all, I suppose.'

'Oh, speaking of your Hugo, there's someone here you might like to see,' said Harold. He picked up the phone, spoke a few words into it and a moment later the door opened to admit a smartly dressed woman of perhaps thirty-five, her bobbed blonde hair framing attractive, friendly features which lit up in a delighted smile upon seeing Charles.

'Mr Dufty!' she shrilled.

Charles stood up. 'Caroline,' he beamed, embracing her. 'Lovely to see you. What are you doing here?'

'I work here,' she said. 'Have done for almost five years now. I think Harold here took pity on me when I left Dufty Dufty Popple & Dunn and gave me a job as his PA.'

Harold laughed. 'Caroline may have started as a PA but she's now a qualified estate agent in her own right. Useful member of the firm – though I don't tell her that too often,' he added in a confidential tone. 'She'd probably want more money or something.'

'Do give my regards to Hugo,' said Caroline. 'They were three very happy years I spent as his secretary. Next time I'm in Hockam I'll pop in and say hello to everyone. Must go, I'm showing a couple round that cottage in Hay Green, Harold.'

'Good girl,' replied her boss. 'Turn on the old Adams charm, won't you? If we can shift that place, it'll be champagne all round.'

As the door closed behind her, Harold said: 'Caroline's a first-class worker. Actually, she's outgrown her position here. I wish

I could give her more to do but in the present climate there's just not the work available. I sometimes worry she'll get bored and move on to one of the larger firms – and I suppose I wouldn't blame her if she did.'

Charles nodded. 'Hugo always thought very highly of her. He's never really found anyone to take her place – although, of course, young Trish is coming along well.'

'Yes,' said Harold. 'It was a pity about that junior partner of yours . . . what was his name?'

'Mark Dunn,' supplied Charles.

'That's the fella. He and Caroline had quite a thing going, as I understand it, and when he buggered off to . . . where was it?'

'Spain,' said Charles, his face creasing into a frown. 'He moved to Spain with three friends to open a bar in Benidorm or some such place. Still there, as far as I know, though why he took it into his head to chuck up a promising career in the law for that . . . Well, there it is.'

'Well, wherever it was he buggered off to, Caroline was pretty cut up about it. I gather that's why she left the firm. And I was looking for a PA at the time, so here she is. Still carries a torch for him, I think. Very seldom goes out with anybody else. Thrown herself into her work to forget, I suppose. Which is why it's a pity I haven't got more of it for her to do at the moment.'

Charles was silent for a few moments but then brightened. 'Why don't you open a branch office?' he asked.

Harold blew out his cheeks and considered this. 'Never really thought about it. Wouldn't work, though. We haven't got enough work here as it is.'

'That's because you're one of probably about twenty firms in Walchester. Do you know, we haven't got a single firm of estate agents in Hockam since old Ted Barrows won the lottery and retired to the South of France? Anyone trying to sell a property in Hockam or the surrounding villages has to come to Walchester to find an agent – and then they've got twenty or so to choose from. Why don't you open a small branch office in Hockam? You'd clean up.'

Harold stroked his moustache. 'There's something in that. But then I'd have to set on staff to run it and . . .'

'No, you wouldn't,' countered Charles. 'You've already said that Caroline's outgrown her position here and you haven't got enough for her to do. Why not get her to open a new branch of the firm in Hockam?'

Harold pondered this for a while. 'Good point,' he said. 'But I don't know of any suitable premises there.'

'Yes, you do. There's one on your books to let at the moment. Matter of fact, it's right next door to our offices in the High Street. Prime position. If you were to open a branch there and get Caroline to run it, Dufty's could no doubt put business your way.'

Harold was now sitting bolt upright with a faraway look in his eyes. 'And we could reciprocate when opportunities arose.' He glanced at his watch. 'Look, do you fancy a pint at the Cricketer's Arms down the road?'

Bernard, still slightly bemused some eight hours after his interview, sat, toying with a half of bitter in the lounge bar of the Pig and Whistle, Hockam's ivy-clad High Street inn. Having visited Ben Sharpe, the elderly proprietor of the newsagent's a few doors away, inspected the tiny, two-roomed accommodation above the shop and agreed to take it at what appeared to be a manageable rent, he was now feeling a little swept along by events.

However, he reflected, opening a packet of cheese and onion crisps, his main objective had been achieved – relocation to Hockam. Relaxing into his seat and chewing contentedly, he mused upon the principal motivation for his application to Dufty Dufty Popple & Dunn and his desire to take up residence in this tiny market town, some twelve miles from the bustling city of Walchester, which had been the scene of his boyhood. His reverie was cut short by the entrance into the lounge bar of the aforesaid principal motivation in person.

Joanna Dickinson was looking even more edible than usual as she caught sight of him. Tossing the thick fringe of fair hair from her astonishingly sparkling blue eyes, she made towards him, her long legs clad in tight-fitting jeans.

Seating herself at the rickety table, she directed towards him a smile so radiant that he was obliged to swallow hard, causing the crisp which he had been in the process of munching to lodge in his throat, giving rise to a bout of coughing which attracted amused glances from the three other occupants of the bar.

'Sorry,' he gasped, recovering himself. 'Glad you could come. Got a bit of news!'

The girl's smile faded slightly. 'Oh,' she said, 'I was just going to tell you *my* news. Still, you first.'

There followed a short exchange of polite insistency which ended in Bernard's favour. Drawing himself up in his chair, he announced, portentously: 'I'm moving to Hockam!'

Aware of Joanna's slightly mystifying lack of reaction, he went on: 'Well, we've both had enough of catching the bus to either Walchester or Hockam whenever we want to meet so I decided to do something about it. I kicked Pollock's into touch and, in the space of two days, I've landed a training contract with Dufty Dufty Popple & Dunn and taken a flat over the news-agent's here in the High Street. Now we can see each other whenever we want without one of us having to catch the last bus home. Obviously, we can still have evenings out in Walchester but at least we'll catch the bus together. And I'm sure there's plenty to do here in Hockam.'

Having delivered himself of this, he sat back to take the applause he believed it merited.

'*Hokum*,' said Joanna, her flat tone exhibiting none of the expected emotion.

Bernard screwed up his eyes. 'Pardon?'

'*Hokum*,' she repeated. 'It's pronounced *Hokum*, not *Hockam*.'

'Well, whatever,' he replied. 'I thought you'd be pleased.'

The fringe of fair hair obscured her eyes as she stared at the table in front of her. 'Do you want to hear my news?'

'Yes, of course.' His voice betrayed his disappointment.

'I'm moving to Walchester,' she said without looking up. 'I've at last got a place in Walchester General Hospital and I'm moving into the student nurse's accommodation next week.'

After a long silence, she said: 'I thought you'd be pleased.'

Charles Dufty's presence in the office before three o'clock in the afternoon was a rarity, but he sat now at his desk, his head in his hands, the morning newspaper spread in front of him as the library clock chimed ten. Miss Metcalfe was busying herself at the filing cabinet which stood in a corner of his room, muttering that Mrs Biggs's deeds must be somewhere. 'Probably misfiled,' she tutted.

Charles looked up. 'Good try, Joan, and that would explain the reference to "motorway" but it's too many letters.'

Miss Metcalfe turned to face him. 'Motorway . . . Letters?' she frowned.

'Misfiled – begins with MI – MI – motorway,' he explained. 'But "misfiled" has eight letters. I'm looking for a six-lettered word which could, as you implied, begin with MI.'

His secretary's face cleared. 'Oh, it's your crossword,' she said. 'What's the clue you're stuck on?'

Charles peered at the paper over his half-rimmed glasses. '*Wrongly induced to toboggan on motorway*,' he read.

'Try MISLED,' she suggested and returned to her task.

He threw down his pen. 'Miss Metcalfe, I sometimes wonder at the sheer potency of your intellect. Why am I sitting here pontificating at this fancy desk while you fritter away your powers filing and making tea . . . Oh, speaking of the latter . . .'

'I was just about to put the kettle on, Mr Dufty,' she said, pulling from the deep recesses of the filing cabinet a packet marked 'Mrs Brenda Biggs – Deeds of Rosemary Cottage'.

As she opened the door to go out, Hugo could be heard in reception giving instructions to Trish prior to keeping his appointment with Jonathan Bradshaw QC in chambers. Seeing Charles through the open door, he came in.

'Morning, Father,' he said. 'How did you get on at Rookham and Selby's yesterday?'

Charles leant back in his chair. 'Do you want the bad news, the good news or the even better news first?'

'Give me the bad,' said Hugo, gloomily.

'The premises next door are taken.'

'Ah well,' said Hugo, philosophically. 'Perhaps now wasn't the best time to take on more expense, with the property market the way it is. At least I can tell Helen we tried – she was quite keen on the idea, you know. Anyway, must dash.' He turned to go.

'Don't you want the good news?' called Charles.

Hugo glanced at his watch. 'Well?' he asked.

'The offices next door are to be occupied by a branch office of Rookham and Selby, with whom we are to have a useful association to our mutual benefit – thus countering to some extent the worst effects of the slack property market.'

Hugo closed the door and sat down in front of his father's desk. 'Really? That might be useful – an arrangement like that could lead to more conveyancing business. Mind you, depends on how well we get on with them. You know what some of these estate agents are like.'

'Well,' said Charles. 'That brings me to the even better news. The branch office is to be run by someone with whom we already have a good working relationship – or, at least we had and there's no reason why that shouldn't be the case again.'

'Well, who?' asked Hugo.

'Caroline Adams,' replied Charles.

Hugo's eyes widened. 'Caroline? But how did . . . I thought she . . . ?'

The old man raised his unruly white eyebrows and shrugged. 'Just the way things work out sometimes. You'd better be off, old boy. Don't want to keep old Bradshaw waiting, do you?'

~

Stanley, the Dog and Tadpole's Friday barman, brought fresh drinks to the corner table where he found the two friends chuckling over the chessboard.

'Thanks, Stanley,' wheezed Henry. 'Though I don't think Charles really deserves his whisky.'

'And why would that be, sir?' asked Stanley.

'Because he's a conniving old bugger who's used to getting his own way by whatever means possible.'

'Who, Mr Dufty, sir?' Stanley stepped back a pace in mock outrage. 'I refuse to believe it, sir. A more amenable gentleman I've yet to meet.'

'Thank you, Stanley,' said Charles, adopting a hurt expression. 'As you know, my sole concern is always to ensure that matters are arranged in such a way that everyone is happy. "Getting my own way" as Mr Middleton puts it, doesn't enter into it. Whether I win or lose is of no importance to me. What it is to be misunderstood, Stanley.'

'Quite so, sir,' said the barman, directing a reproachful glance at Henry, clearing the used glasses from the table and pottering back to his bar.

'Well,' mused Henry. 'I suppose you're not such a bad old stick on the whole. I admit you've generally got others' interests at heart.'

'Absolutely,' said Charles, moving his queen four spaces diagonally. 'Checkmate, I think?'

May It Please Your Honour

'Ladies and gentlemen of the jury, I would suggest to you that this witness is, quite deliberately, and for reasons of his own, attempting to mislead this court into believing . . .'

'Objection, M'Lud!'

'Objection sustained, Mr Carstairs, it could be considered that . . .'

'But, M'Lud, I have reason to believe that . . .'

'Shame!'

'Let 'im go on – we all know that bastard's lying!'

'Silence! If there is any more interruption from the public benches, I'll clear the court!'

'Stanley!' called Charles Dufty. 'Can you please close that blasted door? Fellow can't hear himself think in here.'

The barman obediently went over and closed the door, shutting out the increasing decibels from the television in the snug, allowing peace to reign once more in the lounge bar of the Dog and Tadpole. Henry Middleton looked faintly disgruntled. 'I was quite enjoying that,' he complained. 'It was one of the best episodes of Carstairs QC. I remember it from the first time round. Carstairs is defending this electrician chap who's accused of rigging up a device in the bathroom of . . .'

'Bloody racket,' snapped Charles.

Henry turned his attention back to the chessboard. 'Well, I suppose that sort of thing's just work to you; the courtroom confrontation, the cut and thrust of legal argument; the . . .'

'Cut and thrust be buggered. If that lot had simmered down a bit and talked things through it might not have got to court in the first place. Most things don't, you know. There's usually a way of resolving matters to everyone's satisfaction. Had a spot of bother involving a judge myself a few months ago but that was resolved perfectly amicably.'

~

A disinterested observer could have been forgiven for assuming that Sergeant Wilmott of the Herewardshire Constabulary was energetically directing rush-hour traffic. His burly frame swayed heavily from side to side and his arms windmilled furiously, while the expression on his broad, bluff face was one of belligerent authority.

But Sergeant Wilmott was not directing traffic. Indeed, having completed his shift at the station some half-hour previously, he was now standing in the living room of the small, semi-detached house he shared with his wife, dressed in casual shirt, comfortable trousers and carpet slippers, directing his arm-waving operations towards the window which overlooked the back garden.

The scene appeared peaceful, the only movements being a gentle swaying and rustling of leaves in the light evening breeze and an occasional flash of blue and green feathers inside the wire-mesh structure which stood beside the patio and which was the most dominant feature of the little garden. Lying on the cool paving slabs of the patio and staring intently and malevolently at the small inhabitants of this structure was a very large tabby cat, its sleek, bristling body motionless except for occasionally twitching ears, its eyes wide and unblinking.

'Blasted thing!' muttered Sergeant Wilmott, flinging up the sash window and sticking his head out. 'Bugger off!' he shouted, flapping his hand towards the cat. 'Go on, scoot!' The animal remained where it was but slowly turned its steady gaze towards the sergeant, its eyes coolly disdainful. Then, just as slowly, it turned back to resume its watch on the aviary.

His face reddening as his rage increased, the policeman slammed the window shut with a crash which brought his wife, Joan, scuttling in from the kitchen. 'What's happened?' she flustered, and then, seeing her husband's agitation: 'Oh, I suppose it's Miss Metcalfe's cat after the budgies again, is it?' But Sergeant Wilmott was already out of the room, padding purposefully through the kitchen in his carpet slippers and opening the door that led into the garden. In the few seconds that had passed between the window closing and Sergeant Wilmott arriving at the aviary, the cat had risen, stretched luxuriously and strolled to the fence which it surmounted with an effortless bound and disappeared through the cat flap into next-door's kitchen, where its mistress, Miss Metcalfe, had thoughtfully left a saucer of milk.

The sergeant stood by the aviary for some minutes, making clucking, soothing noises and, when he was satisfied that the birds had sufficiently recovered from their ordeal, went back indoors.

'I'll swing for that Miss Metcalfe if she don't keep her ruddy cat in. I've got three prize-winning pairs out there that were ready for breeding weeks ago but there's no way they're going to get anywhere while that . . . blasted . . .'

'It's not Miss Metcalfe's fault, Jack,' soothed his wife as she put on a pan of chips.

'Well, whose fault is it then, Joan? It's her cat. Why can't she have a little bit of consideration and keep the damn thing indoors, instead o' letting it roam around terrorising the neighbourhood?'

'It doesn't terrorise the neighbourhood, Jack,' his wife pointed out.

'Well, it terrorises my birds. Puts 'em right off their laying and everything. I've just about had enough.'

'What are you going to do?' she asked. 'Tackle Miss Metcalfe about it again?'

He sighed. 'No, I've tried that before; she just shrugs and says there's nothing she can do. She keeps saying the cat doesn't actually hurt the birds.'

'Well, it doesn't, does it?' observed Joan. 'It's never got into the aviary or attacked the birds or anything like that, has it?'

'That's not the point, Joan. It frightens them, unsettles them, puts them off their courtship routines. Budgies are sensitive creatures, Joan, and these are prize-winning birds; they're not just household pets in a cage. That's what Miss Metcalfe can't seem to understand. Anyway, I've decided what action I'm going to take.'

He walked back into the living room and Joan followed him, puzzled by the strange steely glint in his eye. After glancing out of the window to make sure the cat had not resumed its customary place, he turned to face her.

'I'm going to consult a solicitor,' he announced, a note of triumph in his voice.

'A solicitor?' echoed his wife.

'Yes, a solicitor. I reckon Miss Metcalfe's infringing my rights in civil law.'

'Rights in civil law?'

'I do wish you wouldn't repeat everything I say, Joan. You do that a lot. It's very irritating.'

'So are you going to see a solicitor about that too then, Jack?' She swept out into the kitchen to attend to the now bubbling chip pan.

'All right, all right,' soothed Jack. 'But I consider that I have a perfect right to breed budgies in my own garden and Miss Metcalfe, by allowing her cat to roam about unattended, is interfering with that right. A solicitor should be able to do something about it.'

'But you don't have a solicitor,' Joan pointed out.

'Well, I've never needed to consult one before, but I know plenty of solicitors. I see them at the station and in court sometimes. I reckon I'll go and see old Dufty down at Dufty Dufty Popple & Dunn. He's getting on a bit but he's not as daft as he looks.' He gazed reflectively out of the window. 'Yes, that's what I'll do, I'll pop in and see old Dufty tomorrow. After all, I . . . GODDAMMIT, IT'S THERE AGAIN!'

He rushed out into the garden, stubbing his toe painfully on the table leg as he went.

'Budgies, you say, Sergeant?' Charles Dufty paused as he sharpened his pencil into his waste-paper bin and peered at Sergeant Wilmott from under snow-white eyebrows.

'Yes, that's right, sir. It's just a . . . well, a hobby, you know; bit of an escape from the rigours of duty, as you might say. It's a recognised interest, you know. And, though I say it myself, I've built up a bit of a reputation in the field – in fact, I've even written a book on the subject. A lot of people don't realise how much is involved, you see; they maybe have a budgie in a cage and they feed it and give it something to play with and they think that's all there is to it, but a budgerigar is a finely tuned, sensitive creature. As I was saying to my wife only yesterday . . . Are you all right, sir?'

Charles had disappeared behind his desk and could be heard groping about on the floor under his chair. The sergeant looked enquiringly at Bernard, the young trainee solicitor who was 'sitting-in' with his principal during the interview. 'I think Mr Dufty's glasses have broken again,' explained the young man. 'Can I help, Mr Dufty?'

The white-haired cranium of the old man appeared over the desk. 'No, it's quite all right, m'boy. Just looking for the little screw that secures one of the arms of my spectacles. It seems to have, er . . . Well, never mind, never mind. Perhaps we can look for it later. If you could just, er . . .'

With the practised assistance of the trainee, Charles was soon ensconced once more in his chair, squinting at Sergeant Wilmott through defective spectacles perched, lopsided, on his nose.

'So. Your neighbour's cat is frightening your budgerigars and causing them to er – ah! There it is!' He pointed to a tiny screw, which lay on the floor near Bernard's left foot. The young man retrieved it and handed it back to his principal who produced a small screwdriver from his top pocket and began the repair.

The sergeant coughed, moved his helmet from his lap to the top of the desk and then back to his lap. 'So, er, do you think there's anything we can do, Mr Dufty?' he asked, at length. 'About Miss Metcalfe's cat, I mean?'

Charles looked up sharply, dropping his screwdriver on the floor as he did so. 'Miss Metcalfe?' he frowned.

'Yes,' nodded Sergeant Wilmott. 'Miss Metcalfe . . . My neighbour . . . the owner of the cat.'

'Hmmmm,' mused Charles. 'Well, I think I should, er . . . I think I should take a note of your address, Sergeant . . .' He took up his newly sharpened pencil and waited.

'My address, sir? Yes, of course, it's 152 Carvers Crescent – that's just off Avonmore Road, down by the . . .'

'Yes, yes, I know where Carvers Crescent is,' said Charles, scribbling furiously. 'So this Miss Metcalfe would live at number . . . ?'

'Number 150, sir; next door to me, you see?'

'And what does she do for a living?'

The sergeant frowned. 'Some sort of secretary, I think, sir. She's always very well dressed when she goes out in the morning. She has a sick mother in hospital, I believe.'

Charles placed his pencil carefully on the desk and sat smiling at Sergeant Wilmott for some moments. 'So, we haven't seen much of each other recently, Sergeant,' he said at length.

'No, that's right, sir. I think the last time we saw you down at the station was when you was acting for old Tom Watts.'

'Yes, of course,' agreed Charles. 'Embezzlement, wasn't it?'

'Flashing in the park,' corrected the sergeant.

The old man nodded solemnly. 'We don't take on a great deal of legal aid work these days. So, how are things at the station?'

'Oh, same as always, sir. Fairly quiet at the moment.'

'Last time we spoke, I seem to recall you were due for a spot of promotion,' observed Charles.

The policeman sighed heavily. 'Sore point, I'm afraid, Mr Dufty. I was due to be made up to inspector two years ago but young Parker got in first. He's over at Stalford now; doing very well, I hear. No, it looks as though I shall be here for the rest of my career; part of the furniture, as it were . . .' His voice trailed off, his usually cheerful features becoming almost wistful.

Charles rose suddenly, knocking over his waste-paper bin. 'Well, never say die, Sergeant. Onwards and upwards, eh? Onwards and upwards. And now, if you'll excuse me, I must be off. Meeting of the Gilbert & Sullivan Society. Bit of a panic. We're putting on *The Mikado* in three weeks' time and our Lord High Executioner has dropped out. We don't quite, er . . . Oh! I don't suppose you, er . . . ?'

Sergeant Wilmott smiled, wryly. ''Fraid not, sir. My wife heard me singing in the bath once and threatened to divorce me.'

'Ah, well, ah well,' shrugged Charles. 'We'll solve the problem, no doubt.'

The sergeant rose, uncertainly. 'And, er, my little problem, sir? Miss Metcalfe's cat, you know?'

The solicitor waved his hand airily. 'Oh, I'm sure we'll be able to come up with something. Young Bernard here's pretty good on animals and things like that. Leave it with me and I'll drop you a line in a day or two. And now, if you'll, er . . .'

He ushered his client out into the reception area where Hugo

Dufty was going over the day's appointments with Conchita, the receptionist.

'Sergeant Wilmott!' said Hugo. 'Haven't seen you since that unfortunate business with, er . . .'

'Tom Watts, sir,' prompted the policeman.

'That's it, Tom Watts – hasn't been misbehaving again, has he?'

'No, no, sir – in fact, I believe he's now studying for the priesthood. No, it's a personal matter I've come about. Mr Dufty Senior reckons he can sort it out for me.'

'Well, I'm sure my father will come up with a solution for your problem – he always does, you know. Good to have you as a client.'

Meanwhile, Charles closed the door and sat down in an armchair by the gas fire. 'Well, Bernard, what do you think?' he asked.

The young trainee scratched his cheek and then passed a hand through his unruly curly hair. 'His next-door neighbour . . . could that be *our* Miss Metcalfe?'

'The very same, unless I'm much mistaken,' Charles confirmed, pressing a button on the intercom and speaking into the machine.

The door opened to admit his secretary, notebook in hand. 'Yes, Mr Dufty?'

'Ah, Miss Metcalfe, I wonder if you'd just take those files and get Trish to put them into storage. Oh, and would you ring Mr Johnson and confirm his appointment for eleven thirty tomorrow?'

'Yes, of course,' she smiled, picking up the files indicated and walking to the door.

Charles raised a finger as a thought struck him. 'By the way, Miss Metcalfe, how's your mother?'

'Oh, not very well,' she replied. 'She's getting more muddled every day. I'm afraid I have to face the possibility that she may never be well enough to come home.'

Charles shook his head slowly and clucked sympathetically. 'I'm sure you must miss having her about the place. Still,' he added, brightening. 'There's always the Judge! How is he these days?'

'Oh, he's very well,' she said. 'I don't know what I'd do without him – even if he does eat me out of house and home! I caught him rummaging in the dustbin for scraps this morning!'

Seeing Bernard's puzzled expression, she chuckled. 'We're talking about my cat, Bernard. His name's Judge Jeffries – you know, the Hanging Judge? I call him that because he presides over my house much as Judge Jeffries must have presided over his court.'

'Magnificent beast,' confirmed Charles. 'Still terrorising the neighbourhood, is he?' he chuckled.

'Oh, he couldn't terrorise anyone,' scoffed Miss Metcalfe. 'He just thinks people are afraid of him. Mind you, he does upset Sergeant Wilmott's budgies from time to time – he's my next-door neighbour, you know. Or, at least, Sergeant Wilmott says he does. But the budgies just make fun of the Judge – they know he can't get to them you see. They're in a cat-proof aviary. Sergeant Wilmott does get a bit upset about it, though. He's very serious about his budgies. But I don't know what I can do about it – short of locking the Judge in all day, and he'd hate that. He's an outdoor cat, you see; likes to roam around, free.'

'Oh, you mustn't do that,' said Charles. 'No, His Honour must do as he pleases. I'm sure Sergeant Wilmott will under-stand. Well, back to work, eh? Onwards and upwards!'

When Miss Metcalfe was gone, Charles again turned to Bernard. 'Well, Bernard, any thoughts?'

A perplexed expression played across Bernard's face. 'I don't really see how we can take on Sergeant Wilmott as a client in this case,' he ventured. 'Particularly as you've just told Miss

Metcalfe that she shouldn't keep the cat in. We've got a bit of a conflict of interest situation.'

'Nonsense, Bernard! We aim to please everyone – Sergeant Wilmott as a client and Miss Metcalfe as a trusted and valued member of staff. We must achieve a solution that's satisfactory to each of them.'

Bernard sighed. 'Well, I haven't really done animal liability in any depth, but I seem to recall something about animals *mansuetae naturae* and *e ferae naturae* and I think a cat is classed as, er . . . Well, shall I get the books?'

Charles had risen during this and was looking at his watch. 'Books?' he snorted. 'Books? We don't need books to deal with a situation like this, boy!'

Bernard's perplexed expression deepened. 'Well, what do we need?' he asked, lamely.

The old man walked to the door. 'Common sense, m'boy!' he boomed. 'Common sense! And,' he added as he was about to leave, 'in this case two tickets to the Policemen's Ball!'

Tapping his nose conspiratorially he closed the door behind him, leaving Bernard to shrug despairingly at his reflection in the dusty mirror over the row of even dustier law books on the mantelpiece.

The Compton-in-Arden Policemen's Ball was a glittering affair by local standards. The Banqueting Room of the Town Hall hummed with genial after-dinner conversation as constables chatted with inspectors, and local tradesmen rubbed shoulders with the Mayor and other dignitaries beneath faded, mock crystal chandeliers, the air redolent with the fragrance of wood smoke from the well-tended blaze in the huge Adam fireplace. Charles was sharing a bottle of claret with his table companion and old friend, Chief Superintendent Grey.

Bernard was seated some distance away at a table with three young police officers whom he knew slightly and two secretaries from a local insurance firm, one of whom he was getting to know rather better. Slightly flushed and waving a glass of port, he was holding forth on the Law of Defamation, his curly hair falling rather limply over his damp forehead. 'Of course, people tend to forget that the most obvious defence to a libel action is that the statement in question was true.'

The secretaries displayed interest and the dark one with long lashes said, 'Oh, so you can say what you like about anybody so long as it's true?'

'Well, yes,' he confirmed, warming to his theme and turning to face the brunette, noticing that her eyes were a particularly deep shade of brown. 'Of course, there are exceptions. Some people are prohitib . . . prohibited from talking about some things even if they're true. For example, statements made by a client to his solicitor are prilivi . . . privileged. Then there's the Offishal Shecretsh Act.' Bernard's tongue seemed, for some unaccountable reason, to be developing a will of its own. 'If you work in the Armed Forces or the Servil Civice . . . sorry, I meant to say Servil Civ . . .'

The rather plump, fair-haired secretary giggled as one of the young constables winked at her and refilled Bernard's glass. 'Come on, Bernie, drink up,' he said. 'You're falling behind, there.'

Before Bernard could resume his discourse, the band struck up and the secretaries were whisked off to the dance floor by two of the policemen, the other wandering off in the general direction of the bar. Peering through the cigar smoke, Bernard focused (with some degree of difficulty) on Charles at his distant table, his white head bobbing as he listened approvingly to the tall, distinguished figure of Chief Superintendent Grey who, curiously, appeared to be singing a song quite unrelated to the tune being played by the band, his hands waving theatrically as he did so. With the intention of joining them, Bernard rose and began to make his way across the crowded room, carefully avoiding the elbows of drinkers and occasionally steadying himself against a convenient table or chair. Suddenly, he felt extraordinarily hot. The smoke-laden air seemed to press in upon him like a damp blanket and the sound of the band took on an unreal quality, as though he were part of someone else's dream. The scene swam before him; he staggered slightly, tripped and subsided backwards on to the lap of a lady councillor who was drinking gin at a nearby table.

Noticing the resulting confusion, Charles beckoned to a waiter, spoke a few words to him and pointed to the stumbling, embarrassed figure of Bernard, who was attempting to apologise to the outraged lady councillor whose lap he had so recently and unexpectedly occupied. Within moments, the trainee solicitor was being discreetly assisted out of the hall and into a waiting taxi, while Charles returned his attention to the musical endeavours of Chief Superintendent Grey.

'Three o'clock precisely, Miss Metcalfe; you never fail, do you?'

She smiled brightly as she placed the cup and saucer on the desk and produced a plate of chocolate biscuits. Charles leant back in his chair and took off his newly repaired spectacles. 'Could you ask young Bernard to slip in? I need a word,' he asked.

'Oh, I'm sorry, Mr Dufty, Bernard's not in today. He phoned in this morning to say he thinks he may have a dose of the flu. Didn't sound very well at all.'

'Ah,' Charles nodded sagely, 'lot of it about, lot of it about.'

Miss Metcalfe busied herself tidying his desk. 'Did you have a nice time at the Policemen's Ball last night?' she enquired.

'Oh, just the usual sort of thing, you know. Work mostly, I'm afraid. Useful, though, useful. These biscuits are excellent! Anything important lined up for today – other than Mr Stanley coming in about his will?'

'No . . . Oh, Mr Knight from the Gilbert & Sullivan Society

phoned yesterday. He seemed very concerned about the forthcoming performance of *The Mikado*. Something about having to cancel the whole thing if a Lord High Executioner can't be found. Could you give him a call? He really did seem very agitated.'

Charles looked up from his crossword. 'Oh, I think we've solved that little problem. I'll give him a ring later on and put his mind at rest.'

She went to the door and turned. 'Oh, and apparently Sergeant Wilmott phoned half an hour ago. Trish took the call. He said to tell you that you needn't take any further action over the little matter he saw you about. Does that mean anything to you?'

'Yes . . . yes, it does. Thank you, Miss Metcalfe.'

She went on: 'Apparently he said something about his long-awaited promotion to inspector and a move to Minsham. It appears he had a phone call from Chief Superintendent Grey first thing this morning. I suppose that means I shall be getting a new next-door neighbour.'

'Ah, yes, I imagine so,' nodded Charles, gravely.

'Still,' she said, her frown clearing, 'at least the Judge won't be teased by those budgies any more!'

The old man beamed at her. 'Of course! Well, well, it's an ill wind etc. etc. eh? Sergeant Wilmott can build a brand new aviary in Minsham and His Honour can roam at will without let or hindrance. Strange how these things work themselves out. Well, back to work. Onwards and upwards, eh? Onwards and upwards!'

∼

'Useful coincidence, Sergeant Wilmott getting his promotion just at the right time,' remarked Henry. 'Incidentally, Chief Superintendent Grey – isn't he a member of that Gilbert & Sullivan Society where you're on the committee?'

Charles nodded. 'He is now.'

'And didn't he play the Lord High Executioner in The Mikado only a few weeks ago?'

Charles nodded again.

'I didn't see it myself,' Henry went on, 'but I remember reading the write-up in the local paper. Grey was singled out for best performance.'

'A role he'd always wanted to play,' said Charles. 'He bided his time, watched for the right opportunity and took it. Lesson there for all of us, eh? Your move, I think.'

Restitutio in Integrum

'Stanley!' Henry Middleton's tone was uncharacteristically peeved as he summoned the Dog and Tadpole's barman to the corner table where he sat with Charles Dufty.

The barman hurried over to stand enquiringly before them.

'Stanley,' began Henry, holding up his gin and tonic for inspection. 'There appears to be some kind of film floating on top of this, can you see, just there . . . Mr Dufty's whisky and water is the same.'

Stanley peered into the glass and took it from him. 'Sorry, sir. Plaster dust. As you'll have seen, we're having a bit of reorganisation behind the bar. They came today and knocked out the wall between the serving area and the storeroom to the side there. It'll mean more space to accommodate everything but the work has produced a bit of mess. We did try to clean everything up as best we could but obviously there's a certain amount of dust still in the air. I do apologise, gentlemen. I'll bring some fresh drinks straight away.'

He pottered off with the glasses. 'Seemed perfectly all right the way things were,' grumbled Henry. 'Why people have to alter things round when they work perfectly well the way they are, I don't know.'

Charles grinned at him. 'You're getting old, Henry.'

'Getting old? I've got old!' said Henry. 'But that's not the point. The point is, if something works, why change it? Nothing to do with age, it's common sense.'

'Things have to move on,' said Charles. 'And we have to keep up otherwise we get left behind. It's the same at the office. The old firm wouldn't have survived fifty years without adapting to new conditions as they arise.'

'I thought you always said Dufty Dufty Popple & Dunn should stay as it is,' said Henry, moving his king pawn two spaces. 'Thought you preferred the status quo – plus ça change, plus c'est la même chose and all that sort of thing.'

'Everything changes,' said Charles. 'Though, I grant you, if you wait long enough, it eventually changes back to where it was before.'

Henry glanced at him. 'You'll be saying next that "what goes around comes around" at which point I shall leave. It's your move.'

~

The High Street of Hockam was beginning to come alive in the hazy morning sunshine and Bernard Summers dodged a deliveryman carrying a tray of bread rolls to the Rialto Café whose proprietor, Ashraf, clad in an apron and carpet slippers, was laying tables for breakfast. Bernard glanced at his watch, ignored the heady fragrance of cooking bacon and hurried past. Half an hour late again. Almost certainly Mr Dufty Junior would have arrived before him and would be waiting to brief him on his duties for the day – mainly the filing, form-filling and assorted errands which had been Bernard's lot since he had joined the firm as a trainee solicitor some six months earlier.

He turned into the alley which led to the cramped car park at the rear of the half-timbered house which served as the offices of Dufty Dufty Popple & Dunn, solicitors and commissioners for oaths, where, as he had expected, Mr Dufty Junior's well-polished saloon was parked, slightly askew, in its usual space. Bernard's eyebrows lifted as he saw that Mr Dufty Senior's elderly estate car was also present – as was a rather racy, low-slung, open-topped vintage sports model with a bag of golf clubs strapped to the luggage rack! He walked over to admire its long, louvred bonnet and sleek lines and was joined by Caroline, the estate agent who had recently taken over the office next door and who shared the little car park with the solicitors.

'Beautiful, isn't it?' said Bernard after a short silence.

Caroline nodded, her blonde hair falling slightly over one eye. 'And I think I know who it belongs to,' she said, quietly.

Bernard looked at her. 'Well? Whose is it then?'

She smiled enigmatically as she turned and walked towards her office. 'You'll find out . . . if I'm right,' she called over her shoulder.

Conchita, the receptionist was applying mascara to her not inconsiderable eyelashes as Bernard entered the firm's little reception area and leant on the desk to peer closely at her. 'You've missed a bit – just there,' he observed. When she ignored him and continued her task, he grinned. 'Did you see the sports car outside?' he asked. 'Little beauty – don't see many of those around here. Any idea who it belongs to?'

Conchita gave a final, satisfied glance in the mirror propped on the desk and carefully replaced her cosmetics in her hand-bag. 'The car, it belong to Mr Dunn,' she explained.

Bernard frowned. 'Who?' he asked.

'Mr Mark Dunn,' she repeated. 'Miss Metcalfe, she say that he work here as a partner until five years ago when he leave the firm and go to Spain with two business partners to open a bar in Benidorm which is near where I live before I come here. He is very nice.'

'Oh, *that* Mr Dunn.' Bernard's frown deepened. 'I've heard Trish mention him. What's he doing here?' Conchita shrugged as the telephone rang and she turned to answer it.

Bernard crossed the reception area and entered the general office which he shared with the secretaries, Miss Metcalfe and Trish, who were in earnest conversation over mugs of tea. The young man awkwardly manoeuvred himself into the chair behind his desk in the corner and shuffled through the papers that Mr Dufty Junior had left for him. After some minutes, fearing he had somehow become invisible, he leant back in his chair. 'Good morning everyone!' he said, rather unnecessarily loudly.

Miss Metcalfe broke off what she was saying to Trish and they both turned to him. 'Oh, good morning, Bernard,' she replied. 'Sorry, we were just . . . talking.'

Trish giggled.

Bernard chucked his pen on to the desk. 'What's going on?'

Both began to talk at the same time until Trish stopped and gestured to the other to continue. 'Haven't you heard?' Miss Metcalfe asked.

'Haven't I heard what?' Bernard was becoming exasperated.

'About Mr Dunn? He might be coming back! He's in with the Duftys at the moment – they're in Mr Dufty Senior's office.' All three turned towards the closed door of the office indicated. 'Apparently,' continued Miss Metcalfe, 'Mark – Mr Dunn, that is – has given up the bar in Spain and moved back here. He rang yesterday and made an appointment to see the Duftys first thing this morning.'

Bernard considered this. 'So he's seeing the Duftys. That doesn't necessarily mean he's coming back to work here. He could be consulting them about . . . well, about business matters. If he's given up his venture in Spain there must be all kinds of formalities to deal with. He's probably just here as a client. Don't you think you're rather jumping to . . .'

Trish cut in: 'Well, I know Mr Hugo is very keen on having him back because he as good as said so after he'd spoken to him on the phone yesterday. And then, just as I was going home last night, I heard him and his father arguing in Mr Hugo's office. So the problem could be old Mr Dufty.'

'Mr Dufty *Senior*,' corrected Miss Metcalfe. 'And I wouldn't describe him as "a problem", Trish. Mr Dufty Senior was always very fond of Mar—, Mr Dunn. In fact when Mr Dunn was an articled clerk here, Mr Dufty Senior had high hopes of him, and when he qualified Mr Dufty Senior handed over some of our most important clients to him.'

Trish again joined in: 'Then, after a couple of years, he was made a partner to replace Mr Pop—'

Miss Metcalfe coughed loudly. 'Trish! You know the rule against mentioning that name in this office. But yes, Mr Dunn was made a partner and proved a great asset to the firm until he suddenly decided to give everything up and go off to Spain with two of his pals from the golf club to open a bar or nightclub or something. Naturally, Mr Dufty Senior was disappointed in him after all he'd done to further his career. Whether he'll be happy to welcome Mr Dunn back into the fold remains to be seen. Now, I suggest we all get on with our work. It's turned ten o'clock and I haven't even started on these letters.' She switched on her computer and bustled about, matching correspondence to files from the cabinet.

'I bet I know someone who'd be happy to welcome him back,' said Trish.

Bernard waited for her to go on but when she turned her attention to arranging the files on her desk, he asked: 'Well, who?'

'Caroline from next door. She was Hugo's secretary before me and I've heard that she and Mr Dunn were beginning to be quite an item before he left and . . .'

'*Trish!*' Miss Metcalfe's tone was brisk. 'Could you be quick and get that tenancy agreement done on the Barstow file? Mr Hugo's seeing him this afternoon.'

Mark Dunn, his fair, wavy hair glinting in the sunlight entering through the leaded light window, had finished speaking and smiled encouragingly across the desk where Hugo Dufty was earnestly addressing his father who sat expressionless next to him. 'Well, I really think we should at least consider Mark's request. After all . . .'

'It's not a request,' Mark was leaning forward now, his even features composed and his voice quiet, reasonable, suggesting a desire to avoid misunderstanding and to ensure that everyone knew where they stood. 'It's a . . . a proposal, if you like. A proposal which you can either accept or reject. All I ask is that you both think about it and let me know your answer when you're ready. I think you already know that I have some small ability in dealing with clients' affairs. I think you also know that I understand and embrace the ethos and culture of this firm – and that, of course, is thanks to you, Charles.' He turned to the old man whose face still betrayed no indication of his thoughts. 'It was your patience,' Mark went on, 'your generosity of spirit and your . . . your unparalleled ability to bring common sense to bear on the most unpromising and sometimes absurd situations, which opened my eyes to . . .'

'Yes, yes, that's all very well.' Charles Dufty spoke for the first time. 'The facts of the matter are that I was your principal and you were my articled clerk, we got on pretty well, you passed your exams and eventually became a partner in the firm in which capacity you were able to contribute significantly to the success of our little undertaking here. You then decided to switch careers and move overseas to take up a business project. That was your prerogative and your decision.'

'A decision of which you disapproved,' Mark reminded him.

'Whether I approved or disapproved was neither here nor there,' observed Mr Dufty Senior. 'You were a free agent. I was your colleague and partner, not your schoolmaster.'

'Agreed,' Mark nodded. 'But you did believe I was misguided in making the decision to throw it all in. And the fact is you were right.' He leant back in his chair. 'Like most very young men, I was impressionable and easily persuaded to join forces with others to go off and conquer new worlds, challenge fresh frontiers, find new foes to fight . . .'

Hugo turned to Charles. 'When you were a young man,

Father, you must have experienced a similar call when you enlisted and were posted to Korea where . . .'

The old man cut him short. 'I didn't enlist, I was called up. And, yes, I was obliged to fight the odd foe here and there – even challenge a frontier or two but, throughout it all, I steadfastly resisted the temptation to open a bar in Spain. Besides, I fail to see how my experiences over half a century ago have any bearing on the issue at hand.'

His son explained: 'I think it helps us to understand Mark's decision to venture forth and . . .'

'Mark's decision to "venture forth", as you put it, is not the issue!' pointed out Charles. 'The issue is Mark's "proposal", as he puts it, to venture *back* and walk into his old job here – as though nothing had happened.'

Mark, still calm and urbane, resumed his attempts to bring reason to the proceedings. 'With respect, Charles, that was not my proposal. I don't expect to be handed back the partnership I relinquished five years ago. Neither do I expect to be taken on in a senior capacity. All I'm suggesting is that you may care to consider giving me an opportunity to use whatever skills you gave me to again make a contribution to the work of the firm – perhaps in a temporary capacity. Simply give me something to do and judge me on my performance. If I prove unequal to the task, then I'll slink off and look for a post as assistant solicitor with a firm in Walchester – I see Pollock's are advertising for something of the sort. On the other hand, if my performance comes up to the required standard, then you may care to take me on permanently in a comparatively junior capacity until I've earned my stripes, as it were. But it's just a suggestion. Naturally, if you don't wish to consider it . . .'

'We *will* consider it, Mark.' Hugo Dufty's tone was conciliatory. 'My father and I will talk about it over the next week and we'll contact you when we've reached a decision. Obviously, I can't promise . . .' There was a knock at the door and Miss

Spiers, the firm's book-keeper appeared, a slanting ray of sunshine glinting off her wire-rimmed spectacles and illuminating her sharp, humourless features.

She addressed herself to Mr Dufty Junior: 'I'm sorry to interrupt, Mr Hugo, but you asked me to let you know immediately if there was no cheque from Mr Phelps in this morning's post. There was not. I felt I should report this to you without delay.'

Hugo passed a hand over his brow, brushing aside a stray lock of dark hair from his slightly damp brow, and sighed. 'Yes, well, er . . . thank you, Miss Spiers. I'll er . . . yes, well thank you.'

She remained in the room. 'Forgive me again for interrupting but could I ask whether we are now going to take some positive action to recover this outstanding sum? The invoices in question now date back some twelve months and the total amount is very considerable.'

'Yes, yes, of course, Miss Spiers.' Hugo's irritation was evident. 'Mr Phelps has really taken this too far. I'll, er . . . I'll come and see you later this morning and we'll go over the matter.'

Miss Spiers withdrew with every appearance of reluctance, leaving the three men in silence. 'Well,' said Hugo, at length, 'I think we all understand your proposal, Mark, and, as I said, my father and I will give it proper consideration and I'll telephone you within a week. Are you in agreement, Father?'

The old man nodded, the three shook hands and Mark walked to the door where he turned. 'Thanks for your time. I appreciate it. If nothing else, it's been a pleasure to visit the old place again.' The door closed behind him leaving Dufty and son to discuss the pressing problem of Mr Phelps and his outstanding indebtedness to the firm.

Mark collided pleasurably with Trish as he turned from closing the door. 'How did it go?' she asked.

'Oh, pretty well, all things considered,' he replied, adjusting his immaculate shirt cuffs. 'Ah, this would be . . . ?' He advanced towards Bernard who rose from behind his desk and took the proffered hand.

Miss Metcalfe appeared from the stationery room. 'Mark, this is Bernard, our trainee solicitor. Bernard, this is Mr Dunn who used to be a partner here.'

Feeling it incumbent upon himself to contribute something meaningful to the conversation, Bernard said: 'I was admiring your car when I got in this morning. She's a beauty, isn't she?'

'Oh, it's just a car,' replied the other. 'Getting a bit elderly now, you know, but it gets me from A to B – and, if I'm lucky, back to A again. If you're interested, I'll show you over it – that is, if you can be spared for a couple of minutes?' Miss Metcalfe smiled approval and the two men walked through reception, Bernard stifling mild, irrational irritation as Mark exchanged a few pleasantries with Conchita in fluent Spanish.

Outside in the car park, Mark indicated the essential features of his precious car while Bernard sat in the passenger seat, asking questions about its specification and performance. At length, Bernard got out and was about to return to work when Mark, now ensconced in the driving seat, called out: 'Oh, by the way, I was wondering – is Reg Phelps a client of the firm?'

'Yes,' answered Bernard, walking back to the car. 'Well, he used to be until recently. I think there's some problem . . . well, I don't know much about it . . .'

'No, obviously I don't expect you to talk about clients and their affairs. It's just that I'm trying to pick up the threads again after so long away. He owns the second-hand-car showrooms in Brook Street, doesn't he?'

'That's right,' confirmed Bernard.

'Thought so. Member of Walchester Golf Club as I recall. Well, must shoot off. See you around, Bernard.' He gunned the motor and engaged reverse gear. 'Oh, incidentally,' he called, over the roar of the engine, 'I'll be in the Pig and Whistle this evening from about eight o'clock. Don't know if you drink there at all but, if you do, we can have a gossip over a pint.'

As the sound of the exhaust died away, Bernard returned through reception where Helen, Hugo's wife, was frowning through the window as the sports car turned on to the High Street and drove past. She turned to Miss Metcalfe who was passing. 'Was that who I think it was?' she asked, quietly.

'That was Mark Dunn,' confirmed the secretary.

Helen's frown deepened. 'I'm surprised he was allowed back into the building after he buzzed off five years ago, leaving everyone in the lurch like that,' she mused, half to herself. 'Mind you, he was always the apple of Charles's eye. Of course, Hugo could never see that. And as for the way he treated poor Caroline – we all thought they were the perfect couple and then he just . . . upped and went. How he can look her in the face after . . .'

She collected herself with an effort. 'Oh, Miss Metcalfe, when Hugo's free, could you remind him I'll be late home tonight. He's bound to have forgotten there's a staff meeting at school this evening. I've left him a steak and kidney pie to heat up – assuming he can remember how the microwave works.' She smiled wryly at Miss Metcalfe. 'Men! Do you know, Joan, I sometimes look at the bright, happy, inquisitive faces of the lads at Hockam Primary and wonder what happens to all that promise between boyhood and manhood.'

The two women exchanged baffled shrugs and Helen left to return to school.

The saloon of the Pig and Whistle was unusually quiet for a Friday night as Bernard caught sight of Mark standing at the bar talking quietly to Caroline Adams who was standing with her head turned slightly away from him, doodling circles on the bar top with her index finger. Sensing his presence would be regarded as unnecessary at that moment, he slipped quietly into the neighbouring snug where four elderly men were seated around a table. After enduring the irritating click of domino tiles on the wooden table top for several minutes, he looked out of the window to see Caroline's retreating form as she made her way through the little beer garden to the street.

He returned to the saloon bar where Mark was now seated on a bar stool, looking thoughtful, while the lovely Adele was expertly pulling a pint of Walchester Pride. Catching sight of Bernard, he shook himself out of his reverie and gestured to the young trainee to join him. 'Make that two, Adele,' he said as Bernard approached.

'Mr Dunn. Hi!' greeted Bernard.

'Mark, please,' insisted the other. 'None of that archaic Mr Dunn stuff. We're not in the office now.'

Bernard grinned as he took up his glass. 'I know what you mean. It's good to spend the evening in the twenty-first century after a day at that place.'

Mark put down his pint and regarded the articled clerk enigmatically. 'Oh, I think you'll find, Bernard, that, despite all appearances to the contrary, the Duftys, both senior and junior, are very much in tune with the . . . zeitgeist of the twenty-first century.' Seeing Bernard's amused expression, he went on: 'You forget, I was with the firm for seven years, man and boy. D'you fancy a packet of crisps or something?'

Bernard shook his head. 'You say they're "in tune" with the modern world and all that but, let's face it, the office is . . . well, it's like a museum. Old man Dufty won't have a computer on his desk and even refuses to carry a mobile phone! Young Dufty, or "Mr Hugo" as we're supposed to call him, is almost as bad – insists on all incoming calls being channelled through reception instead of us having direct lines with voicemail – and I spend half the day filling out forms by hand when it could be done ten times more quickly on-line. I sometimes wonder what I'm doing there. I'm not given anything remotely interesting to do

– how am I supposed to learn how to practise law when I'm treated as a junior filing clerk? I've been there for six months – how the hell did you stick it for seven years?'

Mark thought for a moment. 'By watching,' he said at length.

'Watching?' Bernard's expression was blank. 'You spent seven years watching? Watching what? Paint dry?'

'Watching Charles Dufty at work,' replied Mark. 'I've seen the old man take on cases which most modern firms wouldn't even look at – cases which are clearly incapable of a satisfactory outcome – and, before you know it, problem solved! Very often, he doesn't even appear to have done anything. Events just seem to organise themselves in such a way that everyone comes out a winner. He doesn't use clever legal strategies or try to outwit the opposition – in fact, so far as he's concerned, there is no opposition – just people. A word here, a nod there, a suggestion at the right time, a small adjustment in the right place. You see, he doesn't just take a client's problem and look at it in a vacuum, as it were; he looks at the problem in the context of its real-life setting. He doesn't need a computer for that. All he needs is seventy-nine years of life experience – and he's got that. Yes, I learnt a lot during those seven years watching Charles Dufty at work.'

'Why did you throw it all in and scoot off to sunny Spain?'

Mark shrugged and gave a rueful smile. 'Seemed like a good idea at the time, I suppose.' He sipped his beer, thoughtfully. 'No, it was more than that. I began to feel that I'd never make it in the law. Compared to Charles Dufty – or Hugo, come to that – I was a mere beginner and likely to remain so for some years until I'd acquired the experience, the understanding, the . . . the exposure to life that it takes to practise law the Dufty way. I wasn't prepared to wait so I, as you put it, scooted off to sunny Spain.'

'So, why did you come back? Business didn't work out?'

'Oh, the business did OK – still is, in fact. My partners bought out my share so I had enough to live on for . . . well, until about now, actually. No, I came back because . . . well, there were a number of reasons. There were people I let down when I left.' He was silent for a moment, his thoughts turned inwards. Then he collected himself: 'Not least Charles Dufty. He'd invested a lot of time and money in me – which, I now realise, means that he had faith in my ability to do things his way. I want the opportunity to show him he was right.'

'How are you going to do that?' asked Bernard.

'By showing Charles and Hugo that I'm capable of solving a problem the Dufty way,' answered Mark. 'All I need is a suitable problem – this business about Reg Phelps's unpaid bill, for instance. How much does he owe?' Seeing Bernard's embarrassed shrug, he went on: 'Look, Bernard, I need your help to get my job back. All I need to know is how much Phelps owes the firm in total and his reason for withholding payment. If you're able to provide that information and I can find a way to resolve the situation, then I guarantee you won't be spending your days filling in forms and running errands for much longer. If I can return to Dufty Dufty Popple & Dunn as a partner, then I can make sure you have some real work to do. Between us, we might even make a few changes here and there, eh?'

'But how are you going to resolve the situation with Reg Phelps?' asked Bernard. 'He owes . . .' he lowered his voice: 'He owes the firm £15,000 going back more than a year but he can't pay at the moment because he simply doesn't have the money. Apparently, his partner at the second-hand-car showrooms let him down badly over a deal and buggered off, taking his share of the partnership funds with him. Consequently, Dufty Dufty Popple & Dunn are having to stand out the £15,000 but they can't allow that to carry on indefinitely. I gather Phelps is managing to keep afloat but, unless he gets a bit of luck soon, he's going to have to consider selling up – if only to pay our bill. I don't see how you can resolve that.'

Mark nodded. 'Well, let's look at the problem in the context of its real-life setting. Dufty Dufty Popple & Dunn need payment of the outstanding bills, Reg Phelps needs a bit of a windfall and I need to get back my position with Dufty's. Mmm . . .'

'Well, that's a piece of cake, then, isn't it?' Bernard taunted him. 'The Duftys get paid their outstanding invoices, you get your job back and all that's necessary is for Reg Phelps to receive "a bit of a windfall" to enable him to stump up the £15,000. You've already said you've spent your share of the Spanish project and I'm flat broke, so don't look at me! What have you got in mind – The lottery? Santa Claus? Extortion? Prayer?'

Mark finished his pint, grinned mysteriously at Bernard and rose. 'Must be off – busy weekend. See you on Monday, old boy.'

Ashraf's way with fried eggs was legendary and Bernard was tucking into two of them with four rashers, two pork sausages and a round of fried bread. The tiny café was beginning to fill up with delivery men having finished their Monday morning rounds, local shopkeepers snatching a bite before opening and office workers like Bernard, glancing guiltily at their watches. *Half past nine again*, he thought, mentally resolving to arrive early tomorrow and surprise everyone.

The last morsel of fried bread laced with egg yolk and topped with a sliver of bacon slipped down very satisfactorily and Bernard leant back in his chair, wiping his mouth on his paper napkin. As he did so, he noticed, with mild interest, a small group of people standing together on the pavement fifty yards down the High Street. He finished his mug of tea, paid Ashraf and went out, heading for the offices of Dufty Dufty Popple & Dunn. However, he paused at the entrance, distracted by the hum of voices from the gathering on the pavement, now numbering perhaps a dozen. Curious, he walked towards them, realising they were looking in the widow of Reg Phelps's second-hand-car showrooms on the corner of Brook Street. Drawing closer, he saw that the object of their attention was a car. Not the usual tarted-up family saloon which formed the bulk of Phelps's stock but a sleek, classic, vintage sports car whose clean lines were familiar to Bernard. As he watched, Reg Phelps reached over the windscreen and took off the sign which read £15,000, replacing it with one which bore the legend: SOLD.

'So, Father,' Hugo transferred his smile from Mark, who sat across the desk, and redirected it towards Charles, who sat next to him, his white head bowed, as if in sleep. 'I think we have to admit that Mark has, in the true tradition of the firm, achieved a very satisfactory result for all parties concerned. He has acquired a small interest as sleeping partner in Reg Phelps's second-hand-car business – albeit at the expense of his beloved car – Reg Phelps himself has been enabled to place his finances on a slightly firmer footing and as for us . . .' He held up the cheque for £15,000 which Reg Phelps had brought in some half an hour earlier. 'I suggest we ask Mark to leave us for a few minutes while we discuss possibilities?'

The old man shook his head, slowly without looking up. 'I don't think there's any need for that.' His voice was solemn and his expression unmoved by Hugo's encouraging smile. 'I think it's perfectly plain what we're seeing here,' he said.

'Er . . . what's that, Father?'

The old man's head came up, slowly, his eyes twinkling under their shaggy brows. 'The return of the Prodigal Dunn,' he smiled.

～

Henry finished his gin and tonic and signalled to the barman to replenish their glasses. 'So everyone's a winner, eh? You, the firm, Reg Phelps and this young Mark Dunn fella.'

'For the moment,' agreed Charles, moving his white knight carefully over a line of black pawns. 'For the moment. Checkmate, I believe?'

A Matter of Public Interest

Henry Middleton hung his overcoat on the hatstand, crossed the lounge bar of the Dog and Tadpole and eased himself down at the corner table upon which Charles Dufty was drumming his fingers impatiently.

'Not late, am I?' asked Henry, glancing at his watch.

'No,' replied Charles. 'It's just that I ordered the drinks almost ten minutes ago but Alfred seems otherwise occupied.'

Henry looked towards the bar where Alfred, the ancient reserve barman, was engaged in earnest discussion with a customer concerning the price of pork scratchings. At length, the matter apparently resolved, Alfred brought Henry's gin and tonic and Charles's long awaited whisky and water.

'Evening, Alfred,' said Henry. 'Stanley not in tonight?'

'Oh, he's in, Mr Middleton,' wheezed the old man. 'He's in an important meeting out the back at the moment.' Here he tapped the side of his bulbous nose conspiratorially. 'But he should be back soon. Anything else I can get you?'

'No, that's fine, Alfred. Thanks,' said Charles.

The barman returned, arthritically, to the bar, leaving Charles and Henry to set up the chess pieces and speculate upon the nature of Stanley's 'important meeting'.

Their musings were cut short, however, by Stanley's return from 'out the back', clutching an official-looking clipboard and a banana.

He walked over to their table and greeted Charles and Henry. 'What's that you've got there, Stanley?' enquired Henry.

Stanley held up the clipboard. 'Ah, well, you see, gentlemen . . .'

'No, I think Henry was referring to the banana,' said Charles.

Stanley looked slightly disappointed. 'Oh. Well, I didn't have time for my tea because we've been having meetings out the back with the boss and the brewery representatives since six o'clock – which brings me to this . . .' He again held up the clipboard. 'You see, gentlemen, the Dog and Tadpole has been selected as one of the five candidates to host the next round of the International Pub Quiz League. The boss has deputised me to arrange the layout for the evening. There's going to be a giant plasma screen over here . . .' He consulted the clipboard and waved a hand towards the wall opposite the window. 'There'll be a podium over here for our team and the whole layout of the room is going to be changed to accommodate the spectators and the press and so on. It's really going to put the Dog and Tadpole on the map, believe me. The boss reckons it'll be a real millstone in developing this place. Anyway, must get on.' He bustled off to find some graph paper.

'I think he meant "milestone",' observed Henry.

'Millstone was probably more accurate,' grunted Charles. 'In my experience, these all-singing, all-dancing, action-packed, one-off events are more trouble than they're worth. The disruption they cause is greater than the benefits they produce.'

'Nothing wrong with a bit of fun surely?' said Henry. 'The occasional surge of excitement gives everyone . . .'

'A false picture of who they are,' Charles cut in. 'This is an old-established inn, peaceful, reliable and, in its own way, beautiful. That's what it is and that's what it should remain. Start giving the staff the idea that it's anything else and they'll have no end of trouble coming back to reality when the thing's over and done with. It was just the same with all that nonsense in the town last July . . .'

〜

Something was happening in Hockam.

The morning sun, peeping over the roofs on the east side of the High Street, illuminated the sign above the door of the Rialto Café which appeared to have been newly washed and polished. Ashraf, the proprietor of the establishment, usually at this hour clad in plastic apron and carpet slippers, was serving bacon and eggs, resplendent in crisp white shirt, sleek pinstripe trousers and a strangely incongruous chef's hat; Mrs Bunce, the postmistress, was hurrying to work, her ample frame clothed in a smart, business-like suit; Daniel Frost, the butcher, sporting a straw boater, was arranging a tray of lamb chops with intense concentration and old Ben Sharpe was balancing on a step-ladder, treating the window of his newsagent's to the first wash it had received since its repair following the previous year's visit to the town by Walchester Rugby Club.

At the top of the High Street, an overall-clad workman was descending a ladder, having replaced the missing letter 'M' from the sign above the King's Arms Hotel (an omission also dating from Walchester Rugby Club's memorable overnight stay). And, midway along the High Street between the hotel and the Rialto Café, the half-timbered building which housed the offices of Dufty Dufty Popple & Dunn, solicitors and commissioners for oaths, was buzzing with excitement.

The cause of this unaccustomed enthusiasm was known to everyone except Bernard, the firm's trainee solicitor, who had just entered the building after a fortnight's camping holiday in the Lake District. Slightly bemused by the unusual degree of activity in the High Street, his puzzled frown deepened as he found the little reception area alive with conversation, the spirited nature of which was unusual for a Monday morning.

Trish, Hugo Dufty's secretary, was holding forth, her freckled features even more animated than usual: 'Apparently, they'll be here for most of the week, filming things and interviewing people and whatnot. They're sure to be in the High Street tomorrow because it's market day. I'm having my hair done this afternoon so I'll be out from one o'clock until about three thirty.'

'I presume you'll be taking that as leave?' asked Miss Metcalfe, Mr Dufty Senior's secretary.

Miss Spiers, the book-keeper, polishing her wire-rimmed spectacles, her sharp features reflecting none of the surrounding excitement, put in: 'I rather doubt whether they'll be interested in a small provincial firm of solicitors, Trish. There's nothing out of the ordinary going on here – or at least I hope not!' She replaced her glasses on her nose and stalked off to her tiny office at the back of the building.

Miss Metcalfe watched her go with a wry smile. 'There certainly won't be anything out of the ordinary going on in Miss Spiers's office,' she muttered.

'No,' grinned Trish, 'but I'd have thought they'd be very interested in what we do here – sorting out people's legal problems and that. I wouldn't be surprised if they come and interview us early on – Oh my God! . . . what if they come this afternoon when I'm having my hair done!'

Bernard took advantage of the momentary lull in the conversation: 'Morning everyone – yes, thanks, I've had a very nice holiday.'

'I'm sorry, Bernard,' placated Miss Metcalfe. 'We didn't mean to ignore you, but it is rather exciting, isn't it?'

'I don't know, said Bernard, tetchily. 'I only got back yesterday. What's all this about interviews and filming?'

Hugo Dufty's head appeared round his office door. 'Trish, could you bring in the Drysdale file, please? And, Miss Metcalfe, I believe the Parkinsons are coming in this morning to sign that contract – is it ready yet?'

Both Trish and Miss Metcalfe hurried to do as bidden, leaving Bernard alone with Conchita, the Spanish receptionist, who was seated behind the desk, applying nail varnish with even more care than usual. He leant on the desk, waiting until her task was completed. 'So, what's it all about then?' he asked. 'Everyone seems to know except me.'

She finished putting her make-up away before turning her lustrous eyes in his direction. 'Some people from the television will come to make a documentary about Hockam. It is to be part of a series about English small market towns. They will film us and they will interview us and we will be on the television. It is very exciting, yes?'

'Good Lord!' he exclaimed. 'When are they coming?'

'This week, old lad.' Mark Dunn, the junior partner, emerged from his office, looking even more sartorially elegant than usual, fair, wavy hair freshly cut, shoes gleaming and precisely one inch of shirt cuff showing below each sleeve of his neatly pressed pinstripe jacket. 'In fact, the word is they'll be arriving this afternoon and setting up camp at the King's Arms Hotel preparatory to beginning the process of interviewing the good burghers of Hockam tomorrow.'

The work of the morning proceeded, its customary efficiency interrupted only slightly as members of staff took opportunities to huddle, briefly, in twos or threes to discuss the dizzying possibility of being interviewed for national television or the prospect of seeing a film crew at work *right here* in Hockam High Street.

Lunchtime came as a welcome relief, the hour of comparative freedom allowing the members of the little firm to perhaps drift out into the sunlit High Street for a breath of air, consume sandwiches or, in Hugo's case, catch up with paperwork and make telephone calls, including one to his wife to check that it was tonight that the Johnsons were coming to dinner and another to his father to ascertain that he would not be coming into the office until Thursday afternoon. Replacing the receiver after this last conversation, he rose, left his office and walked to the reception desk, where Miss Metcalfe was carefully arranging a vase of flowers she had purchased from Maisie, the florist, during her lunch hour. She smiled brightly at him: 'I thought these would help to brighten the place up a little.'

Hugo glanced briefly at the unaccustomed floral display and said: 'Could you ask Trish to come in, please, Miss Metcalfe. I need her to put the new filing cabinet in order. Our entire filing system seems to be in a state of disarray recently.'

Miss Metcalfe hesitated as she added another Stargazer lily to her arrangement. 'Er . . . I believe Trish has taken a couple of hours off as part of her leave entitlement, Mr Hugo.'

He frowned and peered at the notice board behind the reception desk where the office holiday rota was pinned up. 'I take it this was arranged very suddenly,' he said. 'Nothing wrong, I hope?'

'No, no . . . I think she has an appointment at the hairdresser's – there was an unexpected cancellation and she . . . well, she likes to look her best,' she finished, lamely.

Hugo nodded. 'Ah, I think I understand. Well, perhaps you wouldn't mind looking at the filing system yourself, Miss Metcalfe – that is, of course, if you've no other urgent, er . . .'

He was interrupted by the street door opening with a crash to admit Bernard. 'They're here!' he said, dramatically, tripping over the doormat. Miss Metcalfe ran to the open door and Mark Dunn, hearing the commotion, emerged from his office and joined her outside on the pavement from where a large, battered crew bus bearing the words '*Media Facilities*' on its side could be seen negotiating the traffic in the congested High Street. This was followed by a second similarly adorned van and a dusty BMW saloon with tinted windows. The little convoy made its way out of sight around the bend in the street and Mark returned to his office, rolling his eyes at Hugo as he went.

'I wonder where they're going?' asked Miss Metcalfe, enabling Bernard to display his recently acquired knowledge.

'The King's Arms Hotel,' he said. 'I happen to know they're staying there while they're in Hockam.'

'Poor Trish will be so cross if they start filming this afternoon while she's not here,' remarked Miss Metcalfe.

'I shouldn't think they'll start until tomorrow,' said Bernard with the air of someone who had the remotest idea what he was talking about. 'They'll need to look around a bit first, you see. Get the measure of the place, sort their equipment out and . . . that sort of thing. Still, just in case, I might slip out down to Clark's this afternoon when I get a minute. If they did happen to drop by this way, I'd hate to be seen on national TV in these shoes. My other pair's at the menders.'

'Miss Metcalfe!' Hugo's voice intruded upon their conversation and they hurried back into reception. 'The filing? When you're ready.'

Filing was not Miss Metcalfe's favourite occupation and the next hour passed slowly as she transferred folders from the old cabinet to the new, adjusting Trish's somewhat idiosyncratic concept of alphabetical order as she did so. At length, she reported completion of the task to Hugo who was staring intently at his computer screen, researching recent changes in the law relating to landlord and tenant in readiness for his two-thirty client. He looked up. 'All finished? Good. Could you ask Bernard to pop in, please? I want him to look up some references for me.'

Miss Metcalfe hurried out to the secretaries' room where Bernard's desk in the corner revealed a noticeable absence of Bernard. A brief search of the offices revealed that the trainee solicitor was not in the building and she was obliged to report the fact to Hugo who enquired as to his whereabouts.

'Well . . . I think he may have just slipped out for a moment to, er . . . well, to buy a new pair of shoes. I think, after his holiday, he felt he needed to smarten up a little and, er . . .'

Her employer sat for a moment, tapping his pen on the desk,

then looked up and spoke quietly. 'When he and Trish have returned, Miss Metcalfe, I'd like to see everyone here in my office.'

'Yes, of course, Mr Hugo. I'll let everyone know straight away.'

Hugo Dufty's office, with its book-lined walls, its dark oak furniture and its double-glazed, leaded light window over-looking the High Street was, like its occupant, deceptive to the uninitiated eye. The piles of papers spread over every available surface in apparent disarray gave an impression of muddle and disorder and yet there was an underlying air of calm reason and purpose. It was, beneath the superficial eccentricity and clutter, a place of honest rationality amidst the chaos of the modern world. It was a quiet place.

Indeed, at this moment, it was very quiet indeed. Hugo sat back in his chair, hands clasped under his chin, eyes shaded by the lock of floppy, still dark hair which fell over his brow, looking steadily at each of his employees in turn as they clustered into the cramped space in front of his desk. At length, his carefully modulated voice broke into the silence: 'I am aware that Hockam is to be visited by a television crew who plan to make a documentary film about the town and its inhabitants. I am also aware that this has engendered a certain amount of excitement among local people. This is perfectly under-standable. I imagine that some of you will be taking an interest in the activities of the television people as they go about their work . . .' Here Miss Spiers, the book-keeper, was heard to cough quietly – a cough which would later be described by Bernard among friends as a *harrumph*.

Hugo continued, unperturbed: 'I can have no objection what-ever to that interest. However . . .' and at this point, he unclasped his hands and placed them, palms down, upon the desk before him, '– I will not, under any circumstances, permit the work of this firm to be disrupted. We will continue to devote the *whole* of our working hours to the service of our clients, television crew or no television crew. It is, in point of fact, extremely unlikely that the planned documentary will be concerned with our work or, indeed, with us, but in the unlikely event that the television people should express an interest in filming in these premises, I think it fair to tell you that I would strongly resist any such intrusion. Do I make myself clear?'

The assembled staff nodded, murmuring assent and, seeing that the meeting was at an end, shuffled off to their respective tasks.

The following day, market day, dawned bright and clear and the work of Dufty Dufty Popple & Dunn proceeded in an efficient, if slightly effervescent manner. The morning's tasks were undertaken willingly and with a light heart as the sunlight streamed through the windows and the bustle of the market outside brought a lively air to even the most mundane of duties.

Towards lunchtime, the tone of the voices in the High Street seemed to undergo a change and the occasional glance out of the windows showed that the usual scattering of market-day shoppers had swelled to something approaching a crowd. The focus of their attention appeared to be located slightly further along the street, tantalisingly beyond the line of sight of the windows in the reception area but, bearing in mind Hugo's instructions, Miss Metcalfe, Trish and Bernard applied themselves diligently to their tasks, giving every appearance of concentrating solely on the job in hand. Hugo was drafting a partnership agreement for the new owners of the bakery, Miss Spiers was ferociously intent upon the quarterly VAT return and Mark Dunn, jacketless and sweating slightly, was just showing out old Mr Jacks whose testamentary instructions he had been taking since ten thirty.

'Goodbye, Mr Jacks,' Mark breezed. 'Fear not, I'll have the

codicil ready for you by next Monday and I'll pop round and go through it with you at about noon.'

The street door closed behind the old man and Mark dived into his office to reappear a moment later, buttoning his jacket and straightening his tie. 'Back about two thirty,' he mumbled to Conchita. 'Lunch appointment.'

Bernard watched through the window as Mark strode past, waving to an acquaintance on the other side of the street. It was almost twelve thirty, the time Bernard usually went to lunch. Waiting the necessary three minutes, he rose from his desk and walked, in a dignified manner through reception and out into the street where he quickened his pace in the direction Mark had taken.

Passing a TV camera set up amid the market stalls and attended by a girl smoking a cigarette and radiating an air of boredom – an impression confirmed by her tee-shirt which carried the legend *I'm bored!* in pink letters – he drew level with the Rialto Café. Through the window he could see Ashraf, his chef's hat now slightly askew, bustling among the crowded tables at one of which, as Bernard had suspected, sat Mark together with a tall, rather pale-faced man intent upon an instrument in his hand which Bernard assumed to be a Black-Berry and an attractive, fair-haired young woman who was nodding at something Mark was saying while glancing around at the occupants of other tables.

Bernard noticed that there were two unoccupied seats at their table and, on an impulse, went in. Feigning surprise at seeing Mark, he made his way over. 'Crowded in here today,' he remarked. 'Do you mind if I sit here? There don't seem to be any other . . .'

'No, sit down, old boy.' Mark waved him to one of the empty chairs. 'Bernard, this is Marianne Jacobs – she and I were at university together. Marianne is the producer/director of the TV crew who are filming a documentary here. I don't know whether you've heard about it?'

'I'd, er . . . I gathered something of the sort was, er . . . Pleased to meet you, Miss Jacobs.'

Marianne directed a radiant smile at him. 'Hello, Bernard.'

'And this,' continued Mark, indicating the tall, pale-skinned man, 'is Jonathan Tukes who's the executive producer.'

Jonathan looked up from his BlackBerry and nodded briefly in Bernard's approximate direction as Ashraf appeared with notebook and pencil. Mark took up the laminated menu card and handed it to Marianne who ordered a salad and offered the card to Jonathan who waved it away. 'I'll just have a coffee,' he said. 'Preferably a wet latte,' he added. Seeing Ashraf's bewildered expression, he sighed. 'Whatever coffee you've got.'

Mark and Bernard ordered the house special, chilli con carne, and Mark turned again to Marianne. 'So, as I was saying, most of the locals you see in here have, at some time, passed through our offices for some reason – whether a business transaction, a house sale or purchase, a dispute over a will, a neighbour dispute, a marriage break-up, a spot of trouble with the police – they all bring their problems to us. In many ways, a lawyers' office is at the very heart of village life in a place like this.'

'I thought Hockam was a town, not a village,' remarked Jonathan.

'*Hokum*,' said Bernard.

Jonathan turned to him, as if noticing him for the first time. 'What?' he snapped.

'*Hokum*,' Bernard repeated. 'It's pronounced *Hokum*.'

Mark laughed. 'The local residents do get a little pernickety about that. And, yes, it is technically a small market town but the community life here more closely resembles that of a village. I certainly feel privileged to be in a position to understand the members of that community and the interaction between them.'

'Must be interesting work,' remarked Marianne. 'Who's that

big guy over there with the moustache and the tattoos, for instance?'

'Greg Boston,' he replied. 'Builder. Looks like a bruiser but in reality he's a pussycat. When old Mrs Dunkerley's garden wall fell down, he spent a weekend rebuilding it and I happen to know he didn't charge her a penny.'

She nodded, picking at the salad Ashraf had just brought, her eyes roaming the neighbouring tables, surreptitiously studying the faces of their occupants. 'And how about the well-dressed chap talking to the blonde in the corner there . . . no, don't tell me . . . the local bank manager?'

Mark smiled at Bernard who was stifling a guffaw. 'Not quite. You don't want to know about Mr Gerard over there. He's well known to the local plod since . . .'

He broke off as a large man in a tee-shirt and jeans with two bulky black boxes slung from his brawny shoulders entered and sat down at the vacant seat at their table. He put the boxes on the floor beside him and stretched his legs out. 'What's the food like?' he asked.

'Right up your street, Bill,' said Marianne. 'Chips with everything.'

'Yeah, but how many chips?' he asked. 'I know these places, you ask for a pie and chips and you get a minuscule pie in a tiny dish and a plate full of bloody lettuce leaves with half a dozen chips on the side.'

Marianne smiled apologetically at Mark. 'This is Bill, our sound man. Bill orders food by weight, you understand. Bill, this is Mark Dunn, a solicitor from Dufty Dufty Popple & Dunn, the firm down the road. He's proving to be a fount of knowledge about the locals. And this is Bernard, who works at the same firm. Mark suggested I pop into their offices this afternoon and meet his partner, Hugo Dufty. There might be some possibilities there for a summing-up piece. What do you think, Jonathan?'

The producer, having gingerly tasted his coffee and hastily

put it down, looked up. 'Why not? You should finish the market piece in a couple of hours if you get going now. I've got a conference call at the hotel at four o'clock so you could go then if you think it's worthwhile. Bill and Dave could go and have a look at that castle or whatever it is you're doing tomorrow afternoon.'

'Manor house,' said Bernard.

Jonathan put down his BlackBerry and turned fully to Bernard. 'What?' he asked, assuming a patient expression.

Feeling himself blush slightly, Bernard explained: 'It's a manor house not a castle. I just thought . . .'

'Whatever,' said Jonathan, turning back to Marianne. 'So let me know whether you decide to do a piece at this Rufty Tufty Diddle & Bunn place.'

Bernard opened his mouth but said nothing.

'OK,' said Marianne. 'Would it be all right if I pop round at about four, then, Mark?'

'Sure,' confirmed Mark, finishing his chilli and ignoring Bernard's raised eyebrows. 'Hugo has a client at two thirty but he'll be finished well before four so I'll see you then. Ask for me at reception. We'd better be getting back, Bernard.'

'Cheers, lads,' said Bill. 'Maybe see you tomorrow, eh?'

The market was still bustling as Mark and Bernard walked back to the office. Apart from the usual shoppers looking for bargains, there were still knots of onlookers, waiting for the return of the film crew whose sole representative at present was still the girl in the *I'm bored!* tee-shirt, guarding the camera and other equipment which littered the pavement.

'I can't believe you've invited this Marianne woman to meet Hugo this afternoon,' said Bernard. 'Particularly after his rant yesterday. She's the . . . producer . . . director thingy of the TV crew, for Christ's sake! Hugo'll probably throw her out – or more likely get me to do it for him.'

Mark chuckled, comfortably. 'Marianne can talk anybody into

anything, old boy. She'll have him eating out of her hand in less than five minutes. Trust me.' Seeing Bernard's doubtful expression, he added: 'You want a chance to be on the telly, don't you?'

As they reached the office, they looked back to see Marianne in conversation with Caroline, the estate agent from the offices next door to Dufty Dufty Popple & Dunn. Caroline appeared to be pointing out the finer features of the Town Hall across the street while Marianne listened with rapt attention.

Bill, the sound man, festooned in wires and cables, was angling a microphone boom over a dazed-looking stall-keeper. A man in an anorak was fiddling with the trolley-mounted camera assisted by the bored girl who was now looking slightly more animated and a young man in an expensive-looking leather jacket and even more expensive-looking hairstyle was leaning on a car bonnet, slightly distanced from the others and speaking into a mobile phone.

Bernard pointed towards the young man. 'Isn't that . . . oh, what's his name . . . that guy who presents that quiz programme . . . used to be on Friday nights?'

'Johnnie Haines,' supplied Mark. 'I suppose he's the presenter in the documentary they're making.'

Marianne saw them and waved, mouthing the words *see you later*. She then made some whispered comment to Caroline and both women laughed uproariously.

At four twenty, the door to the secretaries' room opened and Marianne walked in, closely followed by Mark who waved his hand to take in the scene and explained: 'and this is the secretarial office. You've already met Bernard, our trainee; this is Trish, Hugo's secretary, and over here is Miss Metcalfe, who's secretary to Hugo's father, Charles Dufty, who founded the firm almost fifty years ago and still plays an active part as consultant. Miss Metcalfe also helps me out at those times when Charles is not in the office.'

Marianne flashed a smile, making eye contact with everyone. 'Hi everybody. So this is where the real work goes on, eh?' She winked, knowingly, indicating that she understood and appreciated the importance of capable behind-the-scenes organisation. Predictably, this produced a favourable response and she turned back to Mark. 'Look, I really don't want to get in the way and interrupt everyone's work so if Mr Dufty's free, perhaps we should . . .'

Mark assured her that Hugo was looking forward to meeting her and led her back into the reception area, leaving the door slightly ajar behind him, allowing Bernard, Trish and Miss Metcalfe to eavesdrop unashamedly.

Mark was heard to tap on Hugo's door before opening it and saying: 'Hugo, this is Marianne Jacobs, the friend I mentioned from my university days. I thought, while she's in Hockam . . .'

Marianne's voice was briefly audible before the door closed: 'Mr Dufty, I'm *so* pleased we could meet, Mark has told me so much . . .'

The three occupants of the secretaries' room exchanged apprehensive glances and returned to their tasks.

Wednesday morning's postbag had been unusually light and Miss Metcalfe, having opened the few letters, placed them into a wire filing tray which she handed to Trish who carried it into her boss's office in accordance with established practice.

To her surprise, Hugo, instead of sitting at his desk as normal, was standing by the window, looking out at the sunlit street. As he turned to face her, the filing tray slipped from her fingers, its carefully sorted contents scattering on the carpet.

Hugo's customary slightly crumpled dark blue suit had been replaced by a charcoal grey pinstripe three-piece, across whose waistcoat was displayed a gleaming gold watch chain; his tie was a discreet silver-grey, tied in a Windsor knot and his hair . . . in place of the unruly forelock flopping over his right eye and the stubborn tuft on the crown of his head, there was now a glistening, brilliantined coiffure, swept back elegantly on each side of a carefully judged parting. He stretched out an arm towards the falling papers, a gold cufflink catching the light and a hint of expensive cologne wafting through the air.

Slowly, and with a slightly amused expression on his beautifully shaved face, he raised an admonitory finger towards the unfortunate girl. 'Tut, tut,' he rebuked, gently. 'We don't want any carelessness like that today, Trish. Best behaviour, eh? It's most important that we show the firm in the best possible light when the television people arrive in half an hour. Now, could you ask Miss Metcalfe to ensure that the floral display in reception is in place and that there are no empty coffee cups littering the clients' waiting area as there have been of late? Mr Dunn is aware of the arrangements so I want you all to do whatever he says while the television people are in here with me. There's to be no loitering or getting in their way while they do their work. You and Miss Metcalfe will be at your desks, working and Bernard . . . well, ask Bernard to just stay out of sight – oh, and tell Conchita that I won't be taking any telephone calls for the rest of the morning.'

Trish, recovering herself, picked up the scattered letters, placed them on the desk and hurried out to spread the news to her colleagues.

Hugo's office was filled to capacity with equipment and crew. A bulky camera was set up in the centre of the room, attended by the man in the anorak, assisted by the girl in the *I'm bored!* tee-shirt. Behind the camera was a large metal stand supporting several lamps and a large shiny reflector of some kind. Bill, the sound man, was attempting to insert a small device in Hugo's back pocket and a wire up through his shirt. Marianne was talking earnestly to Johnnie Haines, the presenter, whose face was being powdered by a plump lady with a ponytail and almost every inch of floor space was littered with cables.

When Hugo, too, had received the attentions of the lady with the powder puff, Marianne introduced him to Johnnie Haines who took a seat to the side of the desk. 'Hi, Hugo,' he smiled. 'Bit chaotic in here at the moment, eh?'

Hugo, shifting his position to avoid sitting on the device in his back pocket, looked hesitant. 'Er . . . are we . . . I mean are we . . . on air?'

Marianne laughed. 'No, it's all right, Hugo. We're not *on air*. This is not live, you know, we're just going to record you talking to Johnnie and then we'll cut out anything that doesn't work and save the best bits. Absolutely nothing to worry about. You just chat to Johnnie and ignore all this lot.' She turned an enquiring glance to the man in the anorak who nodded. 'Camera speed,' he said.

She then looked at Bill who had just rigged a boom microphone high over Hugo's head. He fiddled with some knobs on a black box slung on his chest and nodded.

'So, Hugo,' began Johnnie Haines in a quiet, conversational tone, 'it's probably true to say, isn't it, that quite a large proportion of the residents of Hockam have passed through this office at some time?'

'*Hokum*,' said Hugo.

'Cut!' said Marianne. 'Johnnie, it's pronounced *Hokum* – remember?'

'Sorry,' grinned the presenter. 'So, Hugo, it's probably true to say, isn't it, that . . .'

'Cut!' said Marianne, looking at Bill who was holding up a hand and frowning at the window.

'What's that?' he said, glancing at a dial on his black box. In the silence, an intermittent squeaking could be heard from outside. Bill crossed to the window and peered out. 'Yummy mummy with a pram,' he pronounced. 'Could do with a bit of lubrication, by the sound of it. The pram, that is, not the mummy.' Satisfied, he returned to his place. 'Speeding,' he said.

'So, Hugo,' began Johnnie Haines again.

'Cut!' said Marianne. 'Hugo, could you not jump when Johnnie speaks to you. Just relax as though you're having a quiet chat. OK?'

'So, Hugo,' resumed the presenter, his professional smile still intact. 'I expect a lot of the local residents have brought their problems to you here over the years?'

'Cut!' said Marianne. 'Hugo, you aren't answering.'

'I'm sorry, I didn't think it required an answer,' replied Hugo, trying to rearrange the wire under his shirt more comfortably.

Bill was instantly at his side, reconnecting the wire to the device in Hugo's back pocket. 'Best to just leave it alone,' he explained, patiently, then returned to his place. 'OK, sound speeding,' he nodded to Marianne who smiled at Hugo and suggested, 'tell you what, Hugo. Why don't you hold the phone as though you're just finishing a conversation with a client? Then put the phone down and turn to Johnnie who'll take it from there?'

Hugo, sweating slightly, picked up the receiver and said into it: 'Yes . . . er, that's fine, Mr, er . . . I'm sorry, I can't think of a name . . .'

'Cut!' said Marianne. 'You don't need to give a name. Just say goodbye and put the phone down.'

Hugo picked up the phone again, dropped it noisily, retrieved it and was just about to say goodbye to the imaginary caller when the door of the office opened and Mr Dufty Senior entered, saw what was going on and raised both hands apologetically. 'Sorry, didn't know you were all here. I was just looking for a copy of *Kelly's Draftsman*. Make myself scarce.'

He turned to go but Marianne called out. 'Hang on, Mr, er –?'

'Dufty, Charles Dufty,' supplied the old man.

'Mr Dufty, delighted to meet you. I've heard so much about you. I gather you're the founder of the firm?'

'Er, yes. But I really don't wish to intrude. I'll leave you in peace . . . lots to do, you know.'

Marianne hurried after him. 'Mr Dufty, look, I wonder if you could spare half an hour or so. You see we're . . .' The door closed behind them, leaving Hugo, sweating more profusely now and again fiddling with the wire under his shirt.

At length, Marianne returned with Charles who was smiling urbanely and nodding to the crew.

'OK everybody,' said Marianne. 'Slight change of plan.'

～

'So I take it poor Hugo was given the old heave-ho and you replaced him in the starring role?' said Henry.

'Poor Hugo, as you call him, was relieved and delighted to be out of it. Not his cup of tea at all. What are fathers for if they can't extricate their offspring from the odd scrape here and there?'

'Anyway, you got your chance for stardom, eh? But hang on – I saw that programme. Lots of stuff about the market and the manor house and a nice interview with Caroline Adams, the estate agent, but I don't remember seeing you on it.'

Charles finished his whisky and water. 'As has been the case with many artistes before me, Henry, my best work ended up on the cutting room floor. Fancy another?'

The Right to Peaceful Enjoyment

The Dog and Tadpole's Friday bartender walked across from the bar and carefully placed Henry's gin and tonic and Charles's whisky and water on the table. Henry, who had been craning his neck to peer around the strangely deserted lounge bar, asked: 'Where is everybody tonight, Stanley? Place is like a morgue.'

'Ah, apparently, it's an open evening at the golf club, sir. Free drinks from seven 'til eight, I believe. Promotional ruse. They're trying to attract new members. I must say, I was looking forward to you two gentlemen arriving; I was beginning to feel quite lonely.'

'Ah,' said Charles, sipping gratefully at his whisky as Stanley returned to his post. 'Loneliness — now there's a terrible thing.'

Henry nodded agreement. 'Absolutely. And it's surprising how many people suffer from it — sometimes without anyone else realising it.'

'There are times,' observed Charles, warming to the theme, 'when they may not realise it themselves. As a matter of fact, I dealt with a case about a year ago — well, it was Hugo's case originally but he landed me with it — anyway, the client pitched up with a problem involving, as he thought, public nuisance. Turned out the problem was his own loneliness but he didn't realise it.'

'You see, Hugo,' said Claude Barker, 'I live next door to the Malverley Bowling Club and every Saturday they hold what they call a Social Evening on their premises, attended by most of the members and various hangers-on. There's a bar on the premises so I suppose they all get tipsy and there's singing and music and dancing until late. The racket is horrendous. I like to turn in early as a rule but there's no way I can sleep so I just turn up the television and wait till it's all over. It's getting to the stage when I dread Saturdays. What do you, as a solicitor, think I should do about it?'

Hugo Dufty considered the matter carefully and, at length, replied with a question: 'Oo hey hava lihens hor herving alcol and hinging?'

'I believe the premises are licensed, yes, though I don't know the precise terms. How do I find out? You can remove the suction, Angela. Wash out, please, Hugo.'

Hugo accepted the glass, swilled its contents round his mouth and spat into the little basin by the side of the chair. Wiping his mouth with the tissue provided, he swung his legs on to the floor to assume a sitting position. 'Well, why don't you pop into my office and we can have a chat about it?'

'Fair enough,' replied Claude. 'I've got Friday afternoon off while the decorators paint the ceiling in the waiting room. How are you fixed then?'

'Unfortunately, I shall be away on business from Thursday for a few days but I know my father will be free on Friday afternoon. I'm sure he'll be happy to see you. Shall we say three o'clock?'

'That'd be fine. Three o'clock it is. Now you'll need one more appointment to sort out that wobbly crown. Perhaps you'd see Angela on the way out.'

Mr Dufty Senior was troubled. His elbows rested on his desktop, his face buried in his hands, his fingertips absently ruffling his shaggy white eyebrows. He glanced up as his secretary, Miss Metcalfe, entered bearing an armful of files which she proceeded to slot, alphabetically, into the cabinet in the corner of the room. 'You haven't forgotten you've got a Mr Barker coming in at three o'clock, have you, Mr Dufty?'

'A Mr Barker?' repeated Mr Dufty, tugging thoughtfully at his ear. 'No, no, I haven't forgotten, Miss Metcalfe.' He again buried his face in his hands, dislodging his spectacles in the process.

'Nothing wrong, is there, Mr Dufty?' she asked as, with practised ease, she replaced the little screw that fastened the arm of her boss's spectacles and handed them back to him. 'This Mr Barker is a new client, I believe. I hope you're not expecting difficulties with him?'

He sighed. 'An ugly scene, Miss Metcalfe! An ugly scene! How can one be authorised to . . .' He broke off as the telephone rang and Miss Metcalfe answered it briefly and replaced the receiver. 'Mr Barker's here, Mr Dufty. Are you ready to see him?'

'No, not really,' he replied. 'But show him in. This other business will have to wait.'

Miss Metcalfe gave the old man a concerned look but went out and returned with Mr Claude Barker, a tall, smartly dressed man with a shiny bald head and small, delicate hands, one of which Mr Dufty Senior shook before waving him to the leather-upholstered chair in front of the desk and sitting down himself.

'Mr Barker, I gather from Hugo that you've performed wonders with his troublesome molars. I hope we, in turn, can be of some service to you. Hugo mentioned briefly the nature of your, er . . . difficulty, but perhaps you'd like to tell me in your own words.'

'Troublesome neighbours, Mr Dufty. Troublesome neighbours.' He recounted the events which formed the basis of his explanation to Hugo, expanding a little on the weekly inconvenience to him and the high level of public nuisance caused by the Saturday evening revels at the Malverley Bowling Club. 'The sound of these . . . these . . . bowling club members – most of whom are old enough to know better – laughing and singing and . . . generally making fools of themselves. Well, it's . . . it's just . . .'

'An ugly scene,' muttered Mr Dufty, stroking his forehead and staring at his desktop.

'Well, quite,' agreed Mr Barker. 'And I'm hoping you might advise me of what I can do to . . .'

'To put cover on ugly scene.' Mr Dufty's voice was barely audible.

Claude Barker looked closely at him. 'Sorry? . . . I say, are you all right, Mr Dufty?'

The old man looked up quickly, as though waking from a dream. 'What? Oh yes, I'm fine, thanks. Just got something on my mind. The Malverley Bowling Club, you say?' The other nodded and Dufty continued: 'I know the secretary, Frank Knight. He's also on the committee of the Walchester Gilbert & Sullivan Society, you know. We're putting on *The Pirates of Penzance* in September. Don't know whether you're interested in G & S but I could get a pair of tickets for you and your wife, if you . . .'

'I'm not married,' said Claude.

'Live alone?' asked Mr Dufty.

'Yes.'

'Not particularly interested in Gilbert & Sullivan?'

'No, not really.'

'What *are* your interests, Mr Barker?'

'Well, what with the practice, you know, I don't get a lot of time for outside interests.'

'Do you have any family?'

The dentist frowned. 'No, well, a nephew in Canada, but I don't really see . . .'

'Apart from the bowling club, are your other neighbours friendly?'

'Well, I really don't know, we all tend to keep ourselves to

ourselves which, I suppose, suits me. But about this problem
with . . .'

'Any plans to retire?'

Claude seemed taken aback. 'Well, no. That is, I've considered
it from time to time but . . . Well, the practice is my life and has
been for many years. If I gave it up, what would I do?' He shook
himself. 'But, Mr Dufty, I came to see you about the noise from
the bowling club. When I mentioned it to your son, Hugo, he
asked whether the club was licensed. Now, I . . .' He broke off to
stare at Mr Dufty Senior who was sitting bolt upright, staring at
a point some three feet above his client's bald head.

'That's it!' breathed the old man, raising his right forefinger.

'What's what?' asked Claude, slightly alarmed.

'*Licensed!*' cried Dufty. 'Brilliant! Look . . .' He rummaged
among the files littering his desk and uncovered the morning
newspaper folded carefully to reveal the crossword. 'You see –
authorised to put cover on ugly scene – a cover is a *lid*; rearrange
the word scene and you get *cense* – put the lid around the ugly
scene and you get *licensed* – which means *authorised*. Very neat,
that. Very neat indeed.'

Claude stared uncomprehendingly as the old solicitor
chuckled and shook his head over the crossword. 'Mr Dufty,'
he said at length, 'could I remind you that I made an appointment to see you this afternoon concerning a particular
problem which is causing me a great deal of inconvenience. I
would be grateful if . . .'

'Yes, yes, the matter of the bowling club,' Mr Dufty was
collecting himself. 'As I said, I know the secretary and I'm sure
we can come up with a solution that's satisfactory for all parties.
I suggest, I . . .'

'Mr Dufty, with all due respect, I really don't think your
simply having a quiet word with this . . . club secretary or
whoever he is, is going to result in the cancellation of these
Saturday Social Evenings, do you? I'm not here to obtain

satisfaction for all parties, I was thinking more in terms of the legal position. There's no question but that I am being greatly inconvenienced and there must be some legal redress. After all . . .'

Mr Dufty was rising. 'I think we can safely say that a satisfactory solution is to hand, Mr Barker. Can you leave it with me and I'll contact you as soon as I've had an opportunity to put matters in hand. In the meantime, perhaps a pair of those earplug devices you sometimes see people using on aeroplanes might help – purely as a temporary measure, of course. Well, I'll be in touch.'

Tuesday was not Claude Barker's favourite day of the week. There was something about the way that Tuesday was sneaked in between Monday and Wednesday that made one distrust it, he reflected. Monday was the start of the week's work – whether one liked it or not, one had to buckle down and get on with it. Wednesday was the halfway mark – if one had got thus far, one could complete the week. Tuesday, however, was neither fish nor fowl; what was the point of it?

These inconsequential thoughts floated through Claude Barker's head as he squirted the air out of a hypodermic and bent over the open mouth of the first patient of the day. 'Just relax and you'll hardly feel a thing.' The words dropped out unconsciously, the product of over thirty-five years of doing the job. The manner easy and professional, the touch sure and practised as it directed the needle to its precise destination, the mind unstretched and unfettered as it continued to explore the ridiculous banality, the sheer 'Tuesdayness' of Tuesdays.

'There we are, that's the hard part done. Now just lie back and think of England for a few minutes – or better still think of somewhere other than England – the Caribbean, for instance, or the South of France. Where do you usually holiday?'

Having asked the question and thereby diverted the patient's

75

attention from matters dental, Claude returned to his musings on the subject of Tuesdays. They were, after all, such dismal, mean-spirited days with no particular distinguishing character-istics. But there again, the rest of the week wasn't particularly notable for its diversity nowadays – featureless. Except, of course, for Saturdays with their customary racket from the bowling club next door and . . . 'Blast!'

He bent to pick up the hypodermic as his patient was halfway through a description of the Tuscan hotel which he had visited the previous month. 'Sounds wonderful,' Claude enthused. 'I've never been to Tuscany but I've heard it's very beautiful.'

'Wonderful place,' confirmed Frank. 'We've stayed there in the same hotel for the past three years and I can thoroughly recommend it. I could let you have the details . . .'

'Well, that's kind of you,' said Claude, 'but I'm a bachelor, you see, and I usually just have a week in Bournemouth. Little B & B belonging to a former patient. It's very quiet but it suits me. But I'm sure Tuscany is perfect for you and your wife.'

'Oh, no – I've been a widower for about twelve years now. I go to Tuscany with a few friends each year – we're all members of the same club, you see; all either bachelors or widowers and we just enjoy a couple of weeks in peaceful surroundings, good conversation, plenty of good food and the odd drop of vino, perhaps a day's jaunt into Florence to see the sights. I could look out the brochures for the hotel we use if you like,' offered the patient.

'Well, I must admit, I've always wanted to see Florence. The Ponte Vecchio, the Uffizi, the Duomo. Perhaps, one day . . . Open wide, please, that's it. Angela, could you adjust the chair down a little. Now, this won't take long . . .'

Time passed, the silence broken only by the drone of the drill, the gurgle of the suction tube under the patient's tongue and the occasional rattle of instruments on the plastic tray close to Claude's hand.

'Right, that's it, Mr er . . .'

'Knight,' supplied the patient, 'Frank Knight.'

'Mr Knight. Might be a little uncomfortable for a few hours but then you should have no more trouble.'

'Feels absolutely fine,' confirmed the patient, getting up from the chair and taking his jacket from the peg on the door. 'Charles obviously knows a good dentist when he sees one.'

'Charles?' queried Claude.

'Charles Dufty. Solicitor. Dufty Dufty Popple & Dunn in the High Street.'

'Yes, I know who he is but . . .'

'It was Charles who recommended me to you. Said his son Hugo was a changed man since you've been looking after his teeth.'

'Ah, yes. Hugo's been a patient of mine for a few years now. Well, you shouldn't have any more problems with that filling but if you do feel any discomfort just give me a call. We'll drop you a line in twelve months or so to remind you to pop in for a check-up. Perhaps you'll see Mr Knight out, Angela.'

The surgery door closed but opened again briefly and the patient's head appeared briefly. 'I'll try and remember to let you have those Tuscany brochures as soon as I can.'

'Oh, yes . . . but don't go to any trouble . . .' The door closed again and the dentist returned to washing his hands and sorting his instruments ready for the next patient.

Claude completed the washing-up after his Friday evening meal of egg and chips, dried his hands on the damp tea towel and returned to the sitting room where the TV was showing a round-up of the day's news. Resisting the temptation to subside into his customary armchair, he reached for the letter which lay on top of the week's newspapers on the coffee table. He reread its contents:

Dear Mr Barker,

Following our conversation when you visited these offices on the 3rd inst. and our subsequent telephone conversation of today's date, I confirm that an appointment has been made for us both to meet with the secretary of the Malverley Bowling Club on Friday 15th inst. at 8.00 p.m. at the bowling club premises. The purpose of the meeting is to discuss the problems arising from the bowling club's Saturday evening Social Events and I confidently anticipate a satisfactory outcome for all parties. I look forward to seeing you then.

Yours sincerely,

Charles Dufty

Sighing deeply, he walked into the hall, straightened his tie in the mirror and, taking his briefcase from the hall stand, opened the front door and passed out into the front garden, down the path, turned right on to the pavement and, almost immediately, right again through the gates of the Malverley Bowling Club.

Surprisingly, despite having lived in the house next door for over twenty years, this was the first time Claude had trod this gravel drive. Turning the corner around the clubhouse, he saw that the evening sun behind the tall poplars was casting long, graceful shadows across the bowling green. A wooden verandah ran the length of the clubhouse and, through an open door, a murmur of conversation was audible, punctuated occasionally by gentle laughter or the clink of glasses.

His reverie was interrupted by a voice behind him: 'Pleasant evening, isn't it?'

He turned to see an elderly man wearing a panama hat sitting on one of the deckchairs that lined the verandah.

'It is, indeed,' replied Claude, returning his gaze to the smooth expanse of green and the poplars beyond.

The man in the panama continued: 'I often come and sit out

here just to enjoy the view and the air. Don't remember seeing you before. Are you a new member?'

'No, no. Not a bowls player, I'm afraid. No, I'm here on, er . . . on business.'

'Sorry,' the old man raised a hand, 'I just assumed. Actually, I'm not a bowls player either these days. Used to play a bit but the old back's not what it used to be, so now I just come along for the company. They're a good crowd. Nice to have a bit of decent conversation sometimes, isn't it?'

'Ah, Claude. There you are.' Charles Dufty's genial features appeared round the clubhouse door. And then disappeared again. 'Frank,' he called, 'Claude's here. Shall we join him out on the verandah?'

He reappeared with Claude's patient of a few days earlier. 'Claude, I gather you already know Frank here, having very recently replaced a troublesome filling or something. Can I get you a drink?'

Claude shook hands with Frank. 'Er . . . well, I suppose a small glass of white wine would be . . .'

'No sooner said than done.' Charles returned to the clubhouse, leaving Claude and Frank to seat themselves in deckchairs next to the man in the panama. 'Well, I must say, Claude,' said Frank, 'I've had no more trouble from this tooth since you sorted it out for me. I can eat anything now!'

'Oh, so you're a dentist?' said the man in the panama. 'Should have recognised that, I suppose.' Seeing Claude's questioning look, he went on: 'Was in the profession myself for nearly forty years until I retired almost ten years ago. Albert Pinkerton. We must have a chat some time. I'd be interested to hear how things have moved on over the past decade – as I presume they have?'

'Claude Barker,' said Claude, shaking the man's hand, 'and, yes, there have been a number of important developments over the past ten years. Have you heard, for instance about the advances in . . .'

'Ah, so Albert here has spotted a fellow dentist already, I see!' Charles Dufty emerged from the bar bearing a tray of drinks which he proceeded to distribute among the assembled company. 'Takes one to know one, I suppose. Well, while you two debate the respective merits of filling compounds or whatever, Frank and I have a little business to discuss and then it'll be time for our meeting, Claude. I'll give you a shout in five minutes or so, if that's all right?'

Charles and Frank disappeared into the clubhouse leaving the two dentists to compare experiences and swap professional anecdotes. Time passed swiftly and Charles's head soon reappeared around the clubhouse door. 'Ready when you are, Claude,' he smiled, standing back to allow the other to pass into the softly lit bar area. 'Just through there,' he directed, nodding in the direction of a door which stood half open.

Claude entered a small room containing a desk and three comfortable armchairs. The walls were lined with shelves bearing trophies of various shapes and sizes. In one of the armchairs sat Frank Knight who grinned at Claude and motioned him to one of the other chairs. Claude sat down, as bidden, and Charles Dufty claimed the third chair.

Claude nodded to Frank: 'So you're a member here?' he asked.

'Indeed, I am,' replied Frank, holding up a bundle of brightly coloured leaflets. 'And I've remembered to bring those hotel brochures I mentioned to you.'

Claude took them. 'Thank you,' he said, placing them in his pocket. 'That's very thoughtful. I must say, our conversation about Florence has reawakened my interest in Italian art and European history in general – a subject which I've always found fascinating. I may even think about forsaking my usual B & B in Bournemouth next year and holidaying in Tuscany.'

'Splendid idea,' replied Frank. 'Have a look through them and let me know what you think. If you're interested, you might consider joining us next year. Albert, who you've just been talking to, will be coming and one or two others who you haven't met yet.'

'Well, that's very kind of you but I wouldn't want to intrude. I'm not a member of the bowling club, after all and . . .'

'Well, that's very easily rectified, you know. We can sign you up tonight, if you . . .'

Claude held up his hand. 'I'm afraid I've never even held a . . . bowling ball or whatever they're called.'

'That's no obstacle, I can assure you,' chuckled Frank. 'About twenty per cent of the members here are not regular bowlers anyway. They really come along for the social side of things – or at least they have done so up to now . . .' He trailed off with a slightly sad expression.

'Speaking of the social aspect of the club,' began Charles, 'we mustn't forget that Claude and I are here for a reason.'

'Quite,' agreed Claude. 'I understood from your letter, Charles, that we were to meet with the club secretary to discuss the problems associated with the noise from these Saturday evening social events.' He glanced at the empty chair behind the desk. 'I take it the secretary will be joining us?'

'He's here already,' Charles said, inclining his head towards Frank who raised his eyebrows and spread his hands: 'I'm so sorry, Claude, I thought you knew. Yes, I'm currently club secretary, for my sins. And, of course, Charles has explained to me that you live next door and that you are inconvenienced by the noise levels at our little Saturday evening soirees.'

'Well, yes,' Claude confirmed. 'To be quite honest, er . . . Frank, it's getting to the stage where I dread Saturday evenings. I prefer to live quietly and I like to think that I respect the right of others to do the same. It does seem unfair that I am subjected to . . .'

Frank held up a placatory hand. 'I quite agree with you, Claude. It's quite outrageous that you have been inconvenienced to such an extent – and in your own home! Indeed, had I been aware of this, I would certainly have stepped in to find a solution. And I know that my fellow members would share that view. However, such an intervention on my part will, in the event, be unnecessary. You see, tomorrow's Saturday Social Evening will be the last. Indeed, the club will be holding no further organised social events for the foreseeable future.'

Claude's mouth remained open for a moment before he spoke: 'Well, I . . . I wouldn't wish to see your club's social activities cease completely. I'm sure there must be some way of . . .'

'No, no,' replied Frank. 'I assure you the problem is not in any way of your making. You see our entertainments secretary, Albert – the retired dentist you met – announced his intention of standing down some months ago and, unfortunately, none of the members have stepped forward to replace him. Albert had served in the role for some five years and he feels he's getting a bit long in the, er, tooth for it, so to speak. There's a fair bit of work involved, organising the club's social calendar – not just the Saturday evening get-togethers but the various other events which take place all year, corresponding with other clubs to arrange joint activities and so on. Then there's the Christmas and New Year parties and the club's Anniversary Dinner. Obviously, we must all respect Albert's wish to take things easy – he is getting on a bit and his health's not as good as it was – but, in the absence of anyone to step into the breach, the club must abandon its hard-earned reputation as a social as well as a sporting institution. From now on, Claude, the only sound you'll hear from us is the occasional click of bowls on the green.'

There was silence, broken eventually by Charles. 'Well, I'm sorry to hear of the club's difficulties of course, Frank, but this does seem to provide the solution to my client's problem. Claude?'

The dentist sighed heavily and nodded. 'Well, yes it does. Although, I have to say that I'm surprised that none of the members are sufficiently concerned about their club to take on the job of entertainments secretary. I'm quite sure there must be ways of continuing the club's recreational activities while ensuring that neighbouring residents are not overly inconvenienced. I remember, many years ago, I was a member of a local arts appreciation group and, as their social secretary, I was responsible for organising get-togethers and so on and, while some of our events were far from staid, we seldom attracted complaints from neighbours. But, there it is, I suppose. As you say, Charles, from my own point of view, my problem is solved.'

Charles rose. 'Well, thank you, Frank, for explaining the position to us. I don't think we need detain you further.'

Frank walked to the door and saw the other two to the door of the clubhouse. 'I'm so sorry you've been inconvenienced, Claude. If Albert had known about it sooner, I'm sure he'd have taken the matter very seriously and done whatever he could to remedy matters.'

The men shook hands and turned to walk down the verandah steps but Frank called after them: 'Claude, er . . . I don't suppose . . .' He walked down the steps to them. 'I don't suppose you'd be free to pop along tomorrow evening as my guest? As it's the last Saturday Social, I'd very much like to buy you a drink and introduce you to the reprobates who've been unwittingly disrupting your evenings on a weekly basis. They're not really such a bad bunch, you know.'

Claude scratched his nose. 'Well, I think I'm free tomorrow evening. I might just slip round briefly – as it's to be the last time.'

'Splendid!' said Frank. 'We generally kick off at about seven but do pitch up whenever you can. Look forward to seeing you.'

~

Henry Middleton finished his gin and tonic and began to set up the chess pieces. 'So did Claude go to the Saturday Social?'

'Oh, yes,' answered Charles. 'From what I hear, he enjoyed a very pleasant evening. After several "small white wines", he was explaining to Frank how the club's social calendar should be organised and after several more "small white wines" he agreed not only to become a member but also to take on the job of entertainments secretary. After several more "small white wines", he apparently led a group of the younger members in a demonstration of Greek dancing and rounded the evening off by organising a conga line out of the clubhouse, around the bowling green, out of the north entrance, along the road and back via the south entrance. It's your move.'

'Does he still have the surgery in the High Street?' asked Henry. 'I've had a bit of trouble with that bridgework I had done last year in Walchester.'

'No, he sold the practice a few months ago. He's holidaying in Tuscany now, I gather, with Frank Knight and a few other club members.'

Henry moved his king pawn two squares. 'I've a feeling this game could last a bit longer than last week's.'

'Hope not,' said Charles. 'I've a ten-thirty appointment at the office tomorrow. New client.'

'Anything interesting?' asked Henry.

'Could be,' replied Charles, carefully moving his queen knight over his line of pawns. 'This fellow's complaining about the noise on Saturday evenings from the bowling club two doors away from him.'

The Right to Silence

Henry breezed into the lounge bar of the Dog and Tadpole, took off his overcoat and sat down at the usual corner table where Charles broke off from setting up the chessboard to peer over his glasses at his old friend. 'Do I detect a frisson of excitement?' asked Charles. 'You look like my grandson preparing to open his Christmas presents.'

Henry opened his briefcase and drew out a roll of cardboard which he spread out on the table, knocking over most of the chess pieces in the process. 'What do you think of that?'

Charles adjusted his spectacles, peered at the fading school photograph and broke into a broad smile. 'Good God! There's Chunky Charleson . . . and Carrots Campbell – and isn't that Snotty Potterton?'

Henry beamed and nodded. 'We're in it, too – sixth and eleventh from the left, third row. Found it in the attic while I was looking for my old school reports.'

'Why, in the name of all that's rational, were you looking for your old school reports?'

'Ah, well, I've been asked to pop along to Speech Day at the old school next Saturday to spout a few words of wisdom at the assembled company. Thought I'd take as my theme the school motto, "Semper Veritas" – Always the Truth. Stir up a few guilty consciences among the little blighters, eh?'

Charles drew a swift intake of breath. 'Tricky subject, that.'

Henry frowned at him. 'Tricky subject? That's one of the few

85

things from school that's stood me in good stead ever since. What's wrong with telling the truth? You're a solicitor, for heaven's sake – "the truth, the whole truth and so on and so forth" – surely that's exactly what we're supposed to drum into the little stinkers. Why are you shaking your head?'

'Ever heard of the right to silence?' asked Charles, sipping at his whisky and water.

'What's that got to do with anything?' enquired Henry.

'You're an honest man, Henry, but you were a GP for about a hundred and fifty years. Throughout that time, when faced with the family of a patient, were you always willing to trot out the truth about his or her condition?'

Henry blew out his cheeks. 'Well, no, patient confidentiality and so forth. But I never told lies.'

'I'm not advocating telling lies,' said Charles. 'It's just that now and then the best and most honourable course is to say nothing. Dashed complicated business sometimes, as my son Hugo discovered recently. If I were you, I'd choose another topic for your speech – how about "Some Things Are Best Left Unsaid"?'

~

'It's certainly a lovely view,' remarked Emily Jardine as she peered over the top of her reading glasses at the line of wooded hills visible through the bedroom window.

Mrs Frankland beamed widely. 'Yes, Jack and I wake up to it every morning. I must admit we'll miss it.'

'But you're not selling the house,' pointed out Emily, 'only renting it out for a year, as I understand it – you could always move back after that, couldn't you?'

'Yes, but Jack's always had a hankering to retire to the south coast so we're going to rent somewhere down there while we decide whether we want to stay permanently, in which case we'll sell this and buy a place there.'

'Well, I suppose I'm doing the same thing in reverse,' Emily said. 'That's why I'm looking for somewhere to rent in this area. And from what I've seen so far, this house may be just the kind of thing I have in mind.'

'Oh, but you haven't yet seen what I think is the best thing about the house – the kitchen. I've kept that until last. I don't know whether you're interested in cooking?' asked Mrs Frankland as she led the way downstairs and along a passage.

Emily smiled, 'I suppose I ought to be, in view of . . . well . . . is this real parquet flooring, by the way?'

Mrs Frankland looked at her curiously. 'You were about to mention something about cooking?' she said as they entered the spacious, beautifully equipped kitchen. 'You said you ought to be interested in cooking in view of . . .'

'Oh, yes. It's just that my son, Carl, is a chef so, obviously I . . .'

The effect of this upon Mrs Frankland was considerable. Her jaw dropped open and she gazed at Emily, wide-eyed. 'Of course, the name . . . your son is Carl Jardine, the celebrity chef! We never miss his programmes – that one the other week when he was on a cruise ship was just brilliant and that other one when he was at a ski lodge cooking for those youngsters – he's got such a way with him, hasn't he? *Jack!* She called to her husband who was carrying a basket of logs to the sitting room. He appeared in the kitchen doorway. 'I heard,' he said, smiling and advancing towards Emily, hand outstretched. 'Nice to meet you, Mrs Jardine. As a matter of fact, you know our daughter, Kelly, though you wouldn't have realised that's who she was.'

'Oh, yes, of course!' said Mrs Frankland. 'I'd quite forgotten. Kelly is one of the assistants at Melanie's Boutique in Walchester.' Seeing Emily's frown, she went on: 'Kelly's the short, dark one. I gather you're quite a regular there. Kelly often comes round to share some cooking tip of Carl's that you've passed on to her. What a coincidence us meeting.'

Emily's frown deepened. 'I'm sorry, Mrs Frankland, there

must be some misunderstanding. I've never been to – what was it, Melanie's Boutique? In fact, I've only ever been to Walchester a couple of times – I haven't yet moved into the area.'

There followed a short silence, broken by Mr Frankland: 'How very odd. Kelly and the other assistants were quite sure that . . . Apparently, Mrs Jardine – or, at least, the woman who . . . Well, it seems she comes in quite frequently and . . . Well, anyway, have you seen the sitting room yet?'

At this point, Emily was beginning to feel annoyed and could see that her hosts were embarrassed. She therefore excused herself, explaining that she had an appointment to view another property, leaving Mr and Mrs Frankland to wonder what on earth was going on.

Hugo, the younger Dufty of Dufty Dufty Popple & Dunn, solicitors and commissioners for oaths, leant forward in his chair, elbows resting on his desk, chin propped on clasped hands and brow furrowed in concentration as Emily explained the reason for her visit.

As her story drew to a close, Hugo leant back in his chair, swept back a lock of floppy dark hair and exhaled slowly. 'So, on the evidence of Mr and Mrs Frankland, it would seem that someone is . . .'

'Going around pretending to be me!' Emily's anger was now coming to the surface. At first, the Franklands' revelations had been puzzling but her subsequent musings on the subject had given rise to surprise and then to irritation which was now turning to outrage. 'Firstly, why on earth would anyone *want* to pass themselves off as me and, secondly – *how dare they*? It's very disconcerting knowing that, at this moment, some woman is using my name and claiming to be my son's mother! Really, Mr Dufty, this has got to be stopped.'

Hugo nodded. 'Of course, of course, Mrs Jardine. I quite understand how you must feel. However, we must remember that sometimes things are not quite as they appear. If it's the case that an impostor is using your identity for financial gain, for instance, or, by her own actions, endangering your own reputation in some way, then clearly, firm action is needed. But we must first do all we can to establish the facts. At present, all we know is that Kelly Frankland has mentioned certain incidents to her parents who have, in turn, relayed these incidents to you. It may be that Mr and Mrs Frankland misinterpreted something their daughter said or, indeed that Kelly herself misunderstood the woman in the shop.'

'Are you saying I should just assume it was some sort of mix-up and forget about it?' asked Emily, somewhat tetchily.

'No, no!' Hugo assured her. 'On the contrary, I think we should, as I said earlier, do all we can to establish the facts. To that end, may I suggest I talk to Kelly Frankland to ascertain the precise nature of the incidents in question? We will then be in a better position to consider the matter further.'

Emily thought for a moment, then agreed to the arrangement. 'But, Mr Dufty, if I find that someone has been going about claiming to be me and taking my son's name in vain, then I shall expect the full weight of the law to be visited upon their head . . . from a very great height!'

'So you see, Kelly, we seem to have a problem,' said Hugo as he accepted a cup of tea from Mrs Frankland and placed it carefully on the coffee table in front of him.

Kelly was a short, rather pretty girl with long, dark hair which she was now twisting round her fingers as she frowned at Hugo. 'Well, this other woman – your client,' she said. 'You say she claims to be Carl Jardine's mother but how do we know that *she's* not the impostor and that the lady who comes into the boutique is not the *real* Mrs Jardine? We see her quite regularly and she's always really nice. She doesn't brag about her son or anything but we're all fans in the shop and we always ask her what he's up to and she tells us. Once, her mobile rang when she was in the shop and it was Carl on the line.'

'How did you know it was Carl?' asked Hugo.

'Well, because she said "hello, Carl" when she answered the phone. Then she was chatting away for some minutes, asking him what time he was going to be home and stuff like that. Her name *is* Jardine anyway because it's on her cheques and on her debit card.'

'You say she visits the shop quite often?' said Dufty.

'Yes, at least once a week – usually on Friday afternoons and sometimes on other days, too. We always look forward to her coming in, what with her being Carl Jardine's mum and everything. We're always on at her to bring him in with her if ever he's at home and she always laughs and says "well, perhaps one day but he's always so busy filming, you know". She's so nice, Mr Dufty. I really can't believe she's lying to us all – why would she do that, anyway? It's not as though she's using who she is to get free goods or anything. She pays for everything she has.'

Hugo considered. 'You say she usually visits the boutique on Friday afternoons?'

Kelly nodded. 'That's right, so she'll almost certainly be in tomorrow.'

'Unfortunately, I shall be with a client tomorrow afternoon,' said Hugo, 'but would there be any objection if I arrange for someone else from my office to pop round to the boutique at around lunchtime on Friday so as to be there when the lady in question comes in?'

Kelly looked doubtful. 'What would this other person do – would he sort of challenge her?'

'Good Lord, no. Nothing so dramatic. The idea would simply be to observe, to hear anything that's said and be able to identify the lady if necessary in the future. I can assure you there would be no embarrassment or, indeed, any disruption to the business of the boutique.'

'Well . . .' Kelly's tone was still a little dubious but Hugo's smile reassured her. 'All right, then.'

Even for a Friday, Melanie's Boutique was unusually bustling with the female of the species, from teenage girls, hoping to steal a march on their peers by snapping up the latest line in designer jeans, to ladies of 'a certain age' looking for something 'that little bit different' for their nephew's wedding. Kelly Frankland and her two fellow assistants flitted around the cramped space, making a suggestion here, an adjustment there, perhaps offering a complimentary word to a favoured customer.

As Kelly replaced an item in the window, she caught sight of Bernard Summers. She and Bernard had attended the same school, still had several mutual friends and met up occasionally at pubs, clubs or parties. He was standing on the pavement outside, wearing sunglasses and looking vaguely furtive. As she waved to him, he removed his sunglasses and, with a barely noticeable jerk of his head, signalled to her to join him.

Frowning, she looked around to make sure her colleagues were coping and then slipped out through the shop door. Bernard took her arm and led her into the alleyway which led to the small storeroom behind the shop, ignoring her protests to the effect that she was busy and couldn't talk now and, in any case, what did he think he was playing at?

In the more private environment afforded by the alleyway, he again removed his sunglasses and explained to her that he was on an undercover job and needed her help.

She giggled, despite her annoyance. 'What are you talking about? Is this some sort of . . . oh!' Her expression cleared suddenly. 'Hang on, you work at Dufty Dufty Popple & Dunn, don't you? Have you come to spy on that nice Mrs Jardine?'

The young trainee solicitor shushed her, looking furtively around the deserted passage. 'Yes on both counts but I need your help. If I'm going to hear what this woman says, I need to be in the shop but the problem is I'd stand out like a . . . well, like a man in a ladies' boutique.'

Kelly giggled again. 'Well, we could put a wig on you, stand you in a corner and pretend you were a dummy. We could even . . .'

Bernard flushed. Kelly was obviously not appreciating the seriousness of his mission. 'Look, all I need is for you to let me in the back door so that I can watch and listen from the little room behind the shop. When the lady in question comes in, you just give me the nod, OK?'

She rolled her eyes. 'All right, come on then.'

She led him round the back of the building to a door at the side of the storeroom. This led to an even smaller room containing a table and four chairs, a sink and a worktop on which stood an electric kettle, a carton of milk and several chipped mugs. A door with a glass panel provided a view of the shop from which the sound of voices was clearly audible.

'Perfect!' said Bernard, sitting at the table. 'How about a cuppa?'

'Good idea,' agreed Kelly. 'We all have milk and no sugar except Tracey, who takes it black. Careful with the switch on the kettle, it sometimes crackles a bit. See you!' With that, she disappeared into the shop to resume her duties.

Some minutes later, a tap on the glass panel roused Bernard from the reverie into which he had fallen while waiting for the kettle to boil. Kelly's face appeared round the door. 'She's here – Mrs Jardine!' The door closed again.

Bernard rose quickly and peered through the glass. Kelly and another of the assistants were chatting animatedly to a short, rather frail, white-haired woman whose eyes looked tired but crinkled pleasingly at the corners when she smiled. 'I'm only looking today,' she confided to Kelly. 'I'm determined to be strict with myself for a while as a penance for buying that very expensive blouse last week. Mind you, I do like those skirts.'

'Yes, they're lovely,' agreed Kelly. 'New in this week – just your colour as well. Did, er . . . did Carl like the new blouse?'

'Oh, he hasn't seen it yet,' replied the woman. 'He's only just got back from filming in Finland, of all places and I probably won't see him until next week or the week after. He fits me in when he can, bless him. How much are those skirts?'

Bernard pressed his face awkwardly against the glass panel to keep the woman in view as she moved towards the skirt rack in the corner of the little boutique with her back to him. Then she turned to face Kelly who was standing by the door into the back room, holding up an embroidered shawl. Bernard seized the moment and held up his mobile phone, taking a photograph of the woman full face through the glass. She and Kelly chatted for a few more minutes but Bernard had what he needed and left via the storeroom to hurry back to the office where Conchita, the receptionist, and Hugo's secretary, Trish, were huddled in conversation.

'He's so much smaller in real life,' Trish was saying.

'Yes, but he is so good looking,' pointed out Conchita, 'and so charming when he speak and when he smile . . .' She rolled her eyes in a particularly Latin manner. 'He can cook for me a paella any time!'

Bernard broke in upon the girlish laughter. 'So this is how you talk about me while I'm out,' he nodded understandingly. 'Bit rusty on the paella but I can rustle up a passable toad-in-the-hole if you're free this evening, Conchita.'

The girls regarded him with undisguised contempt. 'We were talking about Carl Jardine,' said Trish, 'who is . . .' she paused, theatrically, 'at this moment in with Mr Hugo.'

Bernard frowned. 'Carl Jardine is here?'

'Yes,' answered Trish. 'He rang this morning and asked to see Mr Hugo on an important matter. He arrived about ten minutes ago and he's just gone in to Mr Hugo.'

*

'As I'm sure you'll appreciate, Mr Jardine, I'm not in a position to discuss the matters upon which Mrs Jardine consulted me.' Hugo Dufty's expression was bland and yet indicated quite clearly that he was not, under any circumstances, to be contradicted.

Carl, on the other hand, leant back comfortably in his chair, one arm draped over the back of it, legs crossed, blond head tilted to one side as he gazed at Hugo. 'I'm not here to discuss your conversations with Mrs Jardine, Mr Dufty. It might not have occurred to you that Mrs Jardine may have discussed the matters to which you refer with me, her son, in rather greater detail than with you, her solicitor. My mother is, perfectly understandably, upset that someone is, as she sees it, going around claiming to be her. She is hurt and this concerns me.'

Dufty regarded him carefully and, after a pause, said: 'Clearly, your mother has confided in you and you obviously have her interests at heart. You may be interested to learn that a member of my staff has been carrying out some enquiries this afternoon at the boutique where the woman has been impersonating your mother and I have high hopes that he may have ascertained her identity. Indeed, he may have returned to the office by now – I'll find out . . .' He reached for the internal phone.

'There's no need for that, Mr Dufty. In fact, I would prefer that you drop the matter as from now and carry out no further action in the matter.'

The solicitor paused, his hand resting on the telephone. 'That, I would have thought, Mr Jardine, is for your mother to decide. If she instructs me to drop the matter then so be it, but until then I must carry out my instructions. May I, as a matter of interest, enquire why you are so anxious that the activities of the woman in the boutique should remain uninvestigated?' Hugo rested his elbows on his desk, his hands pressed together and his index fingers resting on the tip of his nose.

After a pause, Carl Jardine replied: 'Because the woman in the boutique is . . . my mother.'

Hugo's head dropped an inch, causing the index finger of his right hand to enter his right nostril. Fumbling in his pocket for a handkerchief, he blinked through watering eyes at the young man. 'Your . . . mother? But . . . who is my client?'

'She's my mother, too,' replied Carl. 'You see, I suppose it could be said that I'm a very fortunate man in that I have two mothers.' Seeing the solicitor's blankly helpless expression, he felt the need to elucidate. Leaning forward and drawing a deep breath, he went on: 'It all began at my father's twenty-first birthday party when he met a girl, Catherine, who fell for his manly charms – he was a good-looking fellow in those days and Catherine was considered by his peers to be quite a stunner, though she was engaged to the second son of the Marquis of Herewardshire. The party got a little bit out of hand and . . . well, a little while later, Catherine discovered she was pregnant. My father was an honourable man and they married some three months before I was born. That was, apparently, how things worked in those days.

'Catherine's former fiancé was, to put it mildly, rather annoyed and made things very difficult for my father in his business activities – he ran a catering firm – and refused to give up his claims on Catherine. The strains on the marriage became intolerable with the result that Catherine left my father – and, indeed, me, when I was barely two years old only to find that the Marquis's son, having wreaked his revenge on my father, emigrated to New Zealand without her to expand the family's shipping company. My father was so traumatised by all that had happened that he moved with me to London, divorced Catherine and married Emily, who brought me up as her own, believing my father to be a widower – a belief fostered by my father.

'My father died five years ago. I happened to find some papers in his study which hinted at the events I've just described and I determined to find out what had happened to Catherine. To cut a long story short, I tracked her down and found that she had been so affected by her marriage, my birth and subsequent events that she had suffered a breakdown and had, for some years, been a patient in a mental institution. Our reunion was an emotional affair and the fact that I was sympathetic and understood her situation meant so much to her that I've carried on seeing her ever since.'

Hugo drew a deep breath. 'So the woman in the shop was, in fact . . .'

'Catherine, my mother,' nodded Carl.

'And Emily, my client, is your stepmother.'

'Correct. Although I've always regarded her as my mother. So, you see, I have, in effect, two mothers, either of whom is perfectly entitled to proclaim herself as such.'

The solicitor rubbed his eyes vigorously. 'But surely Emily must have suspected who the woman in the shop was?'

Carl shook his head. 'Emily always believed Catherine died before she, Emily, married my father. You see, my relationship with Catherine, my birth mother, has been without the knowledge of Emily, my stepmother. I've deliberately kept it that way to avoid hurting either of them. It's worked beautifully for some years now. I'm very fond of both of them and they're each so proud of what I've achieved in my career and . . . But now this business of Emily believing someone – my mother – has been impersonating her has really put the cat among the pigeons.'

Hugo's frown deepened. 'Well, what can I do about it?' he asked. 'Emily has instructed me to look into this imposture business; I now discover that the impostor is, in fact, your mother. I don't feel I can tell Emily that because that would be interfering in a very complex family situation and going against your quite understandable wishes. The problem isn't just going to go away, is it?'

Carl ran a hand through his hair, stared at his feet and

seemed to come to a decision. 'Yes, the problem *is* going to go away, Mr Dufty. Can you meet me in the High Street car park at six this evening? I want to take you for a ride.'

Despite his bafflement at the turn of events, Hugo found himself relaxing into the beautifully upholstered passenger seat of Carl's convertible as it purred smoothly through country lanes. Carl was silent as he drove and Hugo still had no idea where they were going or why. He sensed that all would be made clear in due course and there was no point in trying to accelerate the process by questioning. He contented himself, therefore, by watching the countryside flashing by and enjoying the ride.

At length, Carl swung the car into the drive fronting an impressive half-timbered house, applied the handbrake, switched off the engine and turned to Hugo. 'This is where my mother lives,' he said.

'Catherine?' asked Hugo.

Carl nodded. 'I bought the place for her a few months ago and I come and see her here as often as I can. I'd like to introduce you to her.'

They got out of the car and walked towards the house which Hugo could see was, if not large, very beautiful, with overhanging gables and leaded windows overlooking charmingly laid out gardens. 'Your mother lives here alone?' he asked.

'No, she has company, as you'll see.' Carl knocked on the door which was opened by a middle-aged woman who greeted Carl with a smile. 'I'm so glad you could come. Your mother will be absolutely delighted. I haven't told her you were coming.'

'How is she, Nancy?' asked Carl as they passed into the hall.

'Not too bad, considering. She's tired of course because she had her weekly trip into Walchester this afternoon. She does so love to go shopping at that little boutique in Station Street. They know her there and she has a laugh with the girls. She still looks forward to her Friday afternoon outings. I drove her home about an hour ago.'

She opened a door which led into a spacious, low-ceilinged room, elegantly furnished and lit by firelight from the hearth. In an armchair sat a frail figure with a blanket over her knees, reading a book. She looked up when they entered and her pale features dissolved into a smile as she saw Carl. He crossed the room and kissed her gently on the forehead. 'I gather you've been out on the town again this afternoon,' he scolded. 'Don't you go overdoing it or you'll be too exhausted to entertain me when I call.'

She smiled at him, her faded eyes crinkling at the corners. 'I'll never be too tired to see you, my darling. How was Finland?'

'Oh, OK,' he answered. 'Just the usual stuff, you know. I'll tell you all about it when I come to stay tomorrow.' He turned to Hugo. 'Mum, this is a friend of mine, Hugo Dufty. Hugo, this is Catherine, my mother.'

Hugo approached and took her proffered hand, surprised at its dry frailness. 'It's a pleasure to meet you, Mrs Jardine. And to see your beautiful house.'

'Yes, it is lovely, isn't it?' she agreed. 'Carl's been so good to me. I can't think why, but he has . . .' The woman Carl had referred to as Nancy crossed and, with an air of gentle, profes-sional authority said: 'Come on now, Catherine. It's getting late. Time for your medicine and then to bed. It's been a long day.' She nodded to Carl who again kissed his mother, who closed her eyes tightly as if in pain but put her hand on his arm and squeezed momentarily.

The two men let themselves out and returned to the car where Carl slipped into the driving seat beside Hugo and drew a deep, slow breath.

'Your mother is ill?' asked Hugo, gently.

'She's dying, Hugo. Cancer. The doctors reckon she's got

maybe another three months – though I suspect that may be a little optimistic.'

'I'm sorry.'

Carl started the car, pulled out on to the road and drove in silence for a while.

'So,' he said, at length. 'The problem will very shortly be resolved. The visits to the boutique will cease, there'll be a quiet funeral and that chapter of the family saga will close. Emily will be none the wiser and life will settle down to normal.'

Hugo nodded. 'Whatever *normal* is,' he observed.

Carl stopped the car outside the offices of Dufty Dufty Popple & Dunn and, as Hugo got out, a voice yelled: 'Hey, that's that Carl Jardine off the telly!' A group of young men standing outside the Pig and Whistle opposite nudged each other and one called out: 'Hey, Carl – knock us up a nice steak and kidney pud, eh, mate?'

Carl grinned wryly at Hugo through the open car window. 'That's normal for me. Cheers, Hugo.'

~

The two old men sat in thoughtful silence for several minutes. At length, Henry brightened: 'I know,' he said. 'How about "Silence Is Golden"?'

The Party of the Third Part

Stanley, the Friday bartender in the lounge bar of the Dog and Tadpole, placed the two glasses on the table in front of Charles Dufty. 'There we are, sir, one whisky and water for your good self and one gin and tonic for Mr Middleton – who seems to be a little late this evening, sir.'

'Yes,' said Charles, beginning to lay out the chess pieces, 'he's been away for a couple of days visiting his old army chum Cedric. He only got back today so he's probably feeling a bit the worse for wear.'

'Oh, yes, I recall him mentioning Cedric,' said the bartender. 'It's nice they've kept seeing each other over all this time since they served together. Must be forty or fifty years they've been friends.'

'Oh, they haven't seen each other since they were demobbed. No, they've just kept in touch by post – you know, Christmas cards and the occasional letters swapping old army memories, that sort of thing. This'll be the first time they've met up in all that time. I'll be interested to . . . ah! here he is. So how was the great reunion?'

Henry Middleton slumped into his chair and sat for a moment with his eyes closed. 'You don't want to know,' he said at length.

Stanley discreetly withdrew and, after a decent interval, Charles said: 'Not quite the joyful reunion you expected?'

Henry rested his elbows on the table and his head in his hands. Charles regarded him with a puzzled frown. 'But you were looking forward to seeing him. I thought you'd have so much to talk about, catching up on forty-five years of civilian life. And it's not as though you've become strangers. You've kept in touch regularly by letter. I would have thought you'd have enjoyed meeting his family and seeing how he is after his recent knee operation and what about that extension he's had built on to his house? And what about his wife – wasn't she interested to meet you?'

Henry slowly raised his head from his hands. 'His son hasn't visited him for years – though he does send photos of the grand-children at Christmas; his knee operation has left him lame and complaining; the extension he's had built is to accommodate his collection of army memorabilia which has grown too large to fit in the rest of the house and his wife . . . well, his poor little wife is hardly more than an unpaid domestic servant, pandering to his every requirement and spending the rest of her time dusting his army souvenirs and photographs. She sat in the kitchen all evening while Cedric regaled me with the history of our old regiment and showed me copies of dozens of letters he'd written to old army mates – most of whom I've forgotten and who never replied to his letters anyway.'

The old friends sat in silence for some minutes, reflecting on things in general.

'You know,' Charles said at length, 'I've always thought that you can't know a person by writing and receiving letters. In fact, the only way you can really understand someone is by seeing them in their natural habitat. It's the same with clients. I much prefer to see them at their home whenever possible. That's the only way I can form an accurate impression of who they are and what makes them tick. That's one of the things I always tried to instil into my son, Hugo. And he now tries to drum it into young Bernard, his articled clerk. Actually, Hugo was telling me of a good example of the principle in question only last week.'

~

At the next roundabout, take the third exit. The meticulous, rather bossy voice of the satnav usually irritated Bernard but, on this occasion, he gave the instrument a friendly wink and steered into the right-hand lane as the roundabout in question hove into view. The early evening sun was still peeping over the wooded ridge to his left; the road ahead was clear of traffic; he had, for the first time, been entrusted with the firm's car and all was pretty well with the world as he contemplated the remainder of the day.

Firstly, a brief visit to 'The Oaks', a rather pleasant country house, where he would arrange for its occupants, Mr and Mrs Henshaw, to sign the documents currently reposing in the briefcase on the passenger seat next to him. That done, he would drive into Walchester, pick up Joanna from the nurses' accommodation in Court Street, whence the two of them would proceed to the King's Arms where he would sweep her off her feet with tales of his fascinating work as a trainee solicitor with Messrs Dufty Dufty Popple & Dunn, solicitors and commissioners for oaths. Her coolness since he had moved to Hockam from Walchester before he knew she was moving from Hockam to student nurses' accommodation in Walchester would evaporate in the glow of his charm and wit and they would perhaps go on to a club, and then . . .

Destination! The satnav roused Bernard from his reverie and he peered ahead, seeing through the trees the well-proportioned, mock-Tudor frontage of 'The Oaks'.

The sun was now giving way to dusk as he locked the car, walked to the impressive front door, rang the bell and waited. After several minutes and two more peals of the bell, he stepped back to look up at the house, noticing with a frown that there were no lights visible in any of the windows. He glanced at his watch – seven thirty precisely, the agreed time for his visit. At least, he was pretty sure that was the time stipulated by Mr Dufty Junior when he had handed Bernard the papers, the keys of the firm's car and a clear instruction to the effect that the documents, duly signed by Mr and Mrs Henshaw, must be on his desk first thing tomorrow morning. 'It'll be good experience for you, Bernard,' he had assured him. 'Remember, you learn far more about people when you meet them in their natural habitat, as it were, than you do when they come into the office.'

Further prolonged ringing of the bell and several energetic raps on the door produced no response and it was becoming clear that the Henshaws' natural habitat was to remain uninspected by Bernard on this occasion. He walked back to the car, resolving to call Mr Dufty Junior on his mobile and ask for further instructions. With any luck, the evening could still be salvaged – indeed, he might even be able to pick up Joanna earlier than expected. Getting into the driving seat and leaving the door open, he rummaged in his briefcase for his mobile. It was not there. Getting out of the car, he frisked himself thoroughly, feeling in each of his suit pockets, to no avail. 'Bugger!' he exclaimed to a crow flapping overhead, as he pictured the offending mobile on his desk back at the office.

The situation was now becoming problematic. He could not simply give up on the Henshaws and turn up at the office tomorrow with the documents unsigned; to wait around here in the hope that the Henshaws returned would mean missing his date with Joanna; he had no means of contacting either Hugo Dufty to report in or Joanna to explain the position; and to cap it all, it was beginning to rain slightly. In short, he was . . . But wait; were those headlamps he saw through the trees over there? No, he realised as he walked in the direction of the glimmer; what he could see were the lights of a large house some fifty yards down the lane. He stood, jingling the small change in his pocket as he considered this. Then, making up his mind, he strode off in the direction of the lights, leaving the car on the Henshaws' drive.

The house, when he reached it, appeared relatively modern, not especially large as country houses go, but set in extensive grounds and commanding a pleasant view of the hills beyond. He judged it to be the residence of a successful businessman who, perhaps, commuted daily to Walchester, some ten miles away. The suddenly torrential rain bounced on the paving stones around him as he trudged up the rose-bordered drive towards the lighted front porch and his short ring on the door-bell was answered surprisingly quickly by a tall, slender woman wearing a rather fetching blue housecoat. She was in her early forties, perhaps, with straight fair hair and attractive blue eyes which now looked at him beneath eyebrows arched prettily in surprise.

Bernard shifted uncomfortably under her gaze, dripping rain-water on to the tiled floor of the porch.

'Good evening. Look, I'm really sorry to disturb you but I had an appointment to see Mr and Mrs Henshaw at their house just up the lane but they don't appear to be in. I don't suppose you happen to know . . . ?'

'No, I'm afraid I don't know where they'd be. We don't really know them that well. Sorry.' She smiled apologetically and began to close the door but Bernard persisted:

'Look, I'm sorry again to be a nuisance but I really am in a bit of a spot. I've left my mobile back at my office and I need to make a couple of urgent calls. I don't suppose there's any chance of using your phone? It'd only take a minute.'

She hesitated, drawing her housecoat more tightly round her. 'Well, my husband's . . . oh, I suppose it's all right. Come on in.'

He shuffled his wet feet energetically on the doormat and stepped through into the well-furnished entrance hall. 'I'll be as quick as I can,' he promised as he crossed to the telephone on the corner table. 'Then I'll buzz off and leave you in peace! Sorry about the drips on the carpet, by the way.'

She smiled suddenly, obviously more at ease. 'That's OK. It's pretty horrible out there, isn't it?'

'Yes,' he agreed, picking up the receiver. 'It came on

suddenly. It was fine until . . . er, this seems to be dead – no dialling tone.' He held the receiver towards her.

'Oh, that's always happening,' she said. 'You'll have to use the one on the landing. It's a separate line or something. I don't really understand it. My husband had it put in a few weeks ago. You have to press a button on it I think but it should be OK.'

'Righto. Your husband not in then, I take it?'

'No, he's not actually, although you've only just missed him. He's gone to catch a flight to Edinburgh. He'll probably be ringing me from the airport soon. He usually does.'

'Oh, I see,' he grinned as he mounted the stairs. 'Well, if it rings before I get to it, I'd better not answer it, had I? Be a bit embarrassing trying to explain who I was.'

'I think it probably would be,' she laughed. 'I'll just leave you to it – just give me a call before you go out so that I can lock up.'

'OK, will do!' he called from the landing as he picked up the phone.

It took only moments to establish from Hugo that the Henshaws had phoned after Bernard had left the office to explain that they had been called away unexpectedly this evening but would visit Mr Dufty tomorrow morning to sign the papers. Deciding that it was unnecessary to phone Joanna, he replaced the receiver and began to descend the thickly carpeted stairs but was startled halfway down to hear the click of a key being turned in the lock of the front door. He stood on the stairs, feeling unaccountably uneasy. The door opened and a smartly dressed man of about fifty stepped into the hall. 'It's only me, darling,' the man called out as he closed the door behind him. 'Had to come back for that blasted file on the . . .'

The man froze as he caught sight of Bernard wavering hesitantly on the stairs. There was a hard silence between the two men which seemed to drown the cheerful greeting the woman called out from the sitting room. It was Bernard who, recovering himself, spoke first, attempting a friendly smile.

'Good evening. Hope you don't mind, your wife kindly let me use your phone to call my office – left my mobile behind and er . . . you know how it is. Anyway, I'll clear off and get out of your . . .'

'In there!' The man's voice was harsh and grating but controlled, and he jabbed a thumb in the direction of the sitting room door.

Bernard's smile faded slightly. 'Hang on a second. I hope you don't think . . .'

'Get. In. There!' The voice was louder now but still rigidly under control. Spreading his hands, palms down, in a conciliatory gesture, Bernard did as he was bidden, descending the rest of the stairs and entering the sitting room where the woman had evidently just risen from an armchair and was staring at her husband, her face pale. 'Howard, what on earth's the matter. You surely don't think . . .'

The three stood now, stiffly, in separate corners of the room like characters in a Victorian melodrama, the man staring intently at Bernard. He spoke softly, as if to himself: 'So this is George.'

'Who?' the woman asked in an incredulous tone.

Bernard collected himself and, realising the almost comical absurdity of the situation, fought down a wholly inappropriate urge to giggle. 'The name's Bernard Summers,' he said in as professional a tone as he could manage. 'I'm with Dufty Dufty Popple & Dunn, solicitors, and I had an appointment earlier this evening with your neighbours, Mr and Mrs Henshaw. Unfortunately, they were not in so I rang your doorbell and your wife was kind enough to . . .'

'To let you use the phone. I know, you told me,' snapped the man with a dismissive wave of the hand.

'For God's sake, Howard, who's George?' The woman was now almost laughing.

'Jane, let's cut this out, shall we?' Howard moved to the

drinks cabinet and stood with his back to them as he poured. 'I know about your friend George here.' He turned round, a whisky glass in his hand. 'I damn well ought to know; I wake up in the night often enough hearing you babbling in your sleep "George, George, George" – Good God! I even found his name doodled on the telephone pad the other day. For months now, the whole house seems to have been saturated with the unseen presence of bloody George. How stupid do you think I am!' He slammed the glass on to a coffee table, the amber liquid slopping over the polished surface. 'Well, now we know, don't we? *Now we damn well know!'*

Both Jane and Bernard began to talk at once but Howard silenced them effectively by the quiet, earnest quality in his voice. 'I suggest you both walk quietly out of here and don't come back. I'll have a word with my solicitor in the morning and no doubt you'll wish to do the same. I don't want to see or hear from either of you again.'

He walked to the sitting room door and held it open. 'Now, unless you want this to turn into a sordid brawl, I recommend . . .'

'*Shut up!*' Jane's cry echoed around the room. 'Howard, you're making an absolute bloody fool of yourself. Firstly, if I were . . . well . . . having an affair with someone, would I be likely to scribble his name on telephone pads for you to see? Secondly, take a good look at Mr . . . Summers, here; does he look like the ardent lover, slipping silently into the house at midnight to woo me with his debonair charms? No offence, Mr Summers, but I think you'll agree there is an obvious age difference between us which Howard appears to have overlooked.'

Bernard stood, woodenly, out of his depth, still dripping rainwater on to the Axminster.

'Thirdly,' Jane went on, 'for the last time, Howard, *I don't know any George!* I've never even . . .'

She stopped suddenly, as though remembering something, and a smile began to dance in her eyes, turning eventually into a delighted laugh. 'Oh, Howard!' she giggled. 'You have made an ass of yourself – and in front of Mr Summers here, too – what must he think?'

'Jane, what *are* you talking about?' asked Howard, patiently. Jane's laughter seemed somehow to have blunted the edge of his anger. He was now the harassed but tolerant father figure as she clung to his arm, still giggling girlishly.

'I'm talking about your precious George,' she went on. 'And, what's more, I admit to being totally under his spell – I even dream about him from time to time. Oh, Howard – did it never occur to you? George . . . George Clooney. You know, that dishy film star we saw in – oh, what was the name of that film last summer? Don't you remember me drooling over him in the fourth row of the stalls? You asked me what he'd got that you hadn't and I told you in some detail – and you remember how you proved me wrong later that night?'

Her face was now turned away from Bernard who was by now feeling somewhat surplus to requirements. He shuffled his feet uncomfortably and cleared his throat.

Howard, his face now expressionless, disengaged his arm and crossed again to the drinks cabinet, returning a moment later with two filled glasses, one of which he handed to Jane and the other to Bernard who sipped gratefully at the scotch and soda. Howard then collected his own glass from the coffee table and sank into an armchair, waving to Bernard to do the same. When they were settled comfortably, he spoke, a wry smile hovering uncertainly at the corners of his mouth.

'Mr Summers, it would seem I owe you an apology. As my wife points out, I appear to have made an absolute fool of myself and I . . . bloody embarrassing, isn't it?'

His sudden grin acted as a signal and all three began to laugh, the tension evaporating like summer rain.

'Did you manage to make your phone call OK?' Howard said, at last.

'Yes, thanks. I just needed to let my boss know the Henshaws weren't in, but all's well now. In fact, I'd better be off. I'm supposed to be meeting someone in Walchester in half an hour.'

'Well, you've got bags of time,' Howard pointed out. 'Would you like another whisky, or a cup of coffee or something as you're driving. I feel I really ought to make amends for . . .'

Jane broke in softly before Bernard could reply: 'You'll miss your flight, Howard – in fact, you'll have to drive like the wind if you're going to get to the airport in time to check in.'

'Good grief, you're right!' Howard jumped to his feet. 'Look, I'm sorry, Mr, er . . .'

'It's Bernard,' supplied the other.

'Bernard, I'm sorry I've got to rush off but do accept my apologies for . . '. well, you know.' He collected a file from a bureau in the corner and bade his wife a tender, though hurried, farewell. Bernard also rose and went to the door and a few moments later both men were standing outside on the drive by Howard's car.

'Damn stupid of me, really, sounding off like that,' Howard said, glancing back at Bernard as he opened the car door. 'I've been under a lot of pressure lately and I suppose I worry about Jane being on her own so much. Seeing you there on the stairs, I just jumped to the wrong conclusion.'

'Well, it was quite understandable,' replied Bernard. 'I imagine any married man would get a bit of a shock seeing another man in the house with his wife. I dare say I'd be the same if I were married. Mind you . . . well, it's really none of my business.'

'No, do go on,' said Howard. 'We seem to have dragged you into our business against your will; you're quite entitled to say what you think.'

'Well, I was only going to say that it seems a pity to leave your wife alone at night out here in the country – she must get lonely sometimes. And it's perhaps a little worrying that she's so trusting. When you think about it, I could have been anybody. I mean, had I realised the house was occupied by a woman on her own, I wouldn't have knocked on the door but . . . It must be a worry for you, particularly if you're away a lot.'

'Yes, Jane is trusting,' nodded Howard. 'She tends to credit everyone with the best of motives until proved wrong. And, yes, I am away a lot – sometimes three or four nights a week with meetings, conferences and so on, you know the sort of thing. I sometimes wonder whether it's altogether necessary. They could probably get along just as well without me.'

The ensuing silence was broken by Bernard: 'Well, you'd best be off or you'll miss your flight.'

'True!' said Howard. He got into the car and Bernard walked down the drive to return to his own car at the Henshaws' place, hearing Howard's car start up behind him. A moment later, the car passed him and stopped at the open gates leading on to the lane. Howard's head poked out of the window. 'D'you know what I'm going to do, Bernard?' he said as Bernard drew level with him. 'I'm going to drive to the airport where one of my colleagues is waiting for me and I'm going to hand my papers over to him. And then I'm going to drive straight home to Jane, where I belong. From now on it's strictly nine to five for me. So maybe some good's come of all this, eh?'

Bernard grinned. 'Good idea. Be a nice surprise for your wife. All the best!'

Howard drove off with a cheery wave and Bernard walked on down the lane with a spring in his step. The rain had stopped now and the moon was visible behind the clouds, lending a mottled, silvery sheen to the wet road. 'Bernard Summers,' he muttered with a wry smile, 'marriage guidance counsellor to the gentry!' Reaching the Henshaws' drive, he slipped his hand into his pocket for the car keys and stopped with a puzzled frown. No keys. He must have dropped them somewhere between the car and Howard's house – or possibly inside the house, in which case what was he to do?

Wearily, he turned and retraced his steps, peering at the rough grass at the side of the lane as he went. He remembered that the keys had been in his hand as he walked towards Howard's drive and . . . yes, he had put them in his pocket as he turned through the gate. He may well thoughtlessly have put them into his left-hand trouser pocket in which there was a large hole. The noise of his feet crunching on the gravel would effectively have covered the sound of the keys falling.

He arrived at the entrance to the drive and there, glinting on the gravel, were the keys. Pleased with his newly discovered powers of detection, he stooped to retrieve them and, as he did so, he saw, out of the corner of his eye, the figure of a man flit silently across from the laurels at the side of the house to the front porch. Bernard watched as the door was opened and he caught a glimpse of Jane, silhouetted against the light from the hall.

Her softly spoken words carried well on the still night air: 'George! Thank God you're late. You're never going to believe this, but . . .'

The door closed on the two figures and Bernard straightened up and crept slowly back to the warm familiarity of the firm's car to reflect upon the frustrating tendency of things to be other than as they appear.

~

Henry cleared away the chess pieces after an honourable draw. 'Taught young Bernard a thing or two about life in general, I expect?'

Charles grinned. 'He has been a bit thoughtful for the past few days.'

'Still, I suppose he got to Walchester in time to see this Joanna girl. That probably took him out of himself, eh?'

Charles sighed. 'Sadly, the firm's car broke down on the way there and he had to be towed in to a garage. Ended up getting the bus back to Hockam and retiring to his little room over the newsagent's.'

After a short silence, Henry summoned Stanley for a last refill. 'It's a bugger being young, isn't it?' he smiled.

All That Messuage

'About time!' said Charles Dufty as Henry Middleton took off his overcoat, peered around furtively and crossed the lounge bar to their customary table, carrying a parcel wrapped in decorative paper.

Henry sat down, grinning, and placed the parcel under his chair. 'Sorry I'm late, I had to pick this up on the way here.'

'What is it?' asked Charles.

'Shush,' snapped Henry. 'Stanley's coming,'

The barman walked over and placed their drinks on the table. 'Happy birthday, Stanley,' said Henry, reaching under his chair.

'Thank you, sir,' replied Stanley, smiling broadly. 'And many thanks to both of you for the wonderful present. How you knew I'd always wanted a ukulele I'll never know, but it's been a lifelong ambition of mine to learn the instrument and now, thanks to you gentlemen, I'm able to do so. When you gave it to me when you arrived this evening, Mr Dufty, I can't describe the pleasure it gave me.'

Charles waved away the thanks. 'Least we could do, Stanley. The pleasure you'll derive from your ukulele is as nought compared to the pleasure you've afforded us by your untiring service over the past fifteen years. Enjoy!'

The barman spread his arms in an expression of gratitude and returned to the bar, leaving Henry doubled over, motionless, with one hand beneath his chair.

'So what's in the parcel?' asked Charles.

'Stanley's bloody ukulele,' replied Henry.

'What are you talking about, man? We agreed I'd purchase the instrument and I did so. As you were late, I gave it to him and explained that it was from both of us. Why did you buy another one?'

'Because I assumed you'd forget,' groaned Henry.

Charles picked up his whisky and water and sat back in his chair, a smug smile playing around the corners of his mouth. 'Ever heard of trust, old boy? I said I'd buy a ukulele for Stanley and I did. It's my belief, you know, that half the world's troubles are brought about by a lack of trust. Admittedly, the other half are caused by a lack of trustworthiness, so it sort of cancels out, but, nevertheless, I would have expected a little more faith from so old a friend even if others have less confidence in my ability to deliver the goods. But that's another story.'

～

Hugo Dufty leant his elbows on his desktop and placed his fingertips carefully together in that almost prayerful attitude used by so many of his legal colleagues to convey an impression of grave and learned deliberation – an impression marred somewhat in this case by the fact that Hugo's left elbow rested squarely on the cheese and pickle sandwich he had purchased for lunch.

At length, he spoke: 'May I ask, Mr . . . er . . . Bedford, why this, er . . . property developer has offered to pay such a high price for your house? The figure mentioned is, after all, over twice the ordinary market value of the property.'

Joe Bedford, an electrician of around fifty, turned to his small, sharp-featured wife who sat beside him. 'Have you got that plan, Sarah?' She handed him a folded sheet of paper.

'Now,' Joe began, opening out the paper and spreading it on top of the jumble of files littering the solicitor's desk, 'this is a plan of the new housing estate which this property chap wants to build on the wasteland at the back of our house, but the planning permission is conditional on him putting an access road through here . . .' He stroked a section of the plan with a stubby index finger. 'The only thing stopping him is our house, which is just here. He's been pestering us for months to sell but we've held out because I knew his price would gradually go up, see?'

He grinned at Hugo who nodded understandingly and said: 'And now you've decided to accept his latest offer?'

'Well, wouldn't you?' asked Sarah, leaning forward in her chair. 'It's good money, after all!'

'Oh, quite, Mrs Bedford. I should think you'd be well advised to accept at that figure . . . a very handsome offer – very handsome indeed. I think you said you'd brought the deeds of the house with you?'

'Yes, I got them from the bank this morning,' confirmed Joe, handing over a bulky brown paper parcel bound up with green tape.

Removing his elbow from his sandwich, Hugo untied the tape and drew out the contents of the parcel, spreading them on top of the development plan. 'Now, let me see what we've, er . . . yes, here's the original conveyance to, er . . . yes and we've got the, er . . . Ah! Yes, here's the one we want. Now, I see that you purchased the property some twenty years ago in your joint names.'

'That's right,' agreed Joe, 'just before we got married. That's why the wife's shown under her maiden name.' Mr Dufty nodded as he pored over the deed, reciting its contents under his breath: 'now, whereas by a conveyance dated . . . blah, blah, blah . . . this deed witnesseth . . . blah, blah, blah . . . all that messuage and premises known as number 89 Starling Avenue together with –'

'Ninety-one,' Joe interrupted.

Hugo glanced up: 'I beg your pardon?'

'I said ninety-one – our house is number ninety-one not eighty-nine.'

The solicitor bent over the deeds again, frowned and turned back to the first page. 'Well, according to your deeds, Mr Bedford, you own number eighty-nine.'

Joe shook his head and smiled patiently. 'No, we live at number ninety-on. Number eighty-nine is next door. That's owned by Mike and Julie Phipps – they bought theirs at the same time we bought ours.'

'We got married on the same day,' put in Sarah. 'And we moved in on the same day – it was quite funny, really.'

Hugo was now frowning even more seriously. 'Did you also employ the same firm of solicitors to act for you?' he asked.

'Yes,' affirmed Joe. 'It was your firm, Dufty Dufty Popple & Dunn. I think it was your Mr Popple who dealt with it.'

Hugo nodded and leant back in his chair, which creaked and leaned alarmingly to the right. 'Well, I'm sorry to have to tell you, Mr Bedford, but it seems that there must have been some confusion at the time your instructions were received, with the result that you and your wife own number eighty-nine and Mr and Mrs, er . . . Phipps own the house which you are at present occupying. In other words, number ninety-one is not yours to sell.'

Having delivered himself of this grave pronouncement, Hugo rocked back in his chair, which creaked once more and toppled backwards, depositing him heavily and painfully upon the floor.

Hearing the crash, Hugo's secretary, Trish, ran in and assisted him to his feet. He rubbed the back of his head and picked up a fragment of chair. 'Dear, oh dear. We really must do something about new office furniture, Trish. This kind of thing cannot be tolerated, I suggest . . .'

'But what about our house?' Joe's tone was protesting. 'What about this offer we've had?' Hugo was still rubbing the back of his head. 'Your what? . . . Oh, your house. Yes, well, er . . . I'm very sorry, Mr Bedford, but I really don't see what I can, er . . .'

'You don't see what you can what?' Joe's face was becoming redder by the minute. 'You're a solicitor, aren't you?' he shouted. 'It was your firm that cocked things up in the first place. I stand to lose a shedload of cash and you stand there blathering about office furniture. Well, let me tell you, Mr Dufty *Junior*, you'll be hearing from Pollock's in Walchester – they're proper lawyers. We should have gone there in the first place, Sarah.'

As he stood up and began to gather his deeds from the desk, the door of the office opened and the stooped, bespectacled figure of Charles Dufty appeared. 'Sorry to interrupt, but I just wanted to find – ah! There it is.' He crossed to the bookshelf, selected a copy of *Halsbury's Statutes*, turned to leave but stopped, a smile of recognition illuminating his features. 'It's Mr and Mrs Bedford, isn't it? Never forget a face even after – what is it now – twenty years?'

'You've got a nerve after the trouble your firm's caused us,' growled Joe.

Charles directed a look of interested enquiry at his son who, still fingering a sore patch on the back of his head, outlined briefly the problem. 'So, as I was explaining to Mr Bedford, it's difficult to see what, er . . .'

'Difficult?' The old man's face expressed mild surprise. 'No, it's not difficult. Easily sorted out in no time.'

Joe paused on his way to the door with his wife. 'So you're going to . . . rectify the deeds or whatever and swap the houses into the proper names? Well, you'd better be damn quick about it because this developer chap is champing at the bit.'

'All in good time, Mr Bedford, there's no need to rush these things, you know.'

'There's every need to rush,' Joe yelled. 'If it's not done soon – like now – Mike and Julie Phipps who live next door are going to hear about the developer's offer and if they then find out they own the house he wants to buy, I'm going to lose out.'

The old solicitor eased his frame into a nearby chair, taking off his glasses and polishing them with his handkerchief. 'Mmm . . . who is this developer?' he asked.

'Chap called Peabody. Operates out of London mainly but owns a company in Walchester. But what's that got to do with it? All you've got to do is put right the stupid blundering error Popple made when we bought the house.'

'A very nice house it is, too, I believe. Those properties in Starling Avenue are very much sought after. And the last time I was down there, I noticed that you'd carried out a lot of improvements to the place since you've been in occupation.'

'Too right we have – new double garage, paved drive, conservatory, extended kitchen. We've spent a fortune on it. Unlike Mike and Julie next door, who've let their place go to rack and ruin. Even if the developer wasn't interested in buying it, there's no way I'd let Mike and Julie swan into our place while we moved into their bloody hovel. You'd better get those deeds put straight right now, Dufty, or there'll be real trouble.'

Charles, having polished his glasses to his complete satisfaction, replaced them on his nose and leant back in his chair. 'Well, you know, Mr Bedford, we at Dufty Dufty Popple & Dunn never believe in rushing ahead with the first solution which presents itself. There are always more ways of approaching a problem than the obvious one. Our aim is to ensure that our clients' interests are properly taken care of and we pride ourselves on, er . . . ah! The lovely Trish bearing refreshments.' He waved to the secretary to place the tray on a side table. 'Now, I suggest the first step towards resolving this particular little puzzle is a cup of strong tea and one of these rather splendid chocolate biscuits. Can I interest you, Mrs Bedford?'

Joe let his mouth fall open in an expression of blank astonishment. 'We're in danger of losing the best offer we're ever likely to receive because of your firm's rank incompetence and you sit there drinking tea and munching chocolate bloody biscuits! I don't believe this.'

Hugo, who, now chairless, had perched himself on his desk during the old man's soothing words, now spoke. 'Mr and Mrs Bedford, clearly we must take some appropriate action to remedy any unforeseen and unfortunate consequences which could result from what *appears* to have been an error on the part of this firm. My father will take this matter under his personal control and I can assure you that, whatever action he takes will, without any doubt, produce an outcome which will prove beneficial to *all* parties.'

Joe and Sarah regarded Charles who was balancing his teacup precariously in one hand while brushing crumbs from his tie with the other. Sensing a lull in the conversation, he looked up. 'Well, I'm afraid, I have to leave you all at this point – meeting of the Gilbert & Sullivan Society, you know. I suggest, Mr and Mrs Bedford, that I call in to see you at Starling Avenue . . . shall we say next Wednesday evening at, say, seven? Would that suit?'

'To do what?' asked Joe.

'To provide you with a report on how matters are progressing and, hopefully, to provide the solution to your problem – and, perhaps, to share a pot of tea with you if there should happen to be such a commodity to hand . . . ?' He rose stiffly and moved to the door. 'Wednesday, then?'

Joe nodded dumbly as the door closed.

The glass panes of Joe and Sarah's custom-built conservatory looked out on a thoughtfully landscaped garden, bathed now in the late afternoon sunlight illuminating the rose pergola and casting dappled shadows across the lawn. Sarah handed her husband a gin and tonic and sat beside him on the comfortable sofa. 'Do you think old Dufty *will* sort it out?' she asked.

Joe directed towards her a look of such withering scorn that she flinched. 'Dufty sort it out?' he snorted. 'That old buffer couldn't sort out a bun fight at a nursery school! You saw the way he sat there drinking tea while time was ticking away – Then he toddled off to his Gilbert O'Sullivan meeting or whatever it was. He's past it, Sarah. He doesn't understand that time is of the essence in cases like this. While he's sitting there until next Wednesday, cogitating and dropping biscuit crumbs down his tie, the developer's getting impatient and Mike and Julie are getting more and more likely to rumble that something's up. If they find out that they own this house, we're b—!'

'So what are you going to do?'

'I'll tell you what I'm going to do. I rang Pollock's in Walchester a few minutes ago and I'm going to see them tomorrow morning. They reckon they can put the deeds right pretty well straight away without Mike and Julie being any the wiser. In a day or two, we'll be the rightful owners of this house, number ninety-one, and Mike and Julie will own their house, number eighty-nine. I can then go back to Peabody and accept his offer and by the time old Dufty arrives on Wednesday we'll be home and dry. And, what's more, I'll sting him for the legal costs involved – it was his firm that caused the problem, after all.'

Sarah nodded. 'In a way, I feel quite sorry for Mike and Julie,' she said. 'If they only knew what was going on.'

'Why feel sorry for them, for heaven's sake? Twenty years ago, they thought they were buying the house they've got and we thought we were buying this one. All I'm doing is putting things right so that we all own the house we wanted in the first place. What's wrong with that? In any case, we've spent a fortune on this place over the years, I mean, look at it . . .' He waved an arm to indicate the results of their not inconsiderable expenditure. 'Whereas, those two have done bugger all to improve theirs! Look at them now.'

Joe was craning his neck to peer at the next-door couple in their garden – Mike struggling to remove three weeks' lawn growth with a rusty hand mower and his wife in a floppy sun hat, cutting the first of the season's slightly mildewed roses. 'They just potter about, tweaking things in the garden while their garage doors are disintegrating. They don't think big enough, Sarah. They're small people and always will be.'

'That's not really fair, Joe.' Sarah put down her gin and tonic carefully on one of the coasters on the coffee table. 'Mike's job in insurance doesn't pay much and Julie does what she can by working at the supermarket but they've never had the breaks we've had. I know they admire our house – Julie often says so – but they can't hope to make theirs like ours. They're just nice people doing the best they can.'

'Oh, they're nice enough people in a quiet sort of way but it takes more than nice to make it in today's world, Sarah. I didn't build up Bedford Electrics to what it is now by being nice. I did it by working bloody hard and grabbing opportunities – like this offer from Peabody. There's no way I'm letting that slip through my fingers. I reckon we deserve all the breaks we can get.'

Sarah was standing up now, waving approval at the bunch of roses which Julie was holding up to show her. She turned back to Joe: 'Well, perhaps you're right. It just seems a shame, that's all.' She went to the kitchen to begin preparing dinner.

Charles Dufty did not arrive in his office until midday, the meeting of the Gilbert & Sullivan Society having finished rather later than expected the night before. He sat now, staring at the morning paper. Hugo, who had been searching for a file in the ancient filing cabinet in the corner, turned now, noticing the other's puzzled frown. 'Is there anything wrong, Father?' he asked.

The old man looked up. 'What . . . ? Well, yes, there is, as a matter of fact. You see, I thought it was a simple case of picking out the odd numbered letters in the first phrase but I now see I was mistaken. I'm beginning to think it all hinges on the twin meanings of the word *char*.'

Seeing his son's puzzlement, he explained: 'Nine down. It's the only one I haven't cracked.'

Hugo's expression cleared as he saw that the newspaper on the desk was open at the crossword page. 'Ah! I thought you might have been considering the Bedford case. I really think we should give some urgent thought to that, you know, Father. I spent most of this morning searching the archives for the original conveyancing file but without success – those old files in the cellar are in a dreadful mess. It does appear, though, that the matter was dealt with by Robert Popple and . . .'

Charles looked up sharply. 'I thought we agreed never to mention that name in this office again.'

'Yes, I know but, in this case, we do have a responsibility to find out what we can and if, as appears to be the case, an error was made which affects the title, then we must take all possible steps to remedy the position. This Bedford chap isn't the type to just accept that an innocent mistake was made and leave it at that; he's going to make a lot of noise about it and any resulting adverse publicity could prove disastrous to the reputation of the firm.'

The old man was staring down solemnly, his brow furrowed. After some moments, his expression brightened. 'Domestic!' he chuckled. 'Char, you see. And if you take the first part of the clue *cupolas*, that gives you *domes* and a nervous spasm is a *tic* which gives you . . .'

Hugo slammed the drawer of the filing cabinet shut with a bang which startled even himself. He spread his palms in a placatory manner and took a deep breath. 'Sorry,' he muttered. 'But, Father, I really do feel we should give this some priority. I'm seeing clients all afternoon but perhaps this evening we could spend some time looking into the possibilities and deciding upon a course of action? We might also spend a few moments considering how best to reorganise the archiving in the cellar – not to mention the appalling condition of the office furniture. There really are a lot of things which need attention around the place and my time is so limited at the moment that . . .'

'Yes, yes, my boy. We do need to discuss a number of things – including, of course, Mr and Mrs Bedford's little problem. But I'm afraid I won't be available this evening. I'm attending the Walchester Rotary Club. They meet at the White Horse, you know, and I gather they lay on a slap-up dinner. In any case, there's a chap who's a member there and I need a word with him.'

'But you usually attend the Hereward Rotary Club.'

'Well, mustn't get set in our ways, must we? Onwards and upwards, eh? Onwards and upwards. Clever clue that – *domestic*!'

The younger man ran a hand through his hair and returned to his office, leaving his father chuckling contentedly.

The Wednesday evening rush-hour traffic had cleared by the time Charles turned his elderly Rover away from the main road and into the maze of tree-lined thoroughfares which led to Starling Avenue. Parking outside number ninety-one, he got out and walked up the drive, admiring the immaculately mani- cured front lawn with its central magnolia tree still shedding its petals upon the wallflowers beneath.

Glancing at the slightly ragged privet hedge surrounding the simple but tidy garden fronting number eighty-nine next door, he rang the doorbell. It was answered by a grinning Joe Bedford who ushered him in. 'Well, Mr Dufty. Come on through. Sarah has just made tea – though I'm afraid we haven't got any chocolate biscuits.'

He led the way into the sitting room where Sarah was busying herself with a tray. She nodded briefly to their visitor and then returned to her task, appearing, to the perceptive eye, slightly embarrassed. The solicitor sat down in the chair indicated and Joe, still grinning, took one opposite. 'So, Mr Dufty, you've come to talk about solving our problem, have you? The problem that we were discussing at your office – how long ago was it . . . a week, isn't it?'

'Indeed I have, Mr Bedford, as promised.' He accepted a cup of tea from Sarah. 'I think we should have everything sorted out satisfactorily.'

'Oh yes?' Joe's sarcastic tone was unmistakeable. He was clearly enjoying himself. 'So you've come to talk about how to sort everything out. And when we've talked, we could talk some more and then, possibly, in, say, another week or two or three, there might be some action taken – unless, of course, you need to give your attention to the Gilbert O'Sullivan Club. By which time, of course, the developer will have lost patience, Mike and Julie next door will have discovered they own this house and I'll have lost a very considerable amount of money.' He leant forward in his chair, his expression now almost serious. 'Well, let me show you how things are done in today's world, Mr Dufty . . .'

'Oh, no, Mr Bedford. I really don't think we can wait any longer for a solution, do you? I promised to arrange matters to everyone's satisfaction and that I have done – in accordance with what I understood to be my instructions.'

Joe Bedford's grin became slightly less jubilant. 'Oh, so you've waved your magic wand and sorted it all out, have you? So how have you done that, then? I'm all ears!' He leant back with a slightly exaggerated expression of extreme interest.

'Oh, nothing very dramatic, I assure you, Mr Bedford. Just a little common sense and . . . well, the usual sort of thing, you know.' He picked up his cup and sipped, gratefully, congratulating Sarah on the excellence of her tea. 'Ceylon Orange Pekoe, if I'm not mistaken?' Sarah nodded.

Joe was becoming impatient. 'Look, Mr Dufty, I've got things to do. Why not just tell us what you propose to do and then I'll tell you what I've already done, eh?'

'Well . . .' The solicitor replaced his cup on the table. 'I happen to be a Rotarian – been a member for years. You get to meet a lot of useful people, you know, and convivial surroundings, social intercourse – helps the world go round, don't you agree?'

Joe was fiddling with his mobile phone. 'Look, is this going on for long? I need to make an urgent phone call within the next half-hour or so – to Peabody, as it happens.'

'Ah! Nigel Peabody!' said Charles. 'The very man I happened to bump into at the Walchester Rotary Club last week. Er . . . I wouldn't call him just yet until you've heard what I have to say. You see, he and I had a very productive chat . . . over a particularly fine Chablis, as a matter of fact. Goes so well with a fish course, don't you think? And I was able to point out that the house next door which you own – number eighty-nine, that is – would be a far better candidate for demolition to make way for the access road than this house, number ninety-one – that is, the house you don't own. Firstly, not having been improved and enlarged over the years, it may be slightly cheaper to acquire and, secondly, it would, in some ways, be better situated for the purpose.'

'Better situated?' put in Joe.

'Well, Roger Manning, the chairman of the planning committee, seemed to agree that it is – he also happened to be present at the Rotary Club, you see. So, the outcome is that Peabody now wishes to purchase number eighty-nine – the house you own – at the same figure he quoted to you. So there's no need for any rectification of title. You own number eighty-nine and Nigel Peabody wishes to purchase it at a greatly inflated price.'

Joe turned rather pale and beads of perspiration appeared on his upper lip. It was his wife who pointed out: 'But what about Mike and Julie – they'll be homeless.'

'Not at all, Mrs Bedford. Mr and Mrs Phipps own number ninety-one, don't they? You will presumably be moving to a more desirable residence with the benefit of the substantial proceeds of number eighty-nine, as you planned to do, and Mr and Mrs Phipps will therefore be free to move into number ninety-one, the house you currently occupy and the house which they, in fact, own. Nigel Peabody will be able to go ahead with the planned development, you will go ahead with your plans to move upmarket and Mr and Mrs Phipps will move into their dream house. As I said to you before, we aim to resolve all issues to the satisfaction of *all* parties. I think this does the trick, don't you?'

Joe's mouth was hanging slackly open and he seemed incapable of speech. It was Sarah who spoke first, albeit in a weak voice: 'But . . . but, Joe . . . have Pollock's done what they said they would?' Joe nodded, his shoulders sagging. 'So that means we now own this house,' she went on. Joe nodded again.'

Charles broke the almost palpable silence. 'I'll be, er . . . Oh, that was your doorbell, should you, er . . . ?' He rose and followed Sarah into the hall where excited voices could be heard as she opened the front door. 'I won't intrude any further as you have visitors,' he insisted, shaking her hand and slipping out as Mike and Julie burst in, both talking at once. When they reached the living room, Mike's voice prevailed. 'Look, sorry to disturb you both, particularly as you've just had a visitor, but we had to tell someone . . . are you OK, Joe?'

Joe, by now slumped almost lifelessly in his chair, nodded, and Mike went on: 'Well, we had a call just now from this developer chap, Peabucket or something. He wants to buy our house to build an access road and can you guess how much he's offered us?'

But by this time, Jack had lost the will to nod.

~

'Lack of trust, you see?' said Charles.

Henry shifted his feet uncomfortably, rustling against the paper parcel beneath his chair. 'What the hell am I going to do with this?' he grated.

'Well . . . could I suggest you and Stanley get together and master the rudiments of the instrument? Then, in a few weeks' time, a little impromptu concert in the public bar – "Leaning on a Lamp-post", perhaps, or "When I'm Cleaning Windows", that sort of thing . . . Now don't make a scene! . . . You'll break it! . . . A ukulele is a delicate instrument, you know . . . Ouch! . . . STANLEY! . . .'

A Foreign Transaction

Henry Middleton raised his bald head slowly from the chessboard with an irritated expression. 'Charles, I know I'm taking rather a long time over this move but is it absolutely necessary to do that?' he asked.

Charles Dufty stopped drumming his fingers on the table and held up his hands in a placatory gesture. 'Sorry, old boy. Wasn't aware I was doing it.'

Henry resumed his deliberations, only to be disturbed a few moments later by a high-pitched, flute-like note. He glanced up again to see Charles intently rubbing his finger around the rim of his whisky glass, making it resonate. Seeing Henry's look of annoyance, Charles folded his arms immediately and sat up straight, peering intently at the board. Henry again bent over his pieces, moving his lips slightly as he silently plotted his next move.

After a further five minutes, Henry's train of thought was again interrupted, this time by Charles's voice: 'Why don't you bring up your knight to cover your . . .'

Henry slammed his palm on to the table and sat back in his chair. 'Much as I appreciate your advice, old friend, I have always been under the impression that the point of this game is that each player makes his own decisions as to how and, indeed, when to move his pieces, leaving his opponent to do the same. The player who makes the right decisions wins. D'ye see? Perfectly simple, really.'

Seemingly crushed by the other's heavy sarcasm, Charles looked

solemn and made a gesture as if to zip his mouth closed and Henry
returned to the task in hand.

Charles again broke the silence: 'It's just that sometimes one's
thinking can become so focused in a particular direction that the
most obvious way forward is obscured. At such times, an objective
view can provide the solution and matters can proceed.'

Henry put down the pawn with which he had been hesitatingly
toying and motioned to Stanley, the bartender, for refills. When these
had been brought, he settled back with a sigh. 'All right. What's the
story?' he asked.

~

The attractions of Hockam High Street, though many and var-
ied, were really no different from those of any other small
provincial English town. There was the Pig and Whistle, a cosy,
ivy-clad former coaching inn with its welcoming tables set out
on the terrace; the Town Hall, its Doric pillars strangely
incongruous between Marks & Spencer to its left and the post
office to its right; the Rialto Café offering chilli con carne,
cottage pie and soup of the day served by its proprietor, Ashraf,
and a variety of High Street shops including the butcher's, the
baker's and the electricity showrooms to name but a few.

These amenities, while sufficient to entice shoppers and local
residents out for a stroll or a meal with friends, were not of a
nature which would induce holidaymakers and international jet-
setters to divert from more colourful locations and plump for
Hockam as their destination of choice.

However, on this particular Friday, lunchtime shoppers were
surprised by the strains of authentic Spanish flamenco music
drifting in the air and lending a flavour of exoticism to their
workaday tasks. To those walking on the south side of the High
Street, it would have become apparent that the pulsing rhythms
and stirring, if unintelligible, vocals were issuing from a little half-
timbered building between Maisie's florist's and Ben Sharpe's

newsagent's. Closer investigation would have revealed that, behind the front door with its brass plate bearing the inscription *Dufty Dufty Popple & Dunn, Solicitors and Commissioners for Oaths*, the little reception area was being transformed from a place of dignified professional calm into something quite different.

The music issuing from the CD player had prompted Bernard, the articled clerk, to make an attempt at dancing a flamenco with Trish, the young, freckle-faced secretary; the walls were bedecked with red and yellow flags and a long trestle table was being laid by Conchita, the Spanish receptionist, with small plates of assorted titbits while the reception desk was laden with glasses and bottles of Cava and tequila.

The brief appearance of Hugo Dufty's head around his office door produced a quietening effect as Bernard abandoned the flamenco, turned down the music to a slightly more acceptable volume and crossed to the rickety trestle table where he sneaked a sausage-like object from the dish in Conchita's hand, receiving a slap on the wrist for his pains.

'Not bad,' he observed with his mouth full. 'What's with all these little plates of . . . stuff?'

'These are tapas,' explained Conchita. 'In Spain we eat them at lunchtime and sometimes in the evening when we are in a bar.'

'Why are they called tapas?' asked Bernard.

Conchita, pleased to be, for once, the source of information, replied: '*Tapa* is the Spanish for . . . how do you say . . . a top . . . a thing that you put on the top . . .'

'*Tapa* is a lid or cover,' explained Mark Dunn, the junior partner, who had just come into reception from his office. 'They used to serve these bits and pieces on little plates and then serve them on top of your glass – like a lid. Hence *tapas*.'

He then, much to Bernard's irritation, proceeded to chat to Conchita in fluent Spanish until interrupted by Miss Metcalfe, Charles Dufty's personal assistant, who came out of the secretaries' room and turned off the CD player, pointing out: 'She'll be here any minute and, if she hears the music, it won't be a surprise.'

'Good point,' observed Mark. 'Now, I think we should line up over here and keep quiet so that when she comes through the door we can . . . Ah, there you are, Hugo. We thought we'd give her a surprise when she arrives – which should be any minute now.'

Hugo joined the line-up and Charles, his father, also appeared, making a full complement. 'Everything ready, I see,' he smiled, rubbing his hands together. 'We want to make this a proper send-off for her.'

'But she's not actually going for a few weeks yet,' Bernard pointed out. 'So it's not really a send-off, is it?'

Miss Metcalfe explained: 'She's not going to her new home in Spain until the sale of her cottage is completed but this is her last day with the firm so it's a leaving party.'

'I can't believe she's actually emigrating to Spain,' said Trish. 'I always thought of her as . . . well, as somebody who was . . . well, a bit boring really. She's never joined in with anything here and always seemed a bit . . . well, grumpy and old-fashioned. But here she is, selling up and jetting off to live in Spain.'

Bernard nodded. 'Didn't think she had it in her.'

Charles chuckled. 'We shouldn't be too quick to judge people. We think we know someone but we only know what we see on the outside – we don't know what's on the inside, do we?'

'I think she's a very brave lady,' said Miss Metcalfe. 'To leave the cottage she's always lived in and go off to start a new life in a foreign country takes a very special kind of courage. I think she's to be congratulated and she deserves a good send-off with our very best wishes.'

As the chorus of 'Hear, hear!' subsided, Bernard suggested: 'Do you think we should all have a glass of tequila before she comes, just to get ourselves in the mood?'

Hugo was about to make some suitably caustic response when the street door opened to admit Miss Spiers, the book-keeper, and a ragged cheer broke out as everyone rushed to open bottles, pat her on the back and ply her with tapas.

Miss Spiers stood, glass in one hand, plate in the other, her tall, thin frame stiff and motionless, her eyes obscured by the light reflecting off wire-rimmed spectacles, her sharp features arranged into a strangely incongruous, tight-lipped smile.

It was Charles who brought order to the proceedings by stepping into the centre of the room and raising his hand, his short, portly, white-haired figure effortlessly commanding everyone's attention. 'Miss Spiers,' he began in the ensuing silence. 'Or may I, in the circumstances, call you Rosemary?'

There were raised eyebrows all round as people learnt for the first time that Miss Spiers actually had a first name. She nodded graciously towards Charles who continued:

'Rosemary, you have served this firm for over thirty years as our trusted and capable book-keeper. In all that time, you have never taken an unscheduled day off, never wasted time and never shirked your responsibilities. You have come to work each day and given your entire attention to your duties before all else – and those duties have extended a good deal further than looking after the firm's finances. Together with Miss Metcalfe here, you've played an active part in keeping the wheels of the firm turning smoothly; sorting out the holiday rota, organising the cleaners, overseeing the billing system, sourcing and ordering new equipment and furniture – I could go on. You have shown us all the meaning of the word *dedication*. And soon you are to embark upon an adventure which few of us would have the courage – or, indeed, the vision – to undertake. You will be sadly missed here – indeed, I've no idea how we're ever going to replace you – but that's our problem. I know you will be welcomed in your new home, which I understand will be in a villa in the grounds of the house belonging to your niece and her husband in Andalusia, where I'm sure your presence will be as much valued as it has been here in Hockam. You are an example to us all, Rosemary, and we wish you well in your new life in the sunshine. To Rosemary!'

The toast was joined in with enthusiasm and Miss Spiers, seeing that it was incumbent upon her to reply, carefully placed her glass on a nearby table and faced the expectant gaze of her colleagues. 'Thank you all very much,' she began, her controlled, precise tones disappointing some of those present who were, perhaps, anticipating at least some indication that, beneath the formidable, unyielding exterior of the guardian of the firm's finances, beat a warm, human heart, subject to feelings and emotions which others were willing to share.

'You've clearly gone to a lot of trouble,' she continued, peering round at the flags, the balloons and the posters, 'and it's very much appreciated. I have always derived a great deal of satisfaction from my work here and I'm grateful for your interest in my future plans. I wish the firm continuing success and . . . thank you all once again.'

After a momentary pause, the little party continued, though at a slightly less boisterous level, featuring more in the way of intelligent conversation and a civilised exchange of pleasantries. At length, partners and staff drifted back to work and Miss Spiers returned to her little office at the back of the building to complete her handover to Miss Metcalfe, who had been persuaded to look after the financial aspects of the firm until a replacement book-keeper could be found.

Mark Dunn entered as Miss Metcalfe was grappling with the terrors of the quarterly VAT return. 'Sorry to interrupt,' he said. 'Just to let you know, Miss Spiers, that I'm only waiting to hear from your purchaser's solicitor on one or two small points before I prepare the contract for the sale of Butterfly Cottage. All being well, it should be ready for you to sign by the middle of next week. Can I suggest I pop round to see you at, say, four thirty on Wednesday if that's convenient?'

Miss Spiers agreed to the arrangement and returned to Miss Metcalfe and the demanding requirements of Her Majesty's Revenue and Customs.

Butterfly Cottage was well hidden behind ancient oak trees which bordered a stream beside the lane leading from Hockam to Malverley. A small stone bridge over the stream provided access to the front garden which afforded a rough gravel parking patch, on to which Mark's car now drew up.

Taking his briefcase from the passenger seat, he got out of the car and made his way along a short path bordered by carefully tended shrubs to the front door of the little white-painted cottage with its covering of wisteria and early flowering rambling roses. His knock was answered after perhaps three minutes.

This was the first time Mark had encountered an off-duty Miss Spiers and the difference between her more familiar, smartly suited, precisely coiffured person and her present appearance was such that he was momentarily taken aback. Her hair was tied back with a ribbon, she wore a well-used blue jumper over faded, baggy jeans, partly covered by a plastic apron with a front pouch out of which protruded the handles of a trowel and hand fork. Her feet were encased in a pair of grimy trainers. Her wire-rimmed glasses were absent.

'Mr Dunn,' she smiled. 'Sorry I took so long to answer the door – I was doing a bit of pruning in the back garden.' Noting the other's lack of response and slightly open mouth, she added: 'Are you all right, Mr Dunn?'

Mark gathered himself. 'Yes, I'm sorry, I . . . er . . . for a moment I didn't recognise you without your glasses,' he laughed.

'Oh, I only need those for close work,' she said, standing back and opening the door wider. 'Do come in. I'll put the kettle on and we can have a cup of tea.'

The front door led into a small, low-beamed parlour, furnished with a sideboard, a sofa and two armchairs. The centre of the room was occupied by a low table bearing a vase of flowers, several envelopes bearing Spanish stamps and a large book entitled *Great Gardens of Britain*. In the corner stood an upright piano on top of which was a pile of well-thumbed sheet music. Miss Spiers motioned to Mark to sit in one of the armchairs and cleared the table, placing the vase of flowers carefully on the sideboard. 'Will you have enough room to spread your papers on there?' she asked.

Mark assured her that he would and she walked through to the kitchen, taking off her gardening apron as she did so. After taking the contract out of his briefcase and placing it on the table, Mark sat back, noticing, on the mantelpiece, a group of three photographs in gilt frames. One was of a youngish woman with sharp features and a slightly intimidating smile, a second, rather larger than the others, portrayed an elderly, distinguished looking man in evening dress and the third showed a young, swarthy man with his arm around a girl in, perhaps, her late twenties who was holding a baby.

'Ah,' said Miss Spiers on entering with a tray, 'I see you're looking at the family gallery. The elderly gentleman is my late father – he was a barrister – the photograph on the left is of my sister, Daisy, who sadly died twenty years ago, and the little group on the right is my niece, Diane, and her husband, Carlos, with their little daughter, Juanita.'

Mark nodded. 'And it's with Diane and her family that you'll be living in Spain?'

To his surprise, a frown flitted momentarily across Miss Spiers's brow before she nodded and busied herself with the teacups.

'Now,' she said when they were both seated, her manner slipping back into the brisk, professional demeanour with which Mark was familiar. 'I gather that Mr and Mrs Eames have decided, after all, to go ahead with the purchase?'

'That's right,' Mark confirmed. 'As you know, they were initially undecided whether to buy this cottage or another property which they were considering out at Malverley. But, it seems they've now made up their minds that Butterfly Cottage is the home they want so it's all systems go. I imagine that's quite a relief to you as I understand Diane and her husband couldn't have delayed much longer in renting out the villa which you'll be occupying?'

'That's right,' she said. 'They need the rent from that and they said they'd rather have me as a tenant than a stranger. However, it's already taken much longer than we expected to find a purchaser for this place and if the Eameses had backed out, Diane and Carlos would have had to take another tenant for the villa.'

'And your plans to go to Spain would have bitten the dust,' said Mark.

Miss Spiers was silent for a moment. 'It is quite certain that Mr and Mrs Eames are going to buy Butterfly Cottage?' she asked at length.

'Well,' said Mark, observing her closely, 'nothing's certain until contracts are exchanged, of course, and, until then, they could always change their minds . . . as, indeed, could you.'

Miss Spiers gave what seemed to Mark like a short, nervous laugh and turned her attention to the contract which lay on the table.

The necessary papers were soon signed and Mark explained that he would post them to Mr and Mrs Eames's solicitor in the morning and that the deal would be done when their own part of the contract was signed and posted to him. Completion of the sale could then be expected in approximately three to four weeks. Mark gathered up the papers and replaced them in his briefcase. As he did so, a sleek, pure white cat entered the room, paused to direct its steady, oddly unsettling gaze disapprovingly at Mark and then crossed to where Miss Spiers was sitting, rubbing its head against one trainer-clad foot and purring loudly.

'Oh, this is Daisy,' smiled Miss Spiers in response to Mark's enquiry. 'Named after my late sister because she looks rather fierce but is, in reality, a pussycat. We understand each other, don't we, Daisy?' She gently ruffled the fur at the back of the animal's neck.

'You have a lovely home,' said Mark after some moments.

Miss Spiers looked up, smiling at the compliment. 'It is nice, isn't it? But you haven't seen the best part yet. Would you care to see my garden before you go?'

He agreed, eagerly, and she led him through the little kitchen into an even smaller glass conservatory which was packed with plants of all kinds – orchids, fuchsias and many others of whose names Mark was ignorant. As he was bending over a particularly splendid specimen, he heard her open the door into the garden and he straightened to see her standing on the terrace, motionless, with her back to him, looking out at the beautifully ordered panorama of flowerbeds, fruit trees and vegetable plots which stretched down to the copse bordering the property, above which was visible the gently undulating rise of the distant downs.

She seemed, for the moment, oblivious to his presence and he waited for some moments before walking out to stand quietly by her side.

'It's beautiful,' he whispered at length.

Wakening from her thoughts, she turned to face him and he was surprised to see that her eyes were bright with tears. She turned away abruptly and her voice was once again that of the book-keeper at Dufty Dufty Popple & Dunn as she said: 'Yes, it's very pretty, isn't it? It takes a lot of work, of course, to keep it like this but I find it satisfying and, of course, gardening is a useful way to relax.'

'You must spend a lot of time out here,' said Mark.

Her composure now fully recovered, she said: 'Yes, Daisy and I are out here most evenings and weekends during the summer months – except when it's very warm, of course. I do have a tendency to burn in the sun.' She crossed purposefully to a pair of garden shears which lay on the terrace. Picking them up and placing them on a rustic table, she said, over her shoulder: 'I do hope Mr and Mrs Eames take an interest in the garden.'

Mark nodded. 'I hope so, too. By the way, what are you going to do about Daisy?'

She studiously rearranged the shears on the table. 'I haven't decided yet, but there's an animal sanctuary down in Malverley, I'll probably . . .' Seeing a stray leaf on the terrace, she picked it up and placed it with the shears on the table. 'Well, you'll presumably let me know when contracts are exchanged, Mr Dunn, so that I can make all the necessary arrangements to vacate the premises and so on.'

Sensing that his visit was at an end, Mark shook her hand. 'Of course,' he said. 'I'll be in touch immediately there's any news. And, in the meantime . . . please feel free to call me at any time if . . . well, if you have any queries or . . .'

Miss Spiers showed him out through the gate at the side of the cottage and he reversed the car over the little stone bridge, waved to her through the window and drove off.

Caroline Adams laid her knife and fork carefully on her empty plate. 'So, what do you think?'

Mark toyed with the contents of his plate, arranging his remaining chips in a neat, geometric pile on top of his steak. 'Well,' he said at length, 'at the end of the day, you have to do whatever you think best. I mean . . . what does the decision really come down to?'

She frowned at him. 'It comes down to whether I settle on a. another secretary to look after the office side of things, or b. an assistant who I can train up to take on some of my workload, showing potential buyers round properties and so on. I just thought you might be able to shed a bit of light on the pros and cons, after all . . . are you going to eat that or just make pretty shapes with it?'

He looked up. 'Sorry. Well, I suppose it's a question of . . . whether you need . . . I think I'd probably go for b. Unless, of course, you think a. would . . . Do you fancy a dessert?'

She regarded him silently, her intelligent blue eyes slightly quizzical under her blonde fringe. 'Yes, OK,' she said at last. 'I'll go for the summer pudding. How about you?'

He sighed. 'Er . . . yes, I'll probably have that, too.' He caught the eye of the waiter who took the order, cleared away their plates and went back to the kitchen.

'I've got a problem,' he said, breaking a long silence.

'I know,' said Caroline.

'What do you mean, you know?' he said, raising his eyebrows and placing his hands on the table. 'How could you possibly know what I'm thinking when I haven't even mentioned it yet?'

'I don't know *what* you're thinking, but I do know there's *something* on your mind.' She smiled and rested her hand on his. 'Shouldn't we be sharing our problems? Maybe when we've sorted yours out, we could have a crack at mine?'

He smiled back at her and squeezed her hand. 'I'm sorry. You were telling me about this business of needing more help in the office. Have you thought about . . .'

'No, you first,' she insisted. 'Age before beauty and all that.'

He grinned ruefully. 'Well, it's Rosemary Spiers. You know – she's selling Butterfly Cottage and moving to Spain.'

'Yes,' said Caroline. 'Good news about Mr and Mrs Eames, wasn't it? They were really keen on that other property out at Malverley but . . .'

'But you worked the old Adams magic on them and persuaded them to buy Butterfly Cottage instead.'

'Well, that was what you wanted, wasn't it? I understood Miss Spiers had to sell quickly or her plans to move to Spain would have fallen through. They took a bit of convincing, I can tell you, but . . .'

Mark rubbed his eyes and rested his chin on his hands. 'It's not as simple as I thought. I went to see the old girl this afternoon and . . . She doesn't want to move to Spain. She desperately wants to stay in her cottage with her cat and her garden and her . . . well, her life.'

'Oh. So she wants to withdraw from the sale?'

'No.'

Caroline leant back in her chair to allow the waiter to serve their summer puddings. When he had gone, she said slowly and deliberately, as though explaining something to a child: 'So Miss Spiers told you that she doesn't want to sell her cottage but she doesn't want to withdraw from the sale. Perhaps I'm missing something here.'

'No, she didn't tell me any of this,' explained Mark. 'She didn't need to. If you'd seen her in her home, you'd realise it's perfectly obvious. No doubt she accepted her niece's invitation out of family loyalty. But now, having agreed to take on the villa in Andalusia and come this far with the scheme, she feels that she's trapped into continuing and seeing it through. To back out of the sale now would seem – to her – like letting her niece down. And, besides, we've given her a leaving party at Dufty's and everyone's wished her well and congratulated her on her "sense of adventure" and . . . well, she couldn't possibly back out now. But I know for certain that she'll pine for her beloved cottage and her cat and goodness knows how she'll fare in Spain – she even burns in the sun, for God's sake. It's a disaster in the making, Caroline. And I have to sit back and watch it happen.'

Caroline finished her pudding and took a sip of her wine. 'OK, let's look at this sensibly,' she said. 'Miss Spiers really wants to stay in her cottage but feels – understandably in the circumstances – that she's trapped into the course that she's adopted and can't call off the sale. So the sale has to be called off for her.'

Mark shook his head. 'No, it would be completely wrong for me to step in and make decisions for her. She's a grown woman, for heaven's sake. As her solicitor, my job is to carry out her instructions, not to advise her on how or where to live her life. I certainly can't call off the sale for her.'

'Neither can I,' said Caroline. 'But the Eameses could. The place they were looking at in Malverley is still on the market and, frankly, I think it would suit them better. That could solve everything, couldn't it?'

Mark thought. 'Well, yes, but that's not up to you or me, that's up to the Eameses.'

'Of course it is,' she answered. 'But who can tell what may happen? Now – it's my turn. What do you think I should do, take on a secretary or an assistant estate agent?'

Mark smiled at her. 'Let's have coffee and talk it through.'

It was a week later that Miss Spiers again set foot into the offices of Dufty Dufty Popple & Dunn. Dressed as usual in smart business suit and crisp white blouse, her features sharp and expressionless behind wire-rimmed glasses, she sat facing Mark who was leaning back in his chair, one arm resting on his desk.

'I received your letter,' she said, 'from which I understand that Mr and Mrs Eames have decided, after all, not to buy Butterfly Cottage.'

Mark nodded. 'Yes. Caroline Adams, the estate agent, rang me on Monday to say that the Eameses had had second thoughts over the weekend and decided to buy the house in Malverley which, as you know, they had previously been considering. I'm very sorry. But Caroline says their mind is completely made up. I'm afraid this rather messes up your plans. We can put the cottage back on the market, of course and hope that . . .'

'That would be pointless,' said Miss Spiers. 'I telephoned Diane as soon as I read your letter and, while she was naturally disappointed, she explained that they had another tenant ready to move into the villa and, for financial reasons, they could wait no longer. I'm afraid I have no choice but to abandon my plans to move.'

'It must be a great disappointment to you,' said Mark.

'Of course,' she agreed. 'But I fully understand Diane's position – she has no choice in the matter. And neither do I.'

'I'm very sorry,' said Mark, solemnly. 'What will you do now?'

'Mr Dufty has very kindly agreed that I can resume my duties here as from this afternoon. Although he has agreed that I can change to a part-time basis, working mornings only and dealing solely with the book-keeping side of things. I've been suggesting for some time that the firm should employ an office manager to look after the general day-to-day running of the office systems and so forth. Indeed, unless there's anything else we need to discuss, I should really go to my office and find out what's been happening during my absence. I gather from Miss Metcalfe that the quarterly VAT return has still not been submitted.'

'Of course,' said Mark, rising. 'Oh, before you get back to work, I believe Mr Dufty would like to see you in his office.'

Miss Spiers glanced at her watch but followed him into the deserted reception area and through the door which led to an adjoining office, where Charles was waiting with Hugo, Miss Metcalfe, Trish, Bernard and Conchita. Their greeting as she entered, while considerably less noisy than at her leaving party the previous week, was warm, sympathetic and welcoming. Charles spoke on behalf of her colleagues when he expressed their regret that her plans to move to Spain had been so cruelly thwarted by circumstances, but pleasure that the firm was to continue to enjoy the benefit of her services and her company for the foreseeable future. Miss Metcalfe expressed relief that the firm's finances would again be in expert and capable hands and Bernard presented the reinstated book-keeper with a bunch of flowers and, much to her consternation, kissed her on the cheek, to appreciative applause.

It was almost six o'clock that afternoon and the little office at the back of the building was still occupied by its rightful incumbent who was putting the finishing touches to the quarterly VAT return prior to going home to Butterfly Cottage, where Daisy would be awaiting her customary saucer of milk.

Seeing her light still on, Mark popped his head round her door. 'I'm just off, Miss Spiers. Can I leave you to lock up?'

In the middle of adding up a column of figures, she nodded without looking up and he was closing the door when she called: 'Mr Dunn . . .'

He again put his head round the door. Her head remained bowed over the figures.

'Thank you,' she said without looking up.

He smiled, inclined his head and softly closed the door.

~

Henry nodded, sipping at his gin and tonic. 'Poor old Miss Spiers had got herself into a situation and couldn't see the obvious way out?'

'Absolutely.'

'So Mark and Caroline made the decision for her?'

'Couldn't possibly comment.'

'All right,' said Henry. 'As an objective, disinterested party, what move do you think I should make?'

'Take my bishop with your knight which will then cover your queen.'

Henry shrugged and made the suggested move.

Charles then moved his remaining bishop four spaces. 'Checkmate!' he said, taking up his glass and raising it in salute to the gallant loser.

The Condition Aforesaid

Henry Middleton dropped the newspaper which he had been reading and shook his head. 'Serve the blighter right!' he said.

Charles Dufty paused in setting up the chess pieces. 'What serves who right?'

'Fella in the paper. Won over a million on the lottery two years ago, gave up his job and blew the lot on booze, women and loose living. Now he's destitute. Just been convicted of making false statements on his benefits application. What do these people expect? Do they really believe that money on its own is going to produce permanent happiness?'

Charles nodded. 'Yes, they probably do. Like the taking of a "recreational drug", the sudden acquisition of money can give rise to an artificial "high" which, like all things, passes. The resulting "down" then leaves them more depressed than they were before. The fact is that a wet Monday is still a wet Monday whether you're rich, poor, drunk or sober.'

'Avarice can certainly lead people to behave badly,' remarked Henry.

Charles finished setting up the chessboard and sat back in his chair. 'Did I ever tell you about that business at "The Poplars" last summer?'

'What, that big, rambling old place over at West Warpington?'

'That's the place. Used to belong to Clarence Martin until he died. My son Hugo and I were his executors. Old Clarence had amassed *quite a decent amount over the years and, as often happens, "grief-stricken" family members who hadn't seen him for years suddenly appeared out of nowhere like bees round a honeypot. Old Clarence could be an awkward old cuss but he had a sense of responsibility to his family and that was reflected in his will. The thing he failed to take into account was good old-fashioned avarice.'*

Tom Atkins peered around the tiny waiting area, looking for a place to put out the cigarette he had been smoking when he came in. Finding none, he stubbed it carefully on the sole of his shoe and placed the butt in his pocket. He then turned his attention to the dark-haired receptionist who was painting her nails while hunching her shoulder against her ear to support the telephone receiver into which she was speaking rapidly in what Tom judged to be Spanish.

His wife, Olive, laid down the year-old copy of *National Geographic* which she had been frowning at for the past few minutes and looked at Tom. 'Did you bring the letter with you?' she asked.

Tom handed over a folded sheet from his pocket and she read it for perhaps the twentieth time since it had arrived through the letterbox two days earlier. It was from Messrs Dufty Dufty Popple & Dunn and regretfully informed Tom of the death of his Uncle Clarence. It went on to mention a will and suggested that Tom and Olive should call in to see Mr Dufty Junior at their earliest convenience to discuss certain matters.

'Can't you even remember what your Uncle Clarence looked like?' she asked. Tom shook his head. 'I've told you – I only met him once and that was about thirty years ago when I was a kid of ten or thereabouts. All I remember is that he gave me half-a-crown and said that if I looked after it and used it properly, one day it would grow into a fortune.'

'What happened?' enquired Olive.

'I spent it on a penknife and fourteen gobstoppers.'

The receptionist had now paused in her nail painting to listen attentively to the person on the other end of the telephone, leaving a silence punctuated only by the distant clacking of keyboards and the occasional shrilling of a telephone.

'I dropped the penknife down a drain the next day while I was being sick from the gobstoppers,' Tom mused.

At last, the waiting room door opened abruptly and Trish, Mr Dufty Junior's freckle-faced secretary, entered. 'Mr Dufty Junior will see you now,' she smiled and they followed her out.

Hugo Dufty was standing behind his amazingly cluttered desk, tearing up strips of blotting paper and vainly trying to mop up a puddle of coffee which was slowly spreading over the papers in front of him. He looked up brightly. 'Ah! Mr and Mrs Atkins – do sit down – move those files on to the floor, that's right. I'm afraid I've just had a slight, er . . . oops!' He jabbed at a rivulet of coffee which threatened to escape over the edge of the desk. The door burst open again and Trish bustled over to the desk, a file of papers in one hand and a cloth in the other. With practised ease, she brought the situation under control and, in a matter of seconds, the solicitor was seated at his desk, now only moderately damp, leafing through a file of papers before him.

He assumed a professional air and looked very gravely at Tom and Olive for several seconds before speaking. 'Mr and Mrs Atkins, I want you to consider very carefully before answering this question. Is there, in your considered opinion, any reasonable likelihood of a reconciliation between you in the foreseeable future? Think carefully and consider the children.'

There followed a long pause during which Tom opened his mouth to say something but closed it again after a few seconds. It was Olive who at length pointed out, rather lamely: 'We haven't got any children.'

After a further pause, Hugo again scanned his file of papers.

Then he suddenly looked up, gazed at a point in space some inches above Tom's head and dashed to a filing cabinet in the corner, returning to his desk carrying another file of papers which he spread before him. 'Aha!' he cried, 'I think I've solved it – it's Mr and Mrs Atkins of 4 Partridge Drive, isn't it?'

Tom and Olive nodded dumbly.

'Yes, of course,' smiled Hugo. 'Now, I'm glad you called in. I have here your late Uncle Clarence's will, Mr Atkins.' He held up a document, looked at it, put it down and held up another. 'Now, by his will, your late Uncle Clarence appoints my father, Mr Dufty Senior, and myself to be his executors and, after certain small pecuniary and specific legacies, he bequeathes the whole of his estate to you both.'

There was a sharp intake of breath from Tom and Olive asked: 'How much?'

'Well, er . . . it's not possible at this stage to give an accurate figure,' replied Hugo, leafing through the file, 'but I think I can safely estimate the value of the residuary estate, after inheritance tax and administration expenses and so on, at a figure in excess of one and a half million pounds.

'But . . .' he continued hurriedly, seeing Tom's eyes glaze over, 'there is a condition attached to the bequest – though it's by no means, er, an onerous one. You see, your late Uncle Clarence lived at his country house, "The Poplars", with his brother, er . . . your Uncle Matthew, if I may so, er, refer to him. Now, your Uncle Matthew has never enjoyed good health and your late Uncle Clarence always worried about his wellbeing. In his will, therefore, he gives the residue of his estate to you upon condition that you agree to take Uncle Matthew into your home to live with you for the rest of his life and, further, that such arrangement is, from the outset, approved by the executors and by Uncle Matthew himself. If such approval is not forthcoming, the residue of the estate is to be paid to such charity or charities as the executors shall, in their absolute discretion, think fit. Subject to the aforesaid condition, the income from the estate would be made available to you for Uncle Matthew's maintenance and benefit and, upon his death, the capital comprising the residue would be paid over to you.'

'How old is Uncle Matthew?' Olive, as always, went to the heart of the matter.

'Er . . . let me see now . . . yes, Uncle Matthew is now eighty-three. Naturally, he is at present, er, saddened by the untimely death of his brother and it may, therefore, be advisable to, er . . . let things lie for a few weeks to allow him to recover fully. May I suggest that I contact you in approximately one month's time? We can then arrange for you to meet Uncle Matthew either at "The Poplars" or at your own home and, provided you all get along well and the arrangement meets with the approval of Mr Dufty Senior and myself as executors, then Uncle Matthew could move in with you. Would that be satisfactory?'

Tom and Olive looked at each other, then at the solicitor, and nodded agreement.

'Splendid!' said Hugo, rising abruptly to his feet and knocking over his chair. He ushered them to the door. 'You'll find Uncle Matthew a quite charming old gentleman – quite a colourful character in his own way. I'm sure you'll enjoy having him live with you. Well, goodbye. And I'll contact you in about a month's time.'

Tom and Olive walked in silence to their car and it was not until they were safely under way that Tom trusted himself to speak. 'Woo-hoo!' he yelled, 'one and a half million smacker-oonies – we're rich – we're bloody rich, Ollie! And all because of dear old Uncle Clarence, God rest his soul.'

'Never mind about dear old Uncle Clarence,' Olive interjected. 'It's dear old Uncle Matthew we've got to worry about. Have you ever met him?'

'I met him a few times when I was small. He was in the navy then. He used to tell me rollicking tales of the sea, that sort of thing. I seem to remember he went to Australia for a few years before he went to live with Uncle Clarence. Bit of a black sheep really, I think. Still, he can't get up to much mischief at eighty-three, can he? Poor old soul, he's probably bed-ridden most of the time. We can park him in the spare room and he'll be no trouble at all.'

Olive appeared doubtful. 'He could go on for another twenty years,' she pointed out. 'Get his telegram from the Queen and all that. Anyway, we don't know what he's like; he might . . . where are you going – you don't normally turn left here?'

'Where do you think I'm going?' replied Tom. 'I'm going to "The Poplars" like a dutiful nephew to see my dear old Uncle Matthew.'

'But the solicitor said . . .'

'Never mind what the solicitor said; a month's a long time at eighty-three. The old boy could hand in his chips before then and it's goodbye to our fortune. Not likely! We'll go and see him now and by the time old Dufty gets around to doing anything we'll have it all sewn up. In any case, I'm his only remaining family; I ought to go and see him at this sad time – a bit of comfort in his hour of need. Blood's thicker than wossaname and all that.'

'The Poplars' turned out to be a fairly large old stone-built house in the country, approached by a long, potholed drive flanked by overgrown rhododendrons. A smell of dank vegetation pervaded everything. Olive caught her heel on a rough patch of gravel as they walked from the car to the front door. 'Damn!' she snapped. 'Why we had to come traipsing out to this mouldy old ruin I don't know. He probably isn't in, anyway.'

'Come on, Ollie,' soothed Tom. 'Just keep thinking of all that lolly. Here we go!'

He gave two loud raps with the knocker and several large

crows flapped out of a nearby tree, protesting raucously at the noise.

'I told you he wouldn't be in,' complained Olive after a long, expectant pause.

'Well, he can't have gone far at eighty-three,' retorted Tom. 'In any case, I'm sure I heard a sound from inside.' He pressed his ear to the door and listened intently.

'Oh, come out of the way!' Olive pushed past him. Stooping slightly, she lifted the flap of the letterbox and peered in. A stifled squeal issued from her lips and she leapt back with a look of frozen horror.

'Whatsamatta, whatsamatta?' cried Tom, alarmed. Olive merely stood, pointing a wavering finger at the letterbox. Feeling his scalp prickle, Tom gingerly raised the flap of the letterbox and stooped to look in. His anxious gaze was met squarely by a pair of bloodshot eyes almost hidden by a tangle of white eyebrows. The eyes blinked twice before Tom allowed the letterbox flap to drop.

Tom straightened up slowly and drew a deep breath, recovering his composure. 'Well, at least we know he's in,' he murmured.

'He's barmy!' said Olive, loudly.

Tom shushed her frantically. 'He's probably just nervous of unexpected callers,' he reasoned. 'And quite rightly, too – stuck out here on his own, miles from anywhere. We could be anybody.' Putting his face close to the door, he called softly: 'Uncle Matthew, it's me, your nephew, Tom. We've just heard about poor Uncle Clarence and we've come to see if you're all right.'

There was a prolonged silence followed by a violent rattling of chains and bolts and Olive stood back two paces, despite Tom's reassuring smile. At length, the door opened a few inches and a head peered round the edge on a level with Tom's shirt collar. The general appearance of the head was not unlike a very old Cox's Orange Pippin sandwiched between two mop heads – the upper comprising a fringe of frizzy white hair and eyebrows and the lower being the bushiest, spikiest, whitest beard that Tom had ever seen.

Olive giggled and Tom stared as a gnarled hand appeared round the edge of the door immediately below the head, clutching a discoloured clay pipe which it stuck firmly between two rows of broken, yellowed teeth that appeared in the lower mop head. The bloodshot eyes blinked once and a sound issued from around the clay pipe: 'Eh?'

Tom bent his knees to bring his face level with the other and raised his voice: 'It's me, Uncle Matthew, your nephew Tom. Of course, it's a long time since we met – in fact you may not remember me. But I remember you. I can recall you telling me tales of the sea when you were in the navy. This is my wife, Olive. Olive, say hello to Uncle Matthew.'

Olive did as she was bidden and the old head nodded energetically up and down several times.

'Well,' smiled Tom. 'There's a lot to talk about. Would you like us to come in for a while?'

The door opened fully at last to reveal the owner of the head as a little, bent figure in shirtsleeves and baggy trousers held up with braces. He stood back and motioned Tom and Olive in with an exaggerated gesture of a gnarled and sinewy arm, all the while blinking and grinning through the white whiskers and bobbing his head. Shutting the door, he beckoned them to follow him up the dark stairway.

'He's sprightly enough,' murmured Tom.

'He's barmy!' said Olive.

'He's just a bit deaf, that's all,' returned Tom.

The old man led them along the landing towards the open door of a room which, even before he entered it, reminded Tom of the rodent house at the local zoo. He glanced round at Olive who was wrinkling her nose in disgust. As they followed the old man into the room, the reason for the verminous odour became immediately apparent. The walls were lined with roughly constructed cages, cobbled together from tea chests and chicken wire. The murky interiors of these cages afforded glimpses of small, scuttling shapes.

'Ferrets!' said Tom.

'Barmy!' said Olive, obviously intent upon following her own train of thought.

The old man opened one of the cages and drew out a particularly large and evil-looking specimen, which he held up, proudly. ''Oratio!' he wheezed, by way of identification. ''e be a good'un!'

Olive backed away warily to the open door. Tom, on the other hand, advanced with a delighted if somewhat fixed, smile. 'He's a beauty, isn't he? My word, yes . . . who's a fine, handsome fellow then . . . see how he likes his ears ticklAAAGH! . . . He's got a fine set of teeth, hasn't he, Uncle?'

Uncle Matthew's head bobbed even more energetically as he chuckled wheezily through his clay pipe. ''e be a good'un!' he reaffirmed.

Wrapping his handkerchief around his bloodied index finger, Tom got down to brass tacks: 'Well, Uncle Matthew, what are you going to do now poor Uncle Clarence has gone?'

''e be wantin' 'is dinner!' observed Uncle Matthew, replacing Horatio lovingly into his evil-smelling cage.

Realising the extent of Uncle Matthew's deafness, Tom raised his voice to a polite roar: 'I was saying, Uncle Matthew, what are you going to do now that Uncle Clarence has gone? Where are you going to live?'

The old man paused in his ministrations to Horatio, turned to Tom and removed the clay pipe from his mouth. Obviously contact had been established.

'I lives 'ere with me ferrets,' he explained.

'Yes, I know, Uncle,' yelled Tom, compassionately, 'but you can't go on living here on your own, can you? I mean, who'd look after you when you're ill? Who'd cook your meals and do your washing and . . . and all that?'

Uncle Matthew blinked several times and sat down on the rumpled bed which stood by the window. There was a long silence, during which he filled his pipe and then lit it, surrounding himself with clouds of acrid smoke and depositing the spent match among its countless predecessors on the cracked lino.

Tom, sensing that Olive was about to say something, continued quietly: 'Think of the money, love, just think of the money and leave it to me.' She relapsed into a doubtful silence.

'Look, Uncle Matthew,' he continued, in as gentle a tone as he could manage at the top of his voice. 'Why don't you come and live with us? We've got a spare room and we'd love to have you.' Ignoring his wife's choking spasm, he went on: 'You needn't bring anything with you except your clothes; we'll provide everything to make you comfortable. What about it, eh?'

Gurgling, sucking noises issued from the clay pipe and the room slowly filled with tobacco smoke. The strain of shouting was beginning to tell on Tom. He unwound his handkerchief from his finger and mopped his face, leaving a smudge of blood over his left eye. 'You could sit in the garden in summer and we'll fix you up a TV set in your room for when it's raining.'

The smoke thickened, making Tom's eyes smart. He screwed up his courage. 'You can even bring your ferrets with you,' he bellowed, hoarsely, between clenched teeth.

Olive, afflicted with a sudden faintness, subsided heavily upon a nearby wicker chair which emitted a protesting squeak and developed a dangerous list to starboard.

Uncle Matthew removed the pipe from his mouth and looked squarely at Tom. A happy grin spread slowly over his face and Tom noticed with interest that, of the old man's seven teeth, five were broken and the remaining two were worn almost completely away. Then the pipe was replaced in the mouth and Uncle Matthew nodded his agreement to the proposal.

'I know it's not been easy this past five weeks, love.' Tom's tone was sympathetic as he handed his wife her morning cup of tea in bed. 'But we must remember why we're doing it. It won't be for ever and then we can buy a house by the sea and do all the things we've always dreamt about.'

Olive sat up and leant back against her pillow, dabbing at her red-rimmed eyes with a damp handkerchief. 'It's all right for you,' she sobbed, 'you're out at work for most of the day. It's me that has to cope with him and his mad ways and his clutter and his pipes and his . . . his bloody ferrets!' She blew her nose loudly.

'D'you know what he was doing yesterday?' she continued. 'He was digging up that bed of petunias and salvias in the front garden and planting potatoes . . . more potatoes! It wouldn't be so bad if he'd just stay in his room but he's got his gardening tools in the kitchen, his fishing tackle in the dining room and his ferrets in the living room. Now he's started on the garden, we've only got our bedroom left! It's just too much, Tom. I don't know how much more I can take.'

'I know, love, I know,' soothed Tom. 'But think of that house by the sea; a new car; perhaps even a boat, eh? And we'll be able to travel! A cruise in the Mediterranean like you've always wanted. Oh, Ollie, it'll be worth it, won't it?'

She dried her eyes and nodded. 'I suppose so,' she admitted, getting out of bed. 'As you say, it won't be for ever – he *is* eighty-three. Well, let's get dressed and I'll cook breakfast.'

Tom and Olive usually managed to have breakfast without Uncle Matthew, particularly on fine mornings, when he was out in the garden early, replacing the bedding plants with potatoes. 'I never realised you could get so many potatoes in a small garden,' remarked Tom, carrying his empty plate to the sink and tripping over a rusty hoe which was leaning against the garden roller next to the cooker.

Olive had gone to the front door to collect the post and she returned now with an envelope. 'It's from Dufty Dufty Popple & Dunn, the solicitors,' she said.

'Well, open it then,' said Tom, moving a pile of flowerpots from a kitchen stool and sitting down.

Olive did so. 'Mr Dufty Junior is coming to see us at ten thirty this morning with Mr Dufty Senior,' she said with a catch of her breath. 'He says they would like to ascertain whether our accommodation is suitable for Uncle Matthew to live here.'

Tom jumped up, knocking over a sack of leaf mould under the table. 'Right, Ollie! This is it! We've got to show them how well Uncle Matthew has settled in.'

'But the place is a mess!' wailed Olive. 'We'll never be able to clear it all up!'

'No, no, no!' rapped Tom. 'Don't you see – we leave it just as it is! That's the way Uncle Matthew likes it. We let Dufty see how Uncle Matthew's taken over the place – and we also let him see that we're quite happy about it – that's just the kind of thing he'll be looking for!'

'I suppose you're right,' agreed Olive. 'But we ought to smarten Uncle Matthew up a bit.'

Tom considered this. 'Yes, all right then. We'll clean him up, get him into his best suit and dust him off a bit. Come on, we haven't got much time.'

An hour later, Uncle Matthew was sitting on the sofa in the lounge, surrounded by his ferret cages and looking distinctly uncomfortable in his best suit. He had been washed and scrubbed thoroughly and his hair and beard had been brushed until they almost shone. Tom and Olive gave him a last inspection and made one or two final adjustments as the doorbell rang.

Tom straightened his tie, drew a deep breath and walked into the hall, stepping carefully over a box of seed potatoes. He opened the front door. Mr Dufty Junior stood in the porch, accompanied by a tall, distinguished old gentleman in dark overcoat and smart trilby. 'Good morning, Mr Atkins,' smiled Hugo, shaking Tom's proffered hand. 'I'm sorry to drop in on you at such short notice.'

'Not at all,' Tom assured him. 'You're very welcome. And this would be Mr Dufty Senior?' He held out his hand to the elderly gentleman.

Hugo held up a finger. 'Ah, no. Actually, my father wasn't able to come after all; touch of bronchitis, you know. Instead, I thought I'd give you a little surprise. Mr Atkins, this is your Uncle Matthew!'

Tom's smile remained frozen on his face, concealing the confused activity of his brain, as the solicitor continued speaking: 'You see, your Uncle Matthew was discharged from hospital yesterday and I thought it might be a good idea to bring him along to see your wife and yourself in your home so that you can all, er . . . er, may I ask what, er . . .' he trailed off, pointing to the door of the living room, from which was issuing a cloud of pungent smoke. Tom's smile remained fixed as he opened his mouth. 'Tobacco smoke,' he said.

'Ah! . . . Yes, of course,' said Hugo, uncertainly. The tall gentleman coughed once, violently.

'Well . . .' Hugo continued. 'Shall we, er . . .' He waved a hand towards the living room and Tom, still in a dreamlike state and feeling a certain weakness in his lower limbs, led the way along the hall. Assisted by the solicitor, the old gentleman negotiated the box of seed potatoes, some of whose contents were now spilling on to the carpet, and peered into the living room, applying a handkerchief to his nose as the foul-smelling smoke billowed in the air. Olive, who had overheard most of the somewhat disjointed conversation in the hall, was sitting bolt upright in an armchair amidst the ferret cages, an expression of horror frozen on her face.

A sudden scuttling movement from the floor near the sofa

captured everyone's attention. 'What's . . . what's that?' Hugo snapped nervously.

'A ferret,' said Tom tonelessly.

The front door was heard to slam and, through the bay window, Tom, Olive and Hugo watched the old gentleman, trilby clamped on his head, trotting stiffly down the front drive and out of the gate. It was some time before anyone present could think of anything meaningful to say but Tom, at length, established control over his slackly hanging jaw and spoke.

'If that was Uncle Matthew,' he wavered, 'then who . . . is this?' He pointed to the bewhiskered figure sitting on the sofa, dropping pipe ash down his best tie.

Hugo turned from watching his elderly client's rheumatic progress along the pavement outside.

'This . . . ?' he cried, '*this* is Obadiah, your late Uncle Clarence's gardener. He lives in at "The Poplars".'

'Not now I don't,' wheezed Obadiah, knocking out his pipe on the glass-topped coffee table. 'I lives 'ere now . . . with me ferrets.'

~

'So the condition in the will failed and this Tom and Olive Atkins got nothing?' grinned Henry.

'Correct,' confirmed Charles.

'So who did get old Clarence's fortune?'

Charles sipped at his whisky and water. 'Hugo and I, as the executors, used the discretion granted to us by the will to divide the residue equally between two charitable organisations. One of which was the Walchester Care Homes Trust, who used the funds to convert Clarence's old home, "The Poplars", into a beautifully appointed rest home for the elderly.'

'Whose most valued and respected resident was, of course . . .'

'Clarence's brother, Matthew,' nodded Charles.

'What about the other half of the estate?'

'Well,' said Charles. 'Hugo and I thought long and hard about that. As you know, we always try to find a solution which is fair and satisfactory to all parties.'

'So . . . don't tell me . . . you set up a charity to benefit dis-appointed beneficiaries who almost came into a fortune but blew it by being greedy?'

'No,' said Charles, draining his glass. 'We gave it to the West Warpington Retired Gardeners and Ferret-Fanciers' Benevolent Society.'

In Flagrante Delicto

Charles Dufty looked up from the chessboard and raised his hand in the direction of Stanley, the Dog and Tadpole's Friday night barman, who, oblivious of his customers, was intently studying a well-thumbed copy of the Daily Comet. Charles tutted. 'A chap could expire from dehydration in here while Stanley catches up on the latest gossip,' he remarked to Henry.

A disapproving cough from Charles caused Stanley to look up and spring to life, pouring a whisky and water and a gin and tonic and hurrying them over to the two old friends. 'Sorry, gents,' he said. 'I was just reading about some bloke in Perth who gave up playing the bagpipes because his wife developed a sensitivity to noise. Apparently he's been playing the pipes all his life and won all kinds of awards for it – he was even asked to play for the Queen at Balmoral – but when he found it was affecting his wife's health, he vowed never to play again and gave his pipes away to his cousin . . . just like that. Must have been a terrible sacrifice for him.'

'Terrible sacrifice for his cousin's wife as well, I imagine,' remarked Henry, sipping gratefully at his gin and tonic as Stanley returned to the bar.

Charles chuckled. 'It's surprising what lengths people will sometimes go to to protect those they love,' he observed.

'If I'd been playing the bagpipes all my life, I'd find it a blessed relief to stop, never mind a sacrifice,' countered Henry.

Charles shrugged. 'That which is a relief to some would be a sacrifice to others. Different strokes for different folks, eh?'

∼

The clientele of the Duck and Dive in Walchester were known as a lively crowd, particularly on Saturday nights when its premises afforded a popular meeting place for the town's younger inhabitants to gather and cast aside the cares of the week, prior to moving on to one or other of the two nightclubs in the vicinity.

Thursday evenings, however, were usually comparatively uneventful and the few groups enjoying a quiet drink in the lounge bar looked up in mild surprise as sundry squeals and shrill laughter issued from the adjoining private room, whose door had opened briefly to admit a good-looking young man in jeans and sweater, carrying an attaché case. Then the door closed behind him and the drinkers in the lounge bar returned to their conversations.

Around the table, which stood in the centre of the private room behind the closed door, were assembled a number of brightly attired young women whose heads were adorned by a variety of coloured wigs, party boppers and sparkly Stetsons, and whose eyes followed the young man who crossed the room with his attaché case and entered another small room, smiling knowingly at the girls before he closed the door behind him.

'I know him,' shrilled Trish, secretary to Hugo Dufty of Dufty Dufty Popple & Dunn, above the chorus of whoops and hollers induced by the young man's smile. 'That's Harry Alcock. I went to school with him.'

'Is that really his name?' yelled Tracey.

'Yeah,' confirmed Trish. 'He used to be a window cleaner in Hockam but he's doing strippagrams now to earn more money but he's not getting many bookings. I told him he needs to advertise more.'

A commotion broke out on the other side of the table as

Tracey, in her excitement, spilled a full glass of white wine over the pink party wig of her sister Patsy, whose forthcoming wedding was the reason for the celebrations. The young woman sitting opposite Patsy rummaged in her handbag, her pink and white bunny ears bobbing as she produced her mobile phone and took a picture of Patsy, her wig dripping Chardonnay over her smudged mascara. 'I'm taking this to school after half-term and pinning it on the notice board so the kids in 4A can see teacher letting her hair down!' she shrieked, producing howls of laughter from the assembled company, including Patsy, who removed the wig, wrung it out and replaced it on her head, slightly askew.

By now, a song from *The Full Monty* had begun to issue from the CD player in the corner and, as it increased in volume, the door of the little changing room opened slowly and all eyes turned towards it.

Outside in the lounge bar, Ronnie Davenport, cub reporter with the *Walchester Advertiser*, was seated at a table, sipping his drink and chatting to Rick Hart, a photographer with the same weekly periodical. Rick had slipped off his shoes to rest his feet after a hard day covering the visit of a minor royal to the town. He moved his camera case from the table and placed it on the floor, took up his pint and leant back, grinning towards the door to the private room, behind which was audible, over the music, a chorus of cheers and applause.

'If we'd known the duchess was going to come out the front door of the Town Hall, we needn't have shinned over the wall at the back,' mused Ronnie. 'You wouldn't have sprained your ankle and we might have got a bloody picture.'

'Nobody tells us anything,' muttered the photographer. 'That's the trouble. If we knew what was . . . what's the matter?'

Ronnie was twisting round in his chair, looking at a smartly dressed, middle-aged woman who was passing through the lounge bar and walking towards the private room. She opened the door and entered. A noticeable increase in decibels greeted her before the door closed.

Ronnie turned back to his companion, frowning thoughtfully. 'That's Mrs Dufty, my old teacher,' he said. 'She's headmistress of Hockam Primary. I think she's married to Hugo Dufty, senior partner of that firm of solicitors on Hockam High Street . . .'

'Dufty Dufty Popple & Dunn,' supplied the photographer.

'That's the one.'

'What's a respectable headmistress doing at a hen party like that?' asked Rick, as the music and screeching laughter from behind the closed door mounted to a shrill crescendo. 'Not the kind of thing that'd do her reputation any good, I'd have thought.'

The two men looked at each other for a moment and then, as one, rose and walked towards the door to the private room, Rick pausing only to pick up his camera case.

Helen Dufty, meanwhile, had been gathered up by the revellers and plonked into a chair at the top of the table, despite her protestations that she had 'only popped in to give her good wishes to Patsy and to make sure the other teachers present were behaving themselves'. A bottle of wine was placed in her hand and her head was furnished with a pair of pink and silver party boppers.

Behind her, the male strippagram artiste was embarking upon the finale of his act. As the music reached a crescendo and segued into 'Rule, Britannia!', he removed his Union Jack boxer shorts and waved them over his head, belting out the chorus in a melodious, if slightly raucous, baritone.

Bewildered by the unexpected scene in which she found herself, Helen turned her head towards the performance as Harry Alcock tossed his boxer shorts in the air in a grand finish, the said garment falling to land draped artistically over Helen's party boppers. Her eyes widened in shock, her spectacles listed to one side and her features froze into a nervous, open-mouthed laugh as champagne corks popped around her.

Unnoticed by those participating in the proceedings, a camera bulb flashed once before the door closed softly.

Shortly after, Helen made her excuses and departed to her sister's house nearby, where she was staying for the week, helping her sister look after the children while her brother-in-law was away on business. There, a soothing cup of hot chocolate and two aspirins were provided for her before she retired gratefully to bed.

The landlord of the Duck and Dive prided himself on the diversity of his customer base and was saying as much to Hugo and Mark as they perched on stools at the bar the day after the foregoing events, enjoying a quiet lunch in between engagements at Walchester Magistrates Court.

'You see,' explained the landlord as he polished a glass, 'although the Saturday night crowd can be a bit lively, they soon bugger off to one of the clubs down the road so we very seldom get any trouble here. Lunchtimes, of course, we get professional men such as your good selves coming in and we try and provide a nice environment for quiet discussion and relaxation in the middle of a hard day.'

'How about evenings in the week?' asked Mark.

'Oh, we're usually pretty busy,' said the landlord. 'But, again, it's mainly just people coming in for a quiet drink with friends and not bothering anybody.

'Mind you,' he continued, applying his tea towel to another glass, 'we do occasionally have the odd private party and they can get a bit loud at times – but they're always in the private room over there so as not to disturb the other customers. Matter of fact, we had one lot in last night – hen party that was and they're the worst. You wouldn't believe what "the gentle sex" get up to when they're all together in a group, like.'

Hugo nodded sagely in agreement. 'It does seem, these days, that girls are taking over from young men in behaving disgracefully in public.'

'Oh, it's not just girls,' said the landlord. 'Last night, for instance, one of the party was a middle-aged woman. I caught a glimpse of her through the door and she looked considerably the worse for wear, I can tell you. Pair of those bobbly things on her head, draped with a pair of Union Jack boxer shorts that the male strippagram fellow had taken off, bottle in her hand, glasses all crooked, lop-sided grin all over her face.'

Hugo shook his head in disapproval and Mark grinned. 'I'd like to have seen that.'

The landlord chuckled. 'You almost certainly will,' he said, leaning closer to them and lowering his voice. 'There were a couple of reporters in here from the *Walchester Advertiser* and they knew who the woman was. Apparently she was the headmistress of that school over at Hockam. Makes you wonder, doesn't it? If that's the kind of example teachers are setting these days, what hope is there for the kids? Anyway, one of the newspaper blokes had a camera and got a photo of her *in flagrante* . . . whatsit. So make sure you get the paper when it's out next week. Should be a laugh.'

Hugo's complexion had now assumed a leaden pallor and he rose and walked, slightly unsteadily, to a table at the other end of the room where Mark joined him after a decent interval.

'Come on, Hugo,' he said. 'It's obviously a mistake. The landlord's got it wrong. That's not Helen's scene at all. In any case, surely Helen was at home with you last night?'

Hugo, still pale, shook his head.

'Well, where was she?' frowned Mark.

'At her sister's,' said Hugo, resting his elbows on the table and massaging his forehead.

'Well, all right, she was at her sister's, so she can't have been here.'

Hugo again shook his head.

Mark stared at him for several seconds, a worried expression on his face. 'Well, if she wasn't with you and she wasn't with her sister, where was she?'

Hugo looked up. 'At a hen party,' he said, a slight tremor in his voice. Seeing Mark's blank stare, he explained: 'One of the young teachers at Helen's school, Patsy, is getting married this weekend and invited her to join a group of her friends, including some of the other teachers and, incidentally, Trish from the office, for a celebratory meal out in Walchester. Helen said that, as she'd be staying with her sister in Walchester over the half-term week anyway, she'd just pop in to wish her well. She assumed – as did I – that the occasion would consist of no more than a quiet meal and an opportunity for her to meet up with some of her staff socially and chat about this and that. There was no suggestion that . . .' He broke off and buried his face in his hands.

Slightly at a loss as to what to say, Mark began: 'It may not be as bad as all that, Hugo. These things are soon forgotten and . . .'

'You don't understand, Mark,' said Hugo, his voice muffled by his hands. 'Helen's school is to receive a visit the week after next by a representative from the Education Department who's to present an award for the best run primary school in the county. It was to be the pinnacle of Helen's career – a just and proper recognition of her years of dedication to the children in her care. When this appears in the paper next week, her career will be ruined – as will her standing in Hockam. It just . . . means so much to her . . .'

The pair sat in silence. After some minutes, Mark collected himself. 'I don't really need to be in court this afternoon; it's your case. If it's all right with you, I have to go and see someone.'

Hugo shrugged and spread his hands in a despairing gesture. 'As you wish,' he breathed quietly.

Mark rose with an air of determination. 'It'll be all right, Hugo. Trust me,' he said, and left.

The general office of the *Walchester Advertiser* was a noisy, apparently shambolic place, its desktops cluttered with computer screens, half-eaten sandwiches, piles of back issues and grimy coffee mugs. Its staff, mainly young men in torn jeans and sweatshirts and girls with determined expressions, either clustered in small, noisy groups, or perched on desks, talking earnestly into telephones. In a corner of the room was a small, glass-partitioned office in which was a desk even more cluttered than its fellows in the general office, behind which sat a short, thin man in shirtsleeves who was now looking at Mark with a disinterested expression.

'Well, what do you want me to do about it?' he asked, offering Mark a cigarette.

'Is it permitted in here?' asked Mark.

'Course it isn't,' replied the editor, lighting up and sitting back in his chair. 'That's why the bloody window's open. So, I ask again, what do you want me to do?'

'Well,' replied Mark, 'for a start, I'd appreciate it if you'd let me know whether or not you're proposing to publish that?' He gestured towards the picture which lay on the desk, featuring Helen Dufty's apparently grinning, underwear-clad face, the dancing, clearly male, figure in the background tastefully airbrushed to preserve a modicum of decency.

'Sure am,' confirmed the editor. 'I've got to put something on the Hockam page and there's bugger all else going on there. Local headmistress caught misbehaving in a public place – that should do the trick, wouldn't you say?'

Mark sighed. 'Look, Freddie, you owe me a favour. You know what happened that time at the rugby club and you also know that you'd have been banged up for criminal damage if it wasn't for me. I think that's worth something, don't you?'

The editor took a deep drag on his cigarette. 'OK,' he said. 'So I owe you a favour and some day I'll repay it – but not by compromising my position as editor of this esteemed and venerable newspaper.' His face assumed a sombre expression. 'I think you'll agree that, as editor, I have an obligation to the readers to present information which affects them and to present it responsibly and in a manner which truly reflects events as they occur.'

'Bollocks,' said Mark. 'In this case, all you're interested in doing is filling a gap on the Hockam page in as titillating a way as possible so as to give the readers a bit of a chuckle over their cornflakes next Friday.'

Freddie scratched his stubbly cheek. 'So what else am I going to fill that gap with? Nothing of interest seems to have happened in Hockam since the pub sign of the Pig and Whistle fell on the Lady Mayoress's head seven years ago. Beats me why the residents don't expire from the sheer boredom of it all. Seriously, Mark, the Hockam page might be only a small part of the paper but it really is a pain in the backside to find something to put in it every week. This thing about the headmistress is something of a gift. I'm sorry she's a friend of yours and all that, but she should have thought before she allowed herself to take part in . . . well, in that!' He indicated the photograph.

Mark was silent for a moment. 'All right,' he began, thoughtfully. 'I understand your problem. You've got to have something to put on the Hockam page. When's the deadline for next week's paper?'

'The paper's put to bed on Wednesday,' said Freddie.

'OK,' said Mark. 'What if a more interesting story comes up before then?'

The editor crossed to the open window and stubbed out his cigarette on the sill, dropping the butt to land among its numerous predecessors on the pavement below. 'Well, there's only space for one story on the Hockam page so if a better story comes along, we'd bin the Helen Dufty thing. But, realistically, Mark, I can't see anything cropping up before Wednesday – unless the local vicar's caught snorting cocaine or something.'

Mark looked at him, an amused smile flickering at the corners of his mouth. 'That's where you're wrong, Freddie, old boy.'

The other looked at him with a suddenly hopeful expression. 'You don't mean the vicar is actually . . .'

'No, no. But if you send your boys over to Hockam village green on Sunday afternoon, I think you'll have a story which will knock this hen party nonsense into a cocked hat.'

Freddie drummed his fingers on the desk, regarding the other steadily. 'OK. I'll send out young Ronnie Davenport and a photographer – they could do with a chance to redeem themselves after the fiasco of the royal visit yesterday. And if the story has legs, I'll publish it instead of the other. But . . .' he added as Mark rose to go. 'It had better be good, otherwise . . .' He picked up the photograph on the desk. 'I wonder where you can get those Union Jack boxer shorts – make a change from boring old navy blue briefs . . .'

But Mark had already left to make some important arrangements.

The area of land referred to as Hockam village green was, in fact, a field bordering a lane which branched off from the lower end of the High Street. Edged on one side by a willow-fringed stream and on the opposite side by a hedge separating it from the cricket ground, the patch had recently been mowed by Jack Paley, who farmed the fields to the west of the village. On the other side of the lane stood the Hockam Hatch, an inn much frequented by the local farming fraternity, and the rickety trestle tables in front of the ancient, ivy-covered building were now fully occupied by Hockam families whose children played noisy games of tag in the Sunday afternoon sunshine, enjoying the festive atmosphere.

The Hockam grapevine was proving a powerful channel of communication as local residents who, having heard of the forthcoming event only the previous day, drifted in groups on to the green, pleased with an opportunity to introduce a little excitement into an otherwise somnolent Sunday afternoon.

The focus of attention was a little knot of people in the centre of the field, clustered around a wooden structure which, on closer inspection, proved to be the village stocks, relocated from their usual place outside the Old Court House. A group of men directed by Constable Hobbs were busy keeping the gathering crowds at a reasonable distance from this central feature, beside which stood Mark Dunn, the Reverend Parker, Doris Chambers (the former Lady Mayoress of Walchester, wearing her customary neck brace) and a tall, slender man whose dark, floppy hair was partly obscured by a brightly coloured hat with three projections, each tipped with a bell which jingled at every movement of the wearer's head. His body was encased in a red- and black-checked jumpsuit and his tightly clad legs terminated in soft shoes (one red the other black) which turned up at the toes. In his hand he carried a short stick, topped with a miniature horse's head.

Hugo, his face flushed with embarrassment, nodded, causing the bells on his hat to jingle as the Reverend Parker explained to him the significance of the court jester's costume. 'So, you see,' said the vicar, 'the three-pointed hat, or *cockscomb* as it was called, symbolised the ears and tail of a donkey – an animal that was considered of low intelligence and a figure of fun – indeed, in the Middle Ages, it was not uncommon for the mentally handicapped to be employed as court jesters, thus providing them with a job. Of course, in these more enlightened times . . .'

Mark interrupted the clergyman's discourse to introduce

Hugo to a young man wearing jeans and a tee-shirt and carrying a notebook. 'Hugo, this is Ronnie Davenport, a reporter from the *Walchester Advertiser*. He's here to cover the event.'

Hugo shook the man's hand while using the other to muffle the furiously jingling bells on his hat.

'Ronnie,' Mark continued, 'perhaps your colleague, Rick, here, would like to take a few preliminary pictures of Hugo while the Reverend Parker explains more about the revival of the ancient village custom we're about to witness.'

Pleased to be given an opportunity to air his not inconsiderable knowledge, the vicar took Ronnie to one side and told him of the tradition dating back to the Middle Ages involving the pursuit and capture of the local lawyer, who would then be dressed as a court jester and placed in the stocks, where the villagers would pelt him with sundry soft fruits as revenge for the fees he had extracted from them over the past year. 'Of course,' laughed the Reverend Parker, 'our revival of the tradition is meant as a good-humoured attempt to remember the past customs of the village and is completely devoid of the prejudice against professional men which existed centuries ago. Hugo, as we all know, is a most respected local figure and has, in my view, very sportingly agreed to participate in the interests of keeping alive the customs and traditions of the past.'

Ronnie broke off from the notes he was scribbling to see Hugo being led by Mark to the furthest perimeter of the green, while Constable Hobbs and his volunteers kept the now considerable crowds confined to the centre of the field.

'Mark . . .' began Hugo as he replaced his hat after bending to disentangle his turned-up shoe from a molehill, 'look, I know you meant well in arranging all this but . . . I've really no experience of this kind of . . .'

'Be strong, Hugo,' said Mark, taking his arm and leading him on towards the edge of the green. 'Just remember why you're doing it. If the *Walchester Advertiser* likes this story, it'll be printed instead of the one about the hen party. Helen's reputation will be safe. That's important to you, isn't it?'

'Yes, of course it is,' replied Hugo, bending to pick up his horse's-head stick and again retrieving his jingling hat. 'But are you sure this is the only way?'

'Yes,' said Mark as they reached the edge of the green and turned to face the distant crowd, presently held back by the outstretched arms of Constable Hobbs. 'Ready?'

Hugo took a deep breath, closed his eyes and nodded, grimacing as his hat jingled merrily. At a signal from Mark, Constable Hobbs stood back from the crowd which surged forward in a laughing mass and made for their quarry, while Rick Hart ran off to the side, adjusting the zoom lens on his camera.

Moments later, Hugo was surrounded by shouting children, followed closely by panting adults who hoisted the solicitor on to their shoulders and ran with him back to the stocks into which his hands and now hatless head were fastened securely. The crowd milled around to face him and the children were armed with buckets and sponges.

'Wait!' shouted Constable Hobbs and a hush fell upon the assembled host. The policeman walked the few yards to where the jester's hat lay, picked it up and walked in a dignified manner to the stocks where he restored the garment to its rightful place atop the perspiring head of Hugo Dufty. 'Don't worry, sir,' he said quietly as he adjusted the hat to a jaunty angle, 'it's all in good fun.' He then walked to one side and gave a thumbs-up to the crowd.

After a further ten minutes or so, the children's sponges were all thrown, the crowd could laugh no more, Ronnie Davenport's notes were made, Rick Hart's pictures were taken and Hugo's humiliation was complete.

On Friday mornings the proceedings at Dufty Dufty Popple & Dunn were usually marked by an air of brisk joviality, common to those who, having toiled through another week, are soon to cast off the restraints of professionalism and relax into the pleasurable freedom of the weekend.

On this particular Friday morning, however, the office of Hugo Dufty was uncharacteristically silent as its occupant sat at his desk with his head in his hands. Opposite him sat his junior partner, Mark Dunn, scanning a copy of the *Solicitors' Journal* without obvious interest.

Hugo raised his head. 'It's usually delivered at about ten o'clock,' he said tetchily.

Mark glanced at his watch. 'It's only five past now. I've asked Miss Metcalfe to bring it in as soon as it arrives. Relax, Hugo. All will be well.'

Hugo replaced his head in his hands and, for several more minutes, the only sound was the ticking of the clock on the mantelpiece.

At length, the door opened and Miss Metcalfe entered, carrying a folded copy of the *Walchester Advertiser* which she placed in front of Hugo before leaving and closing the door behind her.

Hugo, without looking at the newspaper, picked it up and handed it to Mark who turned over the pages until he came to the Hockam feature. Holding the paper in front of him, he was silent for some moments.

'Well?' said Hugo, taking a tremulous breath.

Mark gulped slightly before closing the paper and replacing it on the desk. 'It's all right, Hugo. No mention of Helen or the hen party.'

Hugo breathed out and leant back in his chair.

'Thank God!' he said quietly. 'Mark, I owe you a debt of gratitude. You were right. It wasn't an easy thing for me to do and I shall probably have nightmares about it for some time to come, but my humiliation was worth it. The scheme worked, the newspaper people evidently preferred the story you arranged and, above all, Helen's reputation is safe. Thank you again.'

Mark waved his hands in a modest gesture, picked up the *Walchester Advertiser* and returned to his own office where he sat down and spread the paper on his desk, open at the Hockam section.

He shook his head slowly as he read the headline over the only story on the page: 'STREAKER CLIMBS HOCKAM CHURCH TOWER!' The photograph accompanying the article showed a naked young man prancing on the top of the tower. He was waving a pair of Union Jack boxer shorts above his head in one hand and, in the other was a placard which read: 'HARRY ALCOCK – AVAILABLE FOR CLUBS AND PRIVATE PARTIES *(visit alcockandbull.co.uk.)*'

∾

Henry laughed appreciatively. 'So that poor old son of yours needn't have put himself through all that indignity after all,' he wheezed, wiping his eyes. 'Still, at least he showed willing – made the sacrifice, as it were. He's done it once; he certainly won't need to do it again.'

Charles was solemn. 'Ah . . . well, as a matter of fact, the occasion was such a success that the Parish Council have decided to make it an annual event – on 16 April every year the tradition will be re-enacted. Should stimulate a lot of interest from the surrounding towns and villages. There's even talk of televising it next year.'

Henry's face lit up. 'You mean . . .'

'That's right,' nodded Charles. 'Hugo had better get his jester suit dry-cleaned!'

Stanley, the barman, looked up from his newspaper, startled by the loud guffaws emanating from the chess table in the corner.

Caveat Emptor

~

Stanley, the Dog and Tadpole's Friday barman, trotted over to the corner table in response to Charles Dufty's beckoning finger. 'Evening, Mr Dufty – the usual is it, for you and Dr Middleton?'

'Yes please, Stanley. That's assuming Dr Middleton is going to grace us with his presence – I saw him in the car park a quarter of an hour ago but he hasn't showed up yet.'

'Oh, he's in the public bar, sir,' said Stanley. 'Chatting to Del Handy.'

'My God!' exclaimed Charles. 'I've been stood up! Thrown over in favour of another. Who's Del Handy, anyway?'

'Local odd-job man,' said Stanley with an expression of distaste. 'It was him who fitted that new door in the snug – you know, the one that sticks? I told the boss we should have got a proper firm in but Del did it on the cheap, so . . . Ah, Dr Middleton. Usual gin and tonic, sir?'

Henry Middleton sat down opposite Charles, who was setting up the chessboard. 'Yes, if you please, Stanley,' he said, leaning back and emitting a self-satisfied sigh. Seeing Charles's enquiring glance, he explained: 'I think I've at last solved the problem of my garage roof.'

Charles's reaction was perhaps less enthusiastic than Henry would have wished but he continued, undaunted: 'Damn thing's been leaking for months but when I called in a firm from Walchester to have a look at it they said it needed a complete new roof and quoted me a sum which considerably exceeds the value of the car beneath it.

Anyway, I've just been talking to a local chap in the bar and he said he could repair it perfectly satisfactorily for less than a quarter of what the Walchester firm quoted.'

'Del Handy?' said Charles.

'That's the fellow, do you know him?'

Charles shook his head. 'No, I just heard someone mention his name recently.'

'Well, he seems a reliable sort of chap – says he does a lot of work in Hockam and he's coming to start on my roof next week. Reckons it'll only take him a couple of days. It's good to support local craftsmen whenever possible, don't you think? I've just realised, I left my umbrella in the snug. I'll just pop and get it.' He rose and walked across the room.

'Oh, by the way,' called Charles, 'watch out for the . . .' but his warning was interrupted by a dull thud followed by a muffled curse as the door into the snug reacted to Henry's energetic thud by coming free suddenly and connecting emphatically with his forehead. 'Blasted thing!' he complained. 'I thought this had been fixed last week.'

Henry disappeared into the snug, rubbing his head and muttering about the shoddy workmanship one encountered these days, while Charles, a wry smile playing faintly on his lips, turned his attention to the chessboard.

~

Charles Dufty broke off his conversation with Mrs Bunce, the postmistress, to peer at the sausage roll he had been about to convey to his mouth. The flaky pastry encasing the delicacy within was disfigured by a blob of rust-coloured liquid which had just descended upon it from above. Mrs Bunce followed his upward gaze, her florally embellished Sunday hat tilting to a precarious angle as she did so.

The Reverend Edward Parker, noticing the incident, made his way hurriedly through the throng to the trestle table where Mrs

Bunce and her companion stood. 'I'm so sorry, Charles,' he said, taking the plate with the offending morsel on it and ushering the pair to a safer place away from the new leak which had developed in the roof of the ancient church hall. 'I'm afraid it's raining and we never know where the next seepage is going to manifest itself.' The vicar bustled off to locate yet another bucket to catch the drips while the ladies servicing the refreshment table hastened to cover the cucumber sandwiches and buttered scones with napkins.

Turning to survey the scene from his new vantage point, Charles bumped into a tall, distinguished looking man in, perhaps, his late fifties, his straight back and military bearing slightly at odds with his friendly smile and quiet, urbane tone as he dismissed Charles's apology: 'Not at all. A little crowded in here, eh? But still, it's good to see so many of the congregation gathering after the service. Sign of a thriving community, I always think.'

'Absolutely,' agreed Charles. 'Mind you, it's a pity there isn't somewhere a little more suitable to meet.'

'I must admit,' nodded the other, glancing up at the tangle of old beams and rafters, 'the hall does appear to be in a less than . . .'

'Ah! I was going to introduce you two.' The Reverend Parker hurried over to them, plastic bucket in hand. 'Charles, this is Major General Buller-Meyer, who's only very recently moved into the area. Major General, this is Charles Dufty, solicitor and founder of Dufty Dufty Popple & Dunn in the High Street – a very prominent and respected member of our little community here.'

'Pleased to meet you,' smiled Charles as they shook hands. 'Are you planning to stay in the area or just visiting for a while?'

'Oh no, I'm here permanently,' replied the other. 'Taken the Old Post House out at West Lane, just finished moving in some sticks of furniture and getting settled in. Retired from the army a couple of years ago and feel the need to put down a few roots, you know the sort of thing. Looked at quite a few places around the country and decided that Hockam's the very place.'

'Good, good,' breezed Charles. 'You couldn't have made a better choice – and I think you'll find you'll be made very welcome, Major General. Oh, and by the way, a word to the wise – you may want to know that we pronounce it *Hokum*. Small point but since you're to be one of us, as it were . . .'

The other man grinned. 'Thanks, Charles. Important to get these things right, isn't it? And by the way, it's Jerry – none of that Major General nonsense. All very well in the army, of course, but a bit out of place here in . . . *Hokum*.' The correctly pronounced name evidently gave him pleasure and both he and Charles chuckled appreciatively.

The Reverend Parker, having satisfied himself that his bucket was placed in precisely the right place to deal with the latest leak, rejoined the two men whose conversation had again turned to the church hall's lamentable state of repair.

The vicar sighed deeply. 'When I first moved here some eight years ago,' he said, 'I decided that the complete refurbishment of the hall must take a high priority but . . . as you can see . . .' he waved a hand indicating the leaking roof, rotting window frames, uneven floor and peeling decorations. 'I'm afraid things are still going from bad to worse. It's a constant source of worry.'

'Can't anything be done?' asked Jerry. 'I mean, surely we could at least arrange for a lick of paint and a spot of carpentry work – perhaps a working party of volunteers from among the parishioners or . . .'

The Reverend Parker shook his head sadly. 'We've looked into that and, while there would be no shortage of voluntary help with decoration and so forth, the problems are much more serious. The roof alone, for instance, requires complete replacement and, until that's done, there's no point in redecorating –

rainwater leaking in would stain the walls as soon as they were painted. And then there's the floor and the kitchen. The small meeting room is now completely unusable – all committee meetings have to be held at the vicarage. Virtually the only use for the hall these days is meeting for tea and refreshments after services – and, frankly, I think the time may be coming when that too has to be abandoned. Unfortunately, despite all the efforts of the Church Funds Committee, the money just isn't available.'

Mrs Bunce, having replenished her plate from the refreshment table, joined them to hear the Reverend Parker's tale of despair. 'Take heart, vicar,' she soothed. 'As you know, the Church Funds Committee has been hard at work organising the summer fete next Sunday and I think you're going to be pleasantly surprised. Provided the weather is kind to us, and provided Jack Oates is sufficiently recovered from his gout to set up his horseshoe-throwing stall again, we could raise as much as a thousand pounds.' Her features hardened as she caught sight of Dick Harvard, the local pig farmer. 'Of course,' she continued, rather loudly, 'all that's assuming that people have forgotten about the ill effects they suffered after the hog roast last year.'

Dick Harvard replaced his teacup on his saucer and glowered at her. 'There was nothing wrong with that hog roast,' he called. 'It was just coincidence. Gastro-enteritis can be caused by all kinds of things. And anyway . . .'

'Ladies and gentlemen!' called the vicar, rapping on a nearby trestle table which developed a serious list to starboard. 'I see that time is getting on and I'm sure our loyal workers in the kitchen will want to wash up and get home, so if you'd all like to pop your plates and cups on the table outside the kitchen, we can all, er . . .'

He accompanied Charles and Jerry as they passed through

the door and on to the patch of rough ground which, except in very wet weather, served as a car park.

'I say, can I give you a lift?' Jerry asked Charles who thanked him but explained that his car was parked in the lane outside. He shook Jerry's hand and departed, picking his way over the muddy ruts and waving cheerily to the vicar, who smiled wryly at Jerry.

'Sorry about the little altercation about the hog roast in there. They mean well,' he smiled. 'And they work so hard but . . .' He shrugged, wearily.

Jerry nodded sympathetically. 'Need a heck of a lot of summer fetes to raise the kind of sum you require, eh?'

Seeing the Reverend Parker's mournful expression, he said: 'Look, I'm conscious that I'm a newcomer and so on, and I wouldn't want to muscle in and all that, but I'd really like to help. Why don't I pop in and see you at the vicarage one evening next week and we can discuss ways and means. I'm sure something can be done.'

The vicar looked up, a fleeting ray of hope in his eyes. 'Well . . . I wouldn't wish to . . . I mean . . .'

'How about Wednesday evening at, say, eight o'clock?' said Jerry. 'Unless that's inconvenient, of course, in which case, name your time. And you're welcome to come to the Post House instead if you'd prefer . . .'

'No, Wednesday at the vicarage would be fine. You'd be most welcome – indeed, would you care to come to dinner at about seven?'

'That's most kind,' grinned Jerry. 'I'll be there.'

The firelight lent a pleasingly subdued gleam to the oak panelling lining the walls of the little snug and glittered in the cut glass of the decanter of port from which the Reverend Parker was replenishing Major General Buller-Meyer's glass.

The retired soldier leant back comfortably in the armchair as the vicar placed the decanter on the occasional table between them, poked the fire and settled into his own chair with a weary sigh, his prematurely lined features appearing drawn and tired.

'Hard day?' asked Jerry.

'Well, not hard exactly, just . . . unproductive,' said the clergyman, studying the dark, tawny liquid in his glass. 'I was called out to old Mrs Worrall's cottage this morning but, sadly, she passed away before I arrived. Then I had to intervene in a . . . little dispute concerning the flower rota for next month. This afternoon the Church Funds Committee met to finalise arrangements for the summer fete next Sunday and it appears that three of the stallholders have had to cry off, including Jack Oates whose gout is considerably worse – the poor man does suffer. I really ought to get over and see him tomorrow. I've just realised, you weren't offered the cheeseboard after dinner – would you care for . . . ?'

Jerry showed the palm of his hand to decline the offer and then patted his waistcoat contentedly. 'I'm absolutely up to capacity, Edward. Couldn't cram in another morsel. Dinner was delightful.'

'Yes, Mrs Pendleton can always pull out all the stops when called upon to do so. The steak and mushroom crumble she prepared for the Bishop when he visited last September was superb; he still mentions it now whenever we meet. More port?'

As Edward was replenishing their glasses, a short, middle-aged lady with fluffy white hair entered. 'I'm just off now, vicar. Everything's cleared away and the dishwasher's on. So, unless there's anything else?'

'No, that's fine, Mrs Pendleton. Goodnight and thank you very much.'

She went out but then opened the door again to say: 'By the way, I'll be in at about ten tomorrow morning to do the special bits and pieces if that's all right?'

'Special bits and pieces?' grinned Jerry as the door closed behind her.

Edward laughed. 'That's what we call those.' He indicated the array of glass-fronted cabinets which lined the wall opposite the fireplace and which contained numerous small artefacts and framed documents. 'I'm interested in church history – and in the history of Hockam Church in particular. There has been a church here since the fifth century, you know – though the present building dates largely from 1352. Some of the furniture is considerably later, of course; the rood screen, for instance, was added in the seventeenth century and the marble font is early Victorian. The items in the cabinets there – some of which date from well before the Norman Conquest – are what I call our "special bits and pieces" and Mrs Pendleton lovingly dusts them with great care every month or so. But there I go again! You must forgive me. I'm very much afraid I have a tendency to bore guests with my particular passion.'

'No, no!' protested Jerry. 'As a matter of fact, history has long been an interest of mine – mainly military history, of course, but it's surprising how often the annals of the Church and the military overlap.'

'That's perfectly true,' agreed the clergyman. 'Indeed, the military victory at Milvian Bridge in AD 312 and the consequent Christian conversion of the Roman Emperor Constantine marked a seminal moment in Church history.'

'Quite,' said Jerry, squinting across the room at the items in the glass cabinets. 'If I'm not mistaken, some of those artefacts are of Roman origin.'

The Reverend Parker, delighted with the opportunity to share his collection with a fellow enthusiast, rose and crossed to the cabinets, pointing out various items of interest. The Major General stood next to him, nodding appreciatively at each description.

'And in the frame in the corner there,' went on the vicar, 'is the very document, bearing the signature of Bishop Caleb Smith which granted Hockam Parish Church the status of . . .' He broke off at a sudden intake of breath from Jerry. 'I say, are you all right?'

Jerry was staring at a small bronze cross nestling on a velvet pad towards the back of the cabinet. Pointing at it, he asked, 'Is that . . . ?'

'Byzantine cross,' said Edward, taking out the relic in question and handing it to the other who studied it intently. 'Interesting, isn't it?' continued the vicar. 'Though by no means unique, of course. These bronze crosses were often carried by Byzantine Christian Roman soldiers as an emblem of their faith when they entered battle.'

The relic which lay in Jerry's left hand shone dully in the firelight with a smooth, greenish patina and appeared perfectly plain save for a small blemish in its centre. 'Yes, it's Byzantine,' confirmed Jerry at length. 'But if it's what I think it is, it's by no means an ordinary bronze cross.' With his right hand trembling slightly, he pointed to the blemish which, on closer inspection, appeared to be a tiny, deeply cut inscription which he held up for Edward to see. The vicar peered at it but, unable to decipher the mark, shook his head and looked at the other in puzzlement.

'Where did you get this?' asked Jerry, returning the cross carefully to its resting place in the cabinet.

Edward exhaled, blowing out his cheeks while he thought. 'Well, it was here in the vicarage when I came to the parish eight years ago . . . No, actually, I seem to recall that it was at that time displayed in the church but I brought it into the vicarage to place among the other items here in the cabinets. I'm afraid I've no idea of its provenance. Do you have some reason to believe it could be of particular value?'

Jerry returned to his armchair and took up his glass of port. 'As a matter of fact, I do,' he said. 'Obviously, I'm no expert, but I have seen quite a number of these bronze crosses, most of which are simple and undecorated. A friend of mine who specialises in these things told me of a particular cross which was reputed to have been presented to the Emperor Constantine after his conversion – indeed, my friend showed me a portrait of the Emperor holding the item in question. It's often referred to as "the Milvian Cross" and it bore a tiny inscription. An inscription identical to the one we've just seen.'

Edward leant forward in his armchair. 'You mean . . . ?'

'Well, as I said,' Jerry cautioned, 'I'm no expert. But if I were you, I'd be very careful about leaving the cross in an unlocked cabinet. And I'd think about getting it professionally valued.'

'What sort of value do you think we could be looking at?'

'Well . . . we must bear in mind that I could be wrong but *if* this is the Milvian Cross then I recall my friend mentioning a figure of over £100,000. So it's worth getting it checked out. But to other matters. If you remember, we agreed to discuss the matter of the church hall. As I said, Edward, I'd really like to help in some way.'

'Well, it's very kind of you, Jerry,' said the vicar, poking the fire back to a blaze. 'As I explained to you, the poor state of the hall has been a constant source of worry to me over the past eight years. The problem is, quite simply, cost. To restore the hall to its former glory would, according to the latest estimates, be in excess of £200,000 – possibly more if we include resurfacing the car park. The fact is that such a sum is not available and, frankly, with the resources we have for fundraising, it never will be. I have recently come to the conclusion that there is no practical alternative to demolishing the hall and selling the land for housing. In reality, therefore, my problem is not how to raise £200,000 but how to break it to the parishioners that the hall has to go. That, believe me, is not going to be easy. Any suggestions you can make in that direction would be appreciated.'

The two men were silent for some moments before Jerry said: 'I think you're giving up too easily.'

Edward gave a hollow laugh. 'Jerry, I think after eight long years of organising jumble sales, concerts, horseshoe-throwing events and summer fetes, it's time to call it a day. I'm sorry if I appear cynical but I know when I'm beaten.'

'I understand how you feel,' Jerry sympathised. 'The figure of £200,000 is daunting – a mountain which seems impossible to climb. But if you were to halve that target figure . . . would that seem a little more feasible – particularly if I could help by getting some of my wealthier friends on board?'

Edward considered. 'Yes, but the target has to be £200,000 . . . at least. That's what the repairs will cost. One hundred thousand pounds won't be enough.'

Jerry leant forward, nursing his glass. He appeared to come to a decision. 'If you . . . or rather, *we,* can raise £100,000, I'll match that with a personal donation of another £100,000. How does that sound?'

Edward exhaled deeply. 'Jerry, that's a most generous offer. I hardly know what to . . . Thank you so much.' He took a sip of port, his eyes seeming to brighten considerably. 'Do you know, I think we might succeed after all. One hundred thousand pounds . . .' He mused for some moments. 'We'll need to organise a proper campaign; focus on larger donations; no more jumble sales or passing the plate round in church. Of course, it'll take time . . . possibly several years.'

'Meanwhile,' pointed out Jerry, 'the hall is deteriorating further and building costs are rising. I suppose we could consider expanding our fundraising to Walchester, though of course . . . what is it?'

The vicar stood up suddenly as a thought struck him. 'Wait a minute!' he said. '*The Milvian Cross!* That could solve everything. If, as you say might be the case, that could be sold for £100,000 then, with your matching donation . . .'

Jerry held up his hands. 'Easy does it. Two points to consider: firstly, I could be wrong about the cross – though I fancy I'm not – and secondly, even if the cross *is* worth that much, surely it would be wrong to sell it? The cross has been in the parish for many years – possibly hundreds of years; its rightful place is surely here where it belongs, church hall or no church hall. You, as a historian, must know that to be true.'

'No!' said Edward. 'My personal interest in history is irrelevant. My responsibility as a parish priest is for the present wellbeing of the people of this parish, not for the preservation of relics of the past. A refurbished and fully functional church hall could transform the lives not only of the church members but of the whole village – a meeting place for all, young and old; think of the functions, the activities, the . . . the . . . fellowship and renewed sense of community. This could be the answer to my prayers – the Lord moves in mysterious ways.'

Jerry shifted uneasily. 'I rather wish I hadn't mentioned the cross now,' he said. 'I really don't want to be the cause of the church parting with its most valued treasures for mere money.'

'I disagree, Jerry. I disagree with all my heart. The past must give way to the present. How can we get the cross valued?'

Jerry rubbed his eyes and sighed. 'Well, I could ask the friend I mentioned to come down from London, have a look at it and give us an opinion. But I really must advise that you think very carefully before . . .'

'Do it!' said Edward, imploringly. 'For the sake of the parishioners whom God has entrusted to my care, do it as soon as you can. The hall is crumbling as we speak.'

Jerry rose reluctantly. 'I haven't got his number here but I'll get home and ring him tonight – that's if he's in.'

Edward accompanied him to the front porch where he donned his overcoat. 'I'll do it,' he said, 'but I would urge you not to take any steps to dispose of the cross until you've given it a lot more thought. I'll let you know when I've contacted my friend.'

Edward shook his hand warmly. 'Thank you, Jerry,' he enthused. 'You've given me new hope and I shall always be grateful.'

The village green was bathed in warm sunshine as the summer fete got into full swing. The school orchestra, conducted by Helen Dufty in her capacity as headmistress, struck up a lively medley from *The Sound of Music* and Charles, sporting a straw boater and standing at the front of the little crowd of onlookers, was joined by the Reverend Parker in a state of some excitement. Clearly, he was trying to convey something of importance to Charles but, despite the solicitor's straining ear, the gist of the vicar's discourse was lost in the rising crescendo of 'How Do You Solve a Problem Like Maria?'.

A brief lull occurred while the orchestra geared up for its next number and Charles took advantage of this to explain to the other that he'd only caught the words 'Churchill' and 'general ovation'. The Reverend Parker's brow furrowed for a moment and then cleared. 'No, no. I was saying that the *church hall* project could be saved by a *generous donation* from Major General Buller-Meyer who has offered to personally match whatever we can raise towards the cost of the repairs. This means that, if we can somehow raise £100,000, the work can go ahead. It really is a most handsome gesture by the Major General and brings the prospect of a fully useable church hall so much closer. I really am very excited about it.'

Charles nodded. 'That's certainly a very generous offer by Jerry. Presumably he's aware of the total sum needed?'

'Oh, yes. He and I had a long and very fruitful conversation at the vicarage last Wednesday and he really is very anxious to help – not only by providing the matching donation but also by assisting in the general fundraising effort.'

'Well, the Major General's certainly proving his dedication to the cause,' agreed Charles. 'But, of course, you still have the task of raising £100,000 which, given the local nature of the project, is not going to be easy.'

'Ah!' said the vicar, tapping the side of his nose conspiratorially. 'I think we may have found a short cut as regards that particular problem. You see . . .'

His words were again cut short, this time by the opening bars of 'The Lonely Goatherd', more than adequately backed up by an enthusiastic percussion section on bass drum, tambourines, triangles and cymbals and fronted by a quartet of violinists led by a small girl wearing pigtails and a glare of intense concentration. During the performance, the Reverend Parker wandered off to break his glad tidings to various members of the Church Funds Committee and, as the enthusiastic applause which greeted the final bars died away, a perspiring Helen descended from the podium and joined Charles who congratulated her warmly. 'Absolutely sterling performance by all concerned.'

'Weren't they wonderful?' beamed Helen. 'And they've all worked so hard. Such a pity Jason's drumstick broke David's glasses but that was only enthusiasm, and little Molly on the violin – she'll be playing at the Albert Hall one day, mark my words.'

'And I know the conductor put in a fair bit of work, too,' remarked Charles. 'I imagine you could use a refreshing Pimm's at this point.' He put his arm around his daughter-in-law's shoulders and guided her towards the refreshment tent where they joined the queue of thirsty Hockam residents. As they waited, Charles spotted Jerry Buller-Meyer who, having been served, was carrying his glass towards the open flap of the marquee. Seeing Charles's friendly wave, he walked over and was introduced to Helen.

'Actually, Charles, I could do with a word with you if you'd join me outside when you've got your drinks. And Helen, of course,' he added before negotiating his way through the crowd to the sunlit exit.

He was standing alone near the WI cake stall when Charles and Helen emerged from the refreshment tent. After various pleasantries were exchanged concerning the kindness of the weather and the general gaiety of the occasion, Charles said: 'The vicar has been telling me of your offer of a donation to the church hall project, Jerry. A most generous contribution, if I may say so. Needless to say, Edward is thrilled – as, indeed, are we all.'

The Major General waved away the tribute. 'Did Edward also tell you about the bronze cross?' he asked, with a worried expression. Seeing Charles's puzzled expression, he continued. 'That was what I wanted to see you about. You see, Edward showed me some of the artefacts at the vicarage . . .'

'His special bits and pieces?' smiled Charles.

'That's right. Well, one of them, a bronze cross, is, I believe, of very considerable value – though I certainly wouldn't class myself as an expert. Anyway, I . . . well, I mentioned this to Edward – purely as a matter of interest and said he would be well advised to place it in a place of safety and perhaps get it valued for insurance purposes. The problem is . . .' Here his worried frown deepened. 'Well, the fact is, Edward has got it into his head to sell the thing and put the money towards the church hall fund. He thinks – and he's probably right – that the proceeds of the cross, together with my promised matching donation, would cover the whole cost of the repairs to the hall.'

Charles's face remained expressionless. 'And . . . ?' he prompted.

'Well,' continued Jerry. 'I don't know about you but I feel the cross should stay here in Hockam where it belongs. As I said to Edward, I really don't want to be the cause of the church parting with such an important relic. But Edward really seems to have got the bit between his teeth, as it were, and nothing I say can dissuade him from his intention. I just . . . well, I just don't think it's right. Do you?'

Helen, who had listened quietly thus far said: 'I think Jerry may have a point, Charles. This church hall project does seem to have rather taken over Edward's thinking lately. I don't say he's become obsessive about it but he may have got a little carried away. What do you think?'

Charles sipped reflectively at his Pimm's before replying. 'Edward Parker is a first-class priest,' he said at last. 'At the end of the day, he is the custodian of the church artefacts and if he believes that one or more of them should be sacrificed for the benefit of his parishioners, then who are we to stand in his way?'

The Major General sighed. 'Well, I'm conscious that I'm a newcomer to the community here and I have to bow to your greater understanding of it. At Edward's request, I've invited a friend of mine to come down from London next Saturday. He's an expert in artefacts of this kind and he'll give Edward an opinion as to its authenticity and so forth. I have to say that, in a way, I rather hope the thing turns out to be a fake or something. That would at least lay the matter to rest. I can't help it, but I really wouldn't feel comfortable about the cross being sold. But there it is. Can I tempt you both to a bite to eat from the hog roast over there?'

Hockam Parish Church stood starkly against a lowering afternoon sky, the occasional flash of summer lightning illuminating both it and the neighbouring vicarage, inside which the little snug appeared a very different place from the cosy haven whose comforts had facilitated the discussions of the Reverend Parker and Major General Buller-Meyer only the previous week.

The logs in the grate had not yet been lit and the weak daylight seeping through the rain-streaked window lent a sombre tone to the oak-panelled room as the Reverend Parker ushered in his guests.

'Ah!' said Miles Beddoes, Jerry's friend from London, 'so these are your treasures.'

There was a hint of pride in the vicar's manner as he switched on the nearby standard lamp to illuminate the glass-fronted cabinets and their contents, freshly dusted and polished by Mrs Pendleton. 'I'm afraid most of the items are of little monetary value,' he said, 'but their presence here does give me a great deal of pleasure. Their antiquity seems to impart a . . . a kind of . . .'

'A sense of continuity, linking the past with the present?' suggested Miles, his long fair hair glinting almost redly in the light from the lamp and framing his sensitive features.

'That's it, exactly,' agreed the vicar. 'As a student of history, you obviously appreciate the importance of preserving these relics and understanding what they tell us not just about the past but about who we are.'

Jerry Buller-Meyer stood in respectful silence as the other two chatted knowledgeably about this artefact and that document and it was not until there was a lull in the conversation that he spoke: 'And the particular item on which Edward would like your opinion, Miles, is . . .'

'Of course,' said Edward, reaching into one of the cabinets and retrieving again the little bronze cross which he handed to Miles, who took it carefully and carried it to the standard lamp, by whose light he peered at it intently. He was silent for some moments before taking a jeweller's eyeglass from his pocket and examining the object even more closely. After a long interval, he walked to the window and scrutinised the cross in the day- light, then stroked his hand over it as though it were a kitten and returned it to the vicar. He then drew a deep breath and motioned to the three armchairs set before the fireplace. 'Do you mind if we . . . ?'

'Oh, please do,' said the vicar and the three men settled themselves in front of the unlit fire.

'Well,' said Miles quietly. 'When Jerry invited me down here to look at some "bits and pieces", as he called them, I little dreamt that I would have the honour of holding in my hand an object of such extraordinary significance.'

Jerry leant forward, intently. 'So you think it's . . .'

'The Milvian Cross,' confirmed Miles in little more than a whisper. 'I would wish to have a second opinion, of course, but I don't think there's any doubt. This is the real thing.'

The Reverend Parker's eyes were glistening. 'And as to its value?' he quavered.

'Value?' said Miles. 'You mean monetary value?'

The vicar nodded and Miles raised his eyebrows and blew out his cheeks. 'Well, my interest lies in the historical significance of such items and not in their commercial value but I would think that, if the cross were to be put to auction, it would fetch a sum extending to six figures.'

'One hundred thousand pounds?' said Edward.

Miles nodded. 'At least. I think it fair to say, Reverend Parker, that, in the matter of ecclesiastical artefacts, this rather puts Hockam on the map.'

'*Hokum*,' said Jerry.

Miles turned to him, eyebrows raised. 'I beg your pardon?'

'We locals pronounce it *Hokum*,' explained Jerry. 'Just thought you'd . . .'

'The thing is, Mr . . . er . . . Miles,' put in the vicar, 'at this moment, the parish is in urgent need of funds and, while I absolutely understand the deep significance of the Milvian Cross, my first and only responsibility is to my flock. In that connection, the benefit which could be brought about by the proceeds of the sale of the cross is greater than the pleasure of owning it. I know Jerry here entertains a contrary opinion but I have prayed long and hard on the matter and my mind is made up. Your advice as to how to go about effecting a sale would be appreciated.'

Miles regarded him for a space before replying. 'The cross would need to be taken to London for further examination and official authentication, you understand. Subject to that, if it is your wish then I would be pleased to broker a sale on your behalf.'

'Thank you,' said Edward. 'Bearing in mind that our need for funds is both urgent and pressing, how soon could the cross be taken for . . . what was it you called it . . . official authentication?'

Miles thought for a few moments. 'Well, if time really is of the essence, I could take the item back to London with me tomorrow – Jerry has kindly offered to put me up tonight, you see. I could arrange for the necessary examinations to be carried out within a week and then return it to you, say, next Monday. That is, if you're really serious about this?'

Ignoring Jerry's surreptitious shake of the head, the vicar thanked Miles profusely and agreed to the arrangement. The three men then rose, the cross was placed in Miles's lockable case and he and Jerry took their leave and walked to the car parked outside. Miles got into the passenger seat but Jerry, however, on the pretext of having left something behind, walked back to the front door and motioned to the vicar to follow him inside.

'Look here, Edward,' he began. 'I realise I'm not in a position to influence your decision to sell the cross, but I'm really not at all comfortable with simply handing it to Miles like this. Not that I've any reason to suppose that Miles is anything other than trustworthy – I've known him as an acquaintance for a few years but . . . well, we're dealing with a very valuable item here and . . . well, things can happen . . .' he finished lamely.

'Jerry, I appreciate your concern but, as I made clear earlier, my mind is made up. Time is of the essence. As you said, we've no reason to suspect Miles's integrity and . . . you think I'm being too trusting and naïve?'

'I do, Edward. In fact, I actually believe your actions in simply handing the cross to a comparative stranger verge on the irresponsible.' He saw the vicar's worried frown and gave an exasperated sigh. 'I tell you what. If you're intent on doing this, I'll go to London myself with Miles tomorrow and stay for the week, during which time I propose not to let the cross out of my sight. That would at least give me peace of mind and ensure that nothing untoward happens. I'll come back next Monday – with the cross – and report on events. Then you can come to a decision as to whether or not to take matters further.'

The vicar took his hand warmly. 'Bless you, Jerry.'

The Major General walked down the path towards the waiting car. 'I'll call you when I'm back next Monday and we can meet up,' he called over his shoulder.

Since the small meeting room in the church hall had ceased to be useable, the Church Funds Committee had conducted its monthly Monday meetings around the dining room table at the vicarage, and it was from his seat at the top of that table that the Reverend Parker announced his intention of bringing in a building firm from Walchester to provide a further quote for the repairs to the church hall.

'That's jumping the gun a bit, isn't it, Edward?' said Dougie Bradshaw, the landlord of the King's Arms Hotel. 'Shouldn't we wait until we get the report on this bronze cross before dashing off and getting quotes for building work?'

Jack Oates shifted his left foot, wincing as his gout reminded him of its continuing presence. 'I still don't think we should be even thinkin' of selling that cross thing. It's been in the parish for 'undreds of years and 'ere it ought to stay. We'll be sellin' off the church pews next and replacin' 'em with plastic chairs.' He slammed his hand on the table for emphasis, causing him to wince again.

Mrs Bunce, the postmistress, still recovering from a mild stomach upset after the summer fete, took Edward's side. 'The vicar's already explained his reasons for wanting to sell it and I agree with him. If selling the cross means we can have a nice new hall for everyone to meet in, then we'll all benefit.'

'When are we going to know the results of these tests or whatever?' asked Don Dawson, the proprietor of the off-licence in the High Street. 'I thought Jerry was supposed to be coming back today. Haven't we heard from him yet?'

'No,' replied Edward. 'Well, yes, he is due back today but no I haven't yet heard from him. I tried to telephone him this afternoon before the meeting but the line to the Post House is down again. Something really ought to be done about that; it's been giving trouble for over a year.'

'Well, why not ring his mobile?' suggested John Paisley, the committee's treasurer. 'The sooner we know what we've got and what it's worth, the sooner we can make plans.'

'Because I very stupidly forgot to get his mobile number,' explained Edward.

'Oh, great!' said Don Dawson. 'Jerry's probably at home in the Post House right now, bursting to tell us the news about the cross and can't get through.'

John Paisley glanced at his watch. 'It's eight o'clock now; Jerry's almost sure to be back from London. Why not drive over and see him?'

'As a matter of fact,' said Edward, 'that's what I'd already decided to do. I thought I'd take him a bottle of champagne or something as a thank-you gift for giving up his week to stand guard over the bronze cross.'

'Good idea,' said Don Dawson. 'I'll provide the champagne – I've got a dozen bottles in the car I was going to deliver to the golf club but one less won't matter.'

'That's settled then,' said Edward. 'So, unless there's any other business, I'll drive over to the Post House straight away and, if there's any news, I'll ring round everyone and let them know.'

'I'll come with you,' said John Paisley. 'That is if you can give me a lift home afterwards. My car's in dock.'

The meeting disbanded and Edward and John were soon on their way in Edward's car.

'Actually, I'm looking forward to seeing how Jerry's settled in at the Post House,' said John. 'I hear he's got things pretty well organised there.'

'Yes,' said Edward. 'I popped in not long after he took up residence and admired his taste in furnishings and so on. He was also talking about installing a summer house in the garden and making some other improvements.'

'Good to see the old place being brought to life again,' said John. 'It had been empty for almost a year.'

Turning into West Lane as dusk intensified, Edward switched on his headlights. Soon, he swung the car through the open wrought-iron gates of the Post House. They were disappointed to find the place in darkness.

'Oh,' said Edward. 'It rather looks as though Jerry's not back yet.'

'Well, the gates were open,' said John. 'Maybe he's in one of the back rooms. The lights wouldn't show from the front.'

They got out of the car, walked up to the impressive front door and rang the bell. After a couple of minutes, John applied his ear to the door. 'Ring the bell again,' he said.

The vicar did so and John straightened up. 'I don't think it rang,' he said. 'Let's go around the back.'

The French windows looking out on to the garden were as dark as the rest of the house. 'He's obviously not back yet,' said Edward. 'I'll come back tomorrow and . . .'

'Hang on,' said John, walking to the French windows and

peering in, shading his eyes with his hand. He turned round to face Edward. 'I thought you said he'd got the place nicely furnished,' he said.

The vicar nodded and John motioned to him to look in through the French windows. Edward did as bidden and stepped back, his face pale in the moonlight. 'It's . . . it's empty,' he said.

They stood for a few moments, listening to the breeze rustling the rowan tree under which they stood. Then John roused himself and ran around the house, peering into all the ground-floor windows. 'There's nothing in there,' he panted when he returned. 'Not a stick of furniture in the place. He's gone, Edward . . . as has our bronze cross worth a hundred thousand pounds. We've been had!'

The Reverend Parker sat down heavily on a nearby bench and slowly buried his face in his hands.

'So, you see, Charles, as a result of my unbelievable naïvety and . . . sheer stupidity, the parish has been deprived of our most important and valuable treasure. I telephoned the police last night, of course, to report the matter and now I'm on my way to the station to give a full statement. But I thought I should pop in and see you in your office first to at least explain what had happened. I hold myself fully responsible for all this and I shall, of course, tender my resignation to the Bishop and offer a full apology to the congregation when I preside at my final communion next Sunday.'

Charles shook his head. 'No need for all that,' he smiled. 'We all make mistakes. And, after all, it was only a bronze cross.'

Edward raised his tear-streaked face to look at him. 'Only a bronze cross! Charles, perhaps you don't know but this was not *just* a bronze cross it was . . . it was . . .'

'The Milvian Cross?' said the solicitor.

'Yes,' said the vicar.

'No,' said Charles. 'The item which was in your cabinet of

"special bits and pieces", and with which our friend the Major General – unlisted in the records, incidentally – has now legged it to London with his accomplice, was a fake.'

Edward's face displayed a singular lack of comprehension. 'But . . . how do you know?'

'Because your predecessor, the Reverend Tomlinson, brought the original to me some twenty years ago. When he discovered its value, he was rightly concerned about the dangers of leaving it in the church unattended. We therefore decided to pay for a replica to be made and placed in the church.'

'I . . . but where is the original now?'

Charles rose and walked to a hidden wall safe between a bookcase and a built-in cupboard in a corner of his office. He keyed in a combination, swung open the door and drew out a steel box which he unlocked, opened and placed in front of Edward.

'The Milvian Cross!' breathed the vicar, picking up the little artefact and gazing at it.

'The Milvian Cross,' confirmed Charles. 'Safe and sound and awaiting your instructions for its disposal . . . that is, if you're still of a mind to sell it to pay for the refurbishment of the church hall.'

'What do you think I should do?' asked Edward after a long silence.

'That's up to you,' answered Charles.

The clergyman slowly and reverentially replaced the cross in its steel box, closed the lid and handed it back to Charles. 'There's got to be another way,' he said.

Charles nodded. 'And you're the very man to find it,' he smiled.

~

The two old friends sat in companionable silence for a while before Henry remarked: 'Edward Parker's a good man – though perhaps a little too confident of the virtue of those around him. Still, he seems to have got away with his little . . . lapse of judgement. All's well that ends well, eh?'

Charles nodded. 'Except, of course, for the continuing problem of the church hall. Edward's still saddled with that little conundrum.'

They lapsed again into silence until Henry suddenly brightened. 'Perhaps I should introduce him to Del Handy!'

Charles scratched his cheek, thoughtfully. 'See how he gets on with your garage roof first,' he suggested.

Equity Shall Prevail

Charles Dufty, tiring of trying to catch the unusually harassed barman's eye, gave vent to his irritation. 'Stanley!' he called, slightly more loudly than he had intended.

The unaccustomed volume of this summons caused Stanley to turn sharply from his task of fitting a new gin bottle into its optic, tripping, as he did so, over an empty beer crate on the floor and saving himself from falling full-length by stretching both arms over the bar, precipitating on to the floor a tray of three full pint glasses which he had placed there preparatory to taking them into the snug, where their intended recipients still waited.

Charles and Henry rose stiffly from their corner table and hurried over. 'I say, you all right, old chap?' asked Charles, feeling responsible for the incident.

'Yes, I'm fine, sirs,' the elderly barman assured them, straightening his back with a wince. 'Sorry about the wait. We're a bit short-staffed tonight – bit of a mix-up with the Friday rota. I'm supposed to be covering in here and in the snug. I'll just clear up this mess and . . .'

'Stanley!' This time, the exasperated cry issued from the three thirsty customers waiting in the snug.

'Just coming, gents,' called Stanley, treading on the broken glass on the floor and hesitating between pulling three fresh pints, refitting the gin optic and serving Charles and Henry.

'Look,' said Henry, 'you serve those three in the snug while Charles

and I serve ourselves to our gin and tonic and whisky and water –
we'll put the money in the till.'

'Well, we can't use the till in here, sir. It hasn't been working
properly since last night. John was supposed to do something about it
this morning but he seems to have forgotten. Just put the money on
the bar and I'll take it to the other till in the snug later. So sorry
about the, er . . .' He turned, crestfallen, as the sound of three pairs
of heavy boots leaving the snug by the street door was heard, their
owners clearly having run out of patience.

Several minutes later, Charles and Henry were once again
ensconced at their corner table, drinks in hand, while Stanley busied
himself clearing up behind the bar.

'Seems to me,' remarked Henry, 'that the management here needs
to shape up a bit. Left hand not knowing what the right's up to
springs to mind!'

Charles nodded, sagely. 'A not uncommon situation,' he murmured.

~

The little 'studio flat' above the newsagent's on Hockam High
Street was dappled with such early morning sunlight as was
able to penetrate the grime-streaked window as the alarm clock
rattled its third and final warning. Bernard Summers swung his
legs out of the bed and sat, scratching his rumpled, curly hair
vigorously for some moments before switching on the radio and
padding across the few feet of cracked lino and into the tiny
partitioned alcove which his landlord, the newsagent old Ben
Sharpe, extravagantly referred to as 'the bathroom'.

Emerging five minutes later, shaved and showered, he pulled
on his only clean shirt and donned his second-best suit, as
usual. Yesterday's socks, the least stained of his four ties and
only slightly scuffed black shoes completed his preparations for
the day and he sallied forth to resume his duties as trainee
solicitor at Messrs Dufty Dufty Popple & Dunn a few doors

down the High Street – returning, briefly, seconds later, to turn off the radio, thereby avoiding further complaints from old Ben Sharpe in the shop below.

On his way down the street, he glanced at his watch and turned into the Rialto Café whose friendly proprietor, Ashraf, furnished him with a wrapped bacon sandwich, with which he emerged into the street and continued on his way, enjoying the surprisingly warm morning sunshine.

As he approached the office, his youthful forehead crinkled into a frown as he neared the half-timbered headquarters of Dufty Dufty Popple & Dunn. Outside was a little knot of people, in the midst of which Hugo Dufty, an irritated expression on his sallow features, was pressing a mobile phone to his ear. Around him were gathered Trish, his secretary, Miss Spiers, the part-time book-keeper, and Conchita, the Spanish receptionist, all of whom were exchanging embarrassed glances.

At Bernard's approach, Hugo replaced his mobile in his pocket. 'Bernard!' he called. 'Do you have a key?'

'A key?' said Bernard.

'Yes, a key,' repeated Hugo, in an exaggeratedly patient tone. 'A small, metal device which is inserted into a keyhole to effect entry to . . .'

'No, I've never been given a key. Miss Metcalfe always arrives first to unlock the offices and . . .'

'Well, Miss Metcalfe is not here, is she?' snapped his employer, 'And her mobile appears to be turned off. The only other key holders are Mark – who's attending Malverley Magistrates Court this morning – and myself. Unfortunately, my own key is at home because I came straight here from Walchester where I was staying overnight after a Law Society function.'

'So we can't get in,' explained Trish, somewhat unnecessarily.

Hugo gave an exasperated sigh. 'I have an appointment with an important client who's coming in at ten and I don't propose to see her on the pavement. It's now almost nine forty-five.

Where on earth is Miss Metcalfe?' He took out his mobile phone again and prodded the buttons, shoving it roughly back into his pocket when there was once more no reply.

In a rush of adrenalin, Bernard saw an opportunity to take command of the situation, save the day and increase his standing within the firm. He held up a hand in a calming gesture – he would have held up two but the other was clutching his rapidly cooling bacon sandwich. 'I think I have the answer,' he announced in what he fondly believed to be an authoritative tone. 'I happen to know that the window in the empty room next to Mark's has a defective catch. I think I can get in that way and open the front door from the inside.'

'But that's on the first floor,' Trish pointed out.

Bernard waved a hand dismissively. 'That's no problem. If I go round the back and climb on to the roof of the outhouse in the car park, I should be able to shin up the drainpipe above it and reach the window.' He marched resolutely around the side of the building into the car park, the little group trotting after him.

The outhouse adjoining the building was comparatively easy to scale with the help of a nearby dustbin and, within a matter of minutes, he was standing on its corrugated iron roof, acutely conscious of Conchita's dark eyes watching him with what he perceived as concerned admiration – though, in reality, she was trying not to laugh.

He stuffed his wrapped bacon sandwich deeper into his pocket and looked up, surveying the short length of drainpipe which would provide his route to the window of the empty room. After testing it for stability, he began the climb. When he was adjacent to the window, he leant across and was able to insert his fingers over the sill and, with some difficulty, lift the sash. Ignoring the anxious pleas for caution from below, he then shifted his body precariously towards the open window, and, when he was satisfied he could propel himself head first across the sill, prepared to release his one-handed grip on the drainpipe. Summoning up his courage, he kicked with his feet against the drainpipe and aimed himself through the open window with a manly war whoop which transmuted into an embarrassingly falsetto whimper as his trouser leg caught on a rusty pipe bracket and arrested his progress, so that he landed with his midriff resting on the sill, his upper body hanging inside the room, his left leg dangling outside and his right firmly attached to the drainpipe by his torn trouser leg.

'Er . . . guys . . . I think I'm stuck,' he called, his voice muffled by his jacket which had fallen over his head as he hung upside down over the sill. To his consternation, he could hear no voices from outside. Surely his colleagues could not have abandoned him in this, his hour of need. Abandoning dignity, he called: 'Help! Is anybody there?'

After several uncomfortable minutes, he was relieved when the door of the room burst open and everyone rushed in to seize his shoulders and pull. He shouted over the melee and explained that his right trouser leg was attached to the drain-pipe. Much panic and confusion resulted until junior partner Mark Dunn called to everyone to calm down and leant over Bernard's helpless body to investigate the position.

'There's only one answer,' he said. 'You're going to have to slip your trousers off, old boy.'

This strategy was adopted and, after a few moments, Bernard was seated on the floor of the room, embarrassed, exhausted and trouserless but otherwise intact. Mark ushered everyone out of the room and gave Bernard a wry smile. 'Are you OK?' he asked.

Bernard nodded, rested his head in his hands and exhaled deeply. 'Yeah, just a small cut on my leg. I do feel a bit of a prat, though,' he said. 'I thought for a moment everyone had . . . Wait a minute! I've just realised, you're all inside . . . how did . . . I thought you were . . .'

'My case at Malverley was called off so I came back here – and I've got a key,' he explained, leaning out of the window and dislodging Bernard's trousers from the drainpipe. 'I suggest you put these on, old boy. They're a bit torn but I'm sure the firm will cough up for a new suit – small recompense for a heroic act like that, eh? I'll get Trish to get the first aid kit for that cut. Here, wrap this handkerchief round it for the time being.'

He helped the trainee to his feet and they made their way downstairs where Bernard was greeted with applause and a certain amount of good-natured banter.

'How's Bernard?' Hugo asked as Trish handed him his morning cup of tea.

'Oh, he's OK,' she said. 'He was very brave, climbing up to the window like that. I'm just popping out to the chemist to get him a plaster for the cut on his leg.'

'Where's our first aid kit – I thought it was kept in reception?'

'Well, it is, but there aren't any plasters in it,' she explained.

Hugo sighed and glanced through the file Trish had placed on his desk, his frown deepening. 'This file is for Mr and Mrs Tonks. Where's the file for Mrs Doberman? She's due in at any moment.'

Trish looked puzzled. 'No, it's Mr and Mrs Tonks you're seeing at ten – and you're supposed to be going to see them at their house to have a look at the new fence their neighbour has put up which they think is on their land. It's about ten minutes' drive from here so you're going to be a bit late.'

Hugo reached for his desk diary, looked at it and pushed it towards Trish. 'It's there in black and white,' he snapped. 'Mrs Doberman at ten. There's nothing about Mr and Mrs Tonks. Really, Trish, we must be a little more organised.'

'That's funny,' said Trish. 'I've just checked the diary in reception and that says you're due at Mr and Mrs Tonks's at ten o'clock.' She went into reception and fetched the other diary which clearly showed the appointment with Mr and Mrs Tonks.

Hugo slammed the diary on to his desk. 'Who made this appointment?'

'I did, Mr Hugo. That's why it's in the reception diary.'

'And who made the appointment with Mrs Doberman?'

'Well, that would be Miss Metcalfe; she keeps the diary on your desk.'

Hugo controlled himself with an effort. 'Send Mark in straight away,' he snapped, 'and look out the file on Mr and Mrs Tonks for him – and then go and buy whatever we need for a fully functional first aid kit before Bernard bleeds to death.'

She bustled off and, a moment later, Mark breezed in. 'Trish said you wanted to see me, Hugo. And, by the way, Mrs Doberman's just arrived in reception. It's all go, this morning, isn't it? Funny how sometimes everything . . .' He tailed off, seeing Hugo's impatient frown.

'Mark, I want you to go and see Mr and Mrs Tonks straight away. Trish will give you the file.'

Mark turned to do as bidden but then turned back. 'Ah . . .' he began, hesitantly. 'Bit of a problem there, actually. I've just taken my car into Reg Phelps's garage – clutch trouble.'

'Well, use the firm's car, man. It's in the car park. And would you send in Mrs Doberman?'

Mark looked embarrassed. 'Er . . . problem there as well, I'm afraid. The road tax on the firm's car is two months out of date.'

Hugo's colour was now deepening from red to purple. 'Well, use it anyway – we'll take the risk!' he grated. Before he could say anything else, Trish popped her head round the door. 'Mark,' she whispered. 'We can't find the Tonks file – you haven't got it, have you?'

Before Hugo could speak, Mark bustled Trish out of the room, turning to reassure Hugo that all would be sorted out and promising to send in Mrs Doberman.

By twelve thirty, all files had been located, Mrs Doberman had left the office satisfied, Mr and Mrs Tonks's neighbour's fence had been inspected and Bernard's cut had been dressed. Miss Metcalfe entered Hugo's office bearing a cup of tea and two chocolate biscuits.

He looked up as she came in. 'Miss Metcalfe! Where on earth have you been?'

She looked at him in surprise. 'Half-day's leave, Mr Hugo. The men came to repair my central heating boiler. It's been in the holiday rota for over a week.'

'Miss Metcalfe, I checked the holiday chart on the wall behind the reception desk when I was finally able to get in this morning and your name does not appear on it for today.'

'Oh, that chart on the wall is way out of date. We don't use it any more. The one we use now is in Miss Spiers's office – though, of course, she may not have seen it as she was away all last week.'

Hugo regarded her, breathing heavily. 'Well, why in the name of . . .' He shook his head and leant back heavily in his chair. 'Miss Metcalfe, could you ask everyone to come to my office, please. Right away, if you would.'

He sipped his tea in silence as the staff shuffled in. When all were settled in front of him, he replaced his teacup on the saucer and leant his elbows on the desk, massaging his forehead with his forefingers. 'We have been in the office for just over three hours,' he began, his voice quietly modulated. 'And in that short time we have been locked out because of a mix-up about the holiday rota; Bernard has sustained an injury which we were unable to treat immediately because of an inadequate first aid kit; I have been double-booked because of a serious flaw in the appointments system; files have been temporarily mislaid, and the firm's car has been found to lack a current tax disc. All this before lunch.'

Miss Spiers took advantage of the slight pause to say: 'With respect, Mr Hugo, the holiday rota was only placed in my room a few days ago and I was not informed of . . .'

Hugo held up his hands. 'Let me make it clear that I am not proposing to waste time analysing these events in order to apportion blame. We all have far more important work to do. But the fact is that, for a considerable time now, the day-to-day running of the firm has been . . . how shall I put it?' He placed his fingertips together and considered. '. . . a *shambles*, I think sums it up. As the senior resident partner, I am ultimately responsible for the smooth operation of the firm and I have therefore made up my mind to do something about it.'

The ensuing silence was broken only by the shuffling of feet and Miss Metcalfe's nervous cough. Hugo continued: 'I have decided to set on an office manager to oversee the day-to-day management of the office and to improve efficiency in general. It so happens that a very suitable candidate for such a position was brought to my attention several weeks ago. At that time, I believed we could sort out our problems without assistance but, after the events of this morning, I telephoned the person concerned who, as it happens, is still seeking employment and agreed to visit the office for an interview with me this afternoon at three o'clock. Are there any questions?'

Miss Spiers took off her glasses and replaced them and Miss Metcalfe opened her mouth to speak but then closed it again.

'Very well,' Hugo continued. 'I have entered the appointment in my desk diary. Conchita, would you please see that the appointment for three o'clock is recorded in the reception diary. The applicant's name is Hilary Middleton. And now I suggest we all get back to work.'

Bernard was the first to break the thoughtful silence in the secretaries' office. 'What do you think?' he asked.

'I think it's awful,' Trish said. 'This new woman'll probably boss us all around and tell us what to do.'

Miss Metcalfe began typing letters, her usually friendly face expressionless.

'Even the name sounds ominous,' observed Bernard. '*Hilary Middleton* . . . sounds like a hospital matron in one of those old *Carry On* films. Bet she wears glasses on a chain round her neck.'

'Yes, and has a hairy mole on her cheek!' giggled Trish, glancing at Miss Metcalfe, expecting a rebuke.

Miss Metcalfe, however, continued typing, stony-faced.

'Friend of mine's a trainee at Pollock's in Walchester,' said Bernard. 'He says they've got an office manager there and she makes everyone fill out time sheets so that she can see how they all spend their day. Apparently she even times their tea breaks.'

Miss Metcalfe rose, left the room and went to the back of the building where she found Miss Spiers in her tiny office. She sat down on a stool in the corner. 'That was a bit of a surprise, Rosemary,' she said.

The book-keeper looked up, took off her wire-rimmed glasses, sighed and nodded. 'Yes, it was a surprise,' she agreed. 'To be frank, Joan, I regard it as an insult to both you and me.'

Miss Metcalfe frowned. 'Well, I perhaps wouldn't put it quite that strongly, but I do feel a little slighted. I think Hugo could have at least discussed matters with the two of us before taking a decision to set someone on to take over some of the duties which have always been regarded as ours.'

Miss Spiers nodded. 'Duties which we've carried out over many years – in addition, I may say, to our many other tasks. Admittedly, since I reduced my hours, the bulk of the work has devolved on you, Joan – the holiday rota, the diaries, the filing system and so on, and I think it only reasonable that you should have some assistance, but to simply set on an office manager to take over . . . and without so much as consulting us after all our years of service to the firm.'

Miss Metcalfe looked glum. 'Perhaps the writing's on the wall, Rosemary. Hugo's always going on about "modernising" the firm and bringing in computerised systems and so on. Perhaps we're being phased out.'

'Well, Hugo's got a very back-handed way of going about it,' said Miss Spiers. 'I certainly don't intend to stay on if it means taking orders from this . . . Hilary . . . whatever her name is. I don't see why we should be pushed into the background and trampled over . . .'

'Who's trampling over what?' breezed Mark, entering with a batch of invoices. 'Bernard hasn't been trampling over the roof again, has he?' Sensing that he might have intruded on a private conversation, he handed the invoices to Miss Spiers and smiled weakly. 'Sorry, I'll just go and, er . . . yes, well, see you later.'

Closing the door behind him, he bumped into Hugo carrying a sheaf of files to the archive cellar. The two exchanged apologies and carried on their way but Mark turned and called: 'Oh, Hugo . . . I'm just going for lunch at the Pig and Whistle – fancy a pie and a pint? I could do with a word, actually.'

'Just a half for me,' said Hugo as they stood at the bar.

They carried their drinks to a table and sat down. 'Quiet in here today,' remarked Hugo. 'What was it you wanted to discuss, by the way?'

Mark put down his pint and scratched his cheek thoughtfully. 'I sense unrest in the ranks, Hugo.' Seeing the other's raised eyebrows, he went on: 'Nothing serious, you understand, but I get the impression that the staff are . . . a little apprehensive about this business of taking on an office manager.'

'Oh, that. Well I'm only going to interview an applicant for the post. It's by no means certain that it'll happen. In fact, to be honest, it may not be such a good idea. I perhaps got a little carried away with events this morning and this person was recommended to me a while ago; recently moved into the area, excellent CV, relevant experience etc., so I telephoned and we're meeting this afternoon. But the last thing I want is to upset the staff – I know they're doing all they can. It's just that . . .'

'Things need tightening up, eh? Bringing up to date a bit?'

'Well, yes. I mean, today's disasters were not typical, thank God, but they have emphasised the need for a tighter hand on the reins, as it were. But you and I are stretched to the limit with client work, Miss Spiers is now part-time and Joan Metcalfe, bless her, can't do it all. Maybe an office manager is the answer? I don't know.'

Mark nodded understandingly. 'If we do set anyone on as office manager, they'd have to be a pretty special kind of person. Simply installing new systems and streamlining operations in a small firm like this – well, that's a piece of cake for a suitably experienced person – but to do that *and* get everyone onside and motivated . . . frankly, they'd need to be some kind of genius. But there's no harm in at least looking into it. Would it be of any help if I sat in on this interview this afternoon? Two heads better than one and all that.'

Hugo considered this. 'Well, if you're free this afternoon at three . . .'

'Actually, I've got a new client at three but he's retired and I'm sure he wouldn't mind switching to four. I can give him a call when we get back.'

'Well, if you can reschedule without inconvenience to the client, I see no reason why we shouldn't see this applicant together. Although, like you, I somehow doubt whether it'll work out.'

Miss Metcalfe, Trish and Bernard were diligently toiling in the secretaries' room when, at five minutes to three, a loud and violent sneeze was heard from reception. All three looked up sharply. 'That wasn't her, was it?' said Bernard.

'No, that was a man's sneeze, surely,' said Miss Metcalfe.

'Or a woman with a deep voice,' Trish pointed out, grimacing at Bernard.

'I'm going to have a look,' said Bernard, gathering up a pile of files as cover and marching purposefully out.

He returned a few moments later. 'No, it's a little tubby, bald bloke with runny eyes. No sign yet of Ms Hilary Middleton.' Another even more spectacular sneeze was heard from reception.

'Oh, that'd be Mr Walker, Mark's new client,' explained Trish. 'He's due in at three as well. If Hilary Middleton doesn't arrive soon, she'll be late.'

Bernard grinned. 'Not a very promising start for her, eh? Dear, oh dear.'

Hugo, meanwhile, phoned Conchita to ask her to show in the candidate and she ushered into his office a short, rather stout man holding a handkerchief. His face was round and friendly, despite watering eyes and a slight rash on his cheeks, and his head was almost entirely bald except for a whisp of yellow hair which fell over his brow as he sneezed again, replaced the handkerchief in his pocket and took Hugo's offered hand.

'Mr Middleton,' smiled Hugo, 'this is Mark Dunn, my partner. Do sit down.'

'Tha'k you. Dice to beet you both.'

'Well, now, perhaps we could start by . . .' Hugo was cut short by another sneeze.

'That's some cold you've got there,' Mark commented sympathetically.

The applicant shook his head as he replaced the handkerchief in his pocket. 'Dust,' he explained. 'Bit of an allergy, I'm afraid. Sorry about the sneezing. You were saying, Mr Dufty?'

'Er, by all means call me Hugo.'

The man nodded and smiled cheerfully. 'I'm Bill.'

Hugo consulted his notes. 'I'm sorry, I thought it was Hilary.'

The man winced. 'Bloody silly name – runs in the family, I'm afraid. Everyone used to call me *Hill* for short and that got corrupted to *Bill*, which I much prefer.'

Hugo grinned back. 'Bill it is. I gather you worked for many years in your father-in-law's company, Bill . . . er . . .' he again consulted his notes, '. . . Pilbury's Pies.'

'That's right,' confirmed Bill. 'I married some twenty years ago and my father-in-law wasn't impressed with my status as an impoverished medical student so he offered me a junior position with the company – it's pretty big nationwide.'

Mark nodded. 'Yes, I've seen the products in garages and so forth.'

'Hope you haven't sampled any,' cautioned Bill. 'They're not exactly cordon bleu but they do sell in large numbers. Anyway, my heart wasn't really in medicine so I agreed – much to my father's horror and my wife's delight. I found the work comparatively untaxing and was soon running a branch of the company in Newcastle upon Tyne, which seemed to thrive, and a year or two later my father-in-law set me to opening a branch in Glasgow. Pretty soon, I was managing branches all over Scotland.'

Mark, who had been studying Bill intently, said: 'Clearly, Bill, you've made a success of your career to date but I don't really see how a knowledge of pies, profound or otherwise, qualifies you to manage the running of a firm of solicitors.'

Bill sneezed again. 'Pies? I don't know the first thing about them. My interest lay not in Pilbury's pies but in Pilbury's *people*. You see, I've always taken the view that if people are supported, motivated and enthusiastic about their work, the product of their labours will turn out well – whether that product is pies or . . . or . . . aaa-CHOO! Sorry . . . or adythig else.'

'Why did you leave your father-in-law's company?' asked Hugo.

'Because my wife and I divorced – long story but the decree absolute came through six months ago and, for the first time in my life, I felt free to do what I liked and go where I pleased – no children, you see.'

'And you chose Hockam,' observed Mark. 'Do you mind if I ask why?'

'My father lives here,' Bill explained. 'He is – or rather was – a GP. He's retired now and getting on a bit – in fact, although you'd never know it, he's not in the best of health and he lives alone. I just felt I wanted to be near to him. I think he was disappointed when I gave up my medical studies and . . .'

He was interrupted by the door opening and Charles Dufty's portly frame entering. On seeing Bill, Charles's bushy eyebrows shot up. 'Bill! Haven't seen you for . . . oh, must be five years or more. Remember you stayed with your father for a weekend and he brought you along to one of our Friday evening sessions at the Dog and Tadpole? What are you doing here?'

'Applying for a job,' said Bill, rising and taking Charles's hand with a broad grin. 'Good to see you again, Mr Dufty. Any friend of my father's et cetera . . .'

'Applying for a . . . But I was with Henry . . . sorry, your father . . . a few days ago and he never mentioned it. I thought you were still in Scotland, labouring away for your father-in-law's pie company.'

'Long story,' smiled Bill. 'And Dad didn't mention my applying for a job here because neither of us wanted to pull any strings and all that.'

'Well, well,' bumbled Charles. 'Of course, nobody tells me anything around here, but . . .'

'It only came up today, Father,' said Hugo. 'And I must admit, I hadn't realised that Bill here was Dr Middleton's son.'

Charles looked thoughtful and then collected himself: 'Look, I seem to have barged in and interrupted. I only popped in to find a copy of *Kelly's Draftsman* and . . . Ah! There it is.' He crossed to the bookshelf and took down a dusty volume, provoking another sneeze from Bill. 'Oh dear, still suffering from those allergies, I see. You should see a good doctor about that, you know.'

'Suppose I should,' grinned Bill. 'Do you know of one around here?'

'The best there is,' smiled Charles, taking Bill's hand in both of his. 'I know your father will be delighted to have you closer to him. We all need our families at times.' He glanced at Hugo. 'Although my own family could probably do without me at this particular moment. I'll absent myself and let you all get on. Lots to do, you know.'

The old solicitor left the room, clutching his law book, and Bill resumed his seat, fumbled for his handkerchief and sneezed.

'Well, so much for Hilary Middleton,' remarked Bernard, leaning back in his chair and glancing at his watch. 'It's now almost four thirty.'

Trish paused as she gathered up the mugs for the last brew-up of the day. 'Perhaps she took one look at the old place from outside and decided it wasn't her sort of thing.'

Bernard nodded, handing her his mug. 'Could be. She's probably used to City firms in swish, modern buildings and zombies for staff who'll say "Yes, Miss Middleton" and "No, Miss Middleton" and fit in with her new systems and . . .'

'That'll do, Bernard,' said Miss Metcalfe, carrying on typing. 'We could probably learn a lot from the way they do things in some of the larger firms – though, admittedly, they could learn a lot from the way we do things here. Anyway, she's obviously not coming so perhaps that's the last we'll hear about it. Are you going to put tea in those mugs, Trish, or juggle with them?'

Trish collected herself and made for the door, which opened before she reached it to admit Hugo. 'I thought you might all like to meet Hilary Middleton, our new office manager, who's agreed to start work with us tomorrow,' he said, standing back to allow the successful applicant to enter.

A violent sneeze was heard from the corridor outside and Bill entered, stuffing his handkerchief back into his pocket. 'Sorry, everywod – dust allergy.'

The tubby frame filled the doorway, the tuft of corn-coloured hair falling over the domed forehead, the watering eyes crinkling at the corners as the new office manager smiled around at the room's three bewildered occupants. 'I'm just in time for a brew, by the looks of it.'

Trish closed her mouth and stared at the three mugs she was holding.

'Look, I don't want to hold things up,' Bill continued. 'Why don't I take care of that? Might as well start with the important things – if you can show me where the kitchen is, Trish . . .'

~

'That was on Wednesday,' said Charles. 'It's now Friday and your Bill's got them all eating out of his hand. Don't know how he's done it but even Miss Spiers thinks he's just what the old firm needs. In just two days, he's reorganised the way the staff work and freed up everyone's time so that they can get on with what they should be doing. And, what's more, they're loving it! Wish I knew the secret.'

Henry leant back in his chair and took a long pull at his gin and tonic. 'He likes people,' he smiled. 'Always has. He knows instinctively the right buttons to push to win people over and get them motivated. It was the same when he was at school; the teachers thought he was brilliant and the kids would follow him anywhere – if only out of curiosity.'

Charles nodded. 'Pity about his marriage folding like that.'

Henry's face clouded. 'Sylvia didn't like people,' he said quietly.

215

'She regarded them as . . . well, as pawns in the game of life, to be used and manipulated to gain an advantage and . . . I don't know; takes all sorts, I suppose.' He lapsed into silence.

'Speaking of pawns,' said Charles, sitting up and arranging the pieces on the board. 'Does he still play?'

'Who?' asked Henry, coming out of his reverie.

'Bill!' said Charles. 'Or should I say Hilary? Didn't know that was his name until Hugo mentioned it. What did you saddle him with that for?'

Henry smiled ruefully. 'Runs in the family, I'm afraid. Started with my great-grandfather and every eldest son since then.'

Charles frowned. 'But you're the eldest son and . . .' His face lit up. 'Oh . . . Henry H. Middleton! Never occurred to me to enquire but . . .'

'Yes,' nodded Henry. 'The secret's out. Now let's get on with the game.'

Charles sat back in his chair, grinning. 'Henry Hilary Middleton. How'd you manage to get through school without us finding out?'

'Are we playing chess, or what?' grumbled Henry, studying the board. 'Anyway, what's your middle name? Charles A. Dufty. What's the "A" stand for?'

Charles moved his king pawn two spaces and tapped the side of his nose. 'Chap needs to have some secrets. And he needs to guard them, too – instead of passing them on to his eldest and first-born. Your move.'

In the Presence of Witnesses

Charles Dufty frowned at Henry Middleton who had, after lengthy consideration, moved his king pawn two squares. 'What did you do that for?' he asked.

Henry frowned back. 'What's the matter with that?' he asked.

Charles spread his hands and raised his bushy white eyebrows. 'Nothing at all,' he replied as he took out Henry's castle with his bishop. 'Don't seem to be focusing your brilliantly analytical if somewhat ageing mind on the game tonight . . . something troubling you, old friend?'

Henry sighed. 'As a matter of fact, there is,' he said. 'Does your drink taste all right?'

Charles took a sip from his glass and rolled the liquid round his mouth. 'Bit weaker than usual, now you mention it. Too much water and not enough whisky.'

Henry nodded. 'It's not just me, then. This G and T is almost entirely T . . . Stanley!'

The barman trotted across. 'Gentlemen, what can I get you?'

Stanley listened to Henry's comments concerning the somewhat flaccid nature of their drinks and rolled his eyes towards the bar where a lad of eighteen or so was polishing a glass and looking around the lounge of the Dog and Tadpole with a proprietorial air. Stanley bent close to the two old men and murmured: 'I'm so sorry, gents. It's young Jason over there. He's only been with us a couple of weeks and I'm supposed to teach him how to do the job but he was *getting fed up with collecting glasses and wiping tables. Said he wanted to be a barman not a potboy. So I let him loose on the optics and this is the result. They just don't realise what's involved, do they? They think they can do the job before they've gained enough experience to understand the ins and outs, so to speak.'*

He sighed, gathered up their half-empty glasses and returned to the bar for replacements, leaving Charles and Henry to reflect upon the impetuosity of youth.

'In my day,' said Henry, 'youngsters would accept they knew nothing until instructed by their elders and betters.'

Charles was thoughtful. 'I suspect that's a trick of memory, you know. It seems that way looking back, but haven't young folk always been a bit impatient? And, after all, surely the best way of learning to do something right is to do it wrong and suffer the consequences. Take young Bernard, our articled clerk . . .'

$\sim$

Bernard paused in putting down his half-finished pint on the table as his gaze again turned to the couple sitting at a table in the corner of the lounge bar of the Pig and Whistle.

'Am I boring you, Bernard?' Joanna's tone betrayed irritation.

Bernard started, spilling some of his beer on to the table. 'What? . . . Sorry, Joanna. No, of course you're not boring me, why on earth do you say that?'

The girl's bright blue eyes looked at him searchingly. 'Well, I'm telling you about my latest nursing exam – because you asked me – and you're quite obviously not interested.' Her glance followed Bernard's to the couple at the other table who were deep in conversation.

'Of course I'm interested,' he protested. 'It's just that I know the couple over there – Mark, a chap I work with, and Caroline, the estate agent from the offices next door to ours. I just noticed they were there, that's all. I was listening to every word you said.

You were saying that some of the questions in the exam related to stuff you hadn't done yet and . . .'

'Well, it's boring anyway,' she said. 'Training is boring. You're a trainee solicitor; don't you find it boring training for something? Don't you sometimes long to get on with some real work?'

Bernard puffed out his cheeks. 'Well, my training's well advanced, you know. I'm pretty well at the stage of seeing my own clients and . . . well, practising law.'

She looked faintly amused. 'You were telling me last week that you were fed up with filling in forms and running errands.'

'Well . . . yes, there is still a bit of that but I do have some interesting cases, you know. The law can be pretty exciting. In fact, only the other day I was . . .' His eyes again flicked to the table in the corner where Mark and Caroline had just risen and were about to leave. Mark noticed Bernard and raised a hand in greeting. Bernard waved back. Caroline mouthed the words 'See you tomorrow' as they left.

'Thought you said she worked at the office next door,' said Joanna. 'Why should she see you tomorrow?'

'Well, she often pops into Dufty's – she's an estate agent and . . . what, do you think we're having an affair or something?'

The girl laughed, tossing her fair hair off her forehead. 'Good grief, no. She must be pushing forty. In any case, she and Mark seem to be an item.'

Bernard nodded. 'Well, they used to be but he's been away for five years or so and . . . well, the general consensus in the office has been that she wouldn't be interested in getting back together after he'd dumped her once.'

Joanna looked out of the window to see the pair walking, hand in hand, towards Mark's sports car. 'Well, they seem pretty chummy to me,' she remarked.

Bernard followed her gaze. 'Mmm . . . do you fancy another drink?'

She shook her head. 'No, I need to go and see my mum before it gets too late. My granddad's in hospital and I think she's worried about him.'

'Oh, I'm sorry,' said Bernard, 'I'll walk you there – I still haven't met your mum.'

She untangled her handbag from her chair back and stood up. 'No, it's all right, it's only down the road. And you need to get home – what with all these exciting cases you've got on, you must need to get some sleep. I'm coming to Hockam again on Wednesday. See you here then – if you're free?'

He frowned. 'Yes, of course I'm free. See you on Wednesday. And I hope your granddad's OK.'

He continued to stare glumly at the door which had closed behind her, reflecting upon the complicated nature of the female psyche. At length, he sighed deeply and was preparing to return to his little 'studio flat' above the newsagent's when he was joined by Bill Middleton bearing two full pint glasses, one of which he placed on the table, and sat down opposite Bernard. 'Is that Joanna?' asked Bill, glancing towards the door.

Bernard nodded, accepting the drink gratefully.

'Pretty girl,' said Bill after a pause. 'How long have you been going out with her?'

'Oh, ages. She thinks I'm boring.'

'Why do you say that?'

Bernard took a long pull at his beer and put it down heavily on the table. 'Well, I am boring. I sit there in the office every day, filling in forms and occasionally running errands – she's going out with a bloody office boy. I don't have anything interesting to tell her about. No wonder she's bored – I'm bored! It's about time I had some proper work to do.'

Bill sneezed twice, replaced his handkerchief in his pocket and regarded the other thoughtfully, his eyes watering slightly. 'Have you mentioned this to anyone at the office?' he asked.

'There's no point,' said Bernard. 'I'm supposed to be a trainee solicitor but Hugo treats me like a bloody office boy – when he notices me at all, that is. Mark's not so bad but he's busy with his own caseload and doesn't have any time to spend on the likes of me. I'm seriously thinking of leaving Dufty's and re-applying for a trainee's post at Pollock's in Walchester. They offered me a position before, you know. At least they've got proper training systems in place and there are opportunities to . . . well, to get a taste of proper work.'

The two sat in silence for a while, Bernard glowering moodily at a stained beer mat on the table and Bill deep in thought.

At length Bill finished his drink. 'Well, I've got to go. Said I'd look in on my father – he hasn't been too well, you know.' He rose and picked up his briefcase. 'Look, don't worry about Joanna. I'm sure she doesn't find you boring. And in any case . . . well, I'm probably not the best one to offer advice on the subject of the ladies. Suffice it to say that . . . well, things change.' He sneezed again, waved cheerily and left.

Bernard's desk, wedged into a corner of the currently deserted secretaries' office, was now littered with forms over which hung the trainee solicitor's tousled head as he scribbled a debtor's details on to a county court praecipe, his morning cup of tea cooling at his elbow.

Mark Dunn poked his head round the door. 'Morning, Bernard. Could you nip down to the post office when you've finished whatever that is and hand in this registered letter?'

Bernard nodded without looking up and Mark half closed the door and then opened it again and came in.

'Everything all right?' he asked.

Bernard looked up briefly. 'Oh, same as always,' he said, returning again to his work.

Mark nodded slowly and again went out, only to return a moment later. 'Look, you could do me a favour, as a matter of fact.'

Bernard looked up again, this time with a little more interest, and Mark continued: 'You see, I've just drawn up a will for an old client of the firm who's in Walchester General Hospital. I suspect he's nearing the end. I was going to visit him this afternoon to get him to sign the will before it's too late but I'm pretty fully booked with other clients. Could you go instead?'

Bernard's expression froze. He stared at Mark, opened his mouth to speak and then closed it again.

'Well, a little bird told me you wanted some real work to do,' Mark pointed out. 'This is real work. The poor old boy's on his last legs and is anxious to put his affairs in order. You could be the very man to help him do it.'

'But I haven't really done wills yet – not in any depth, anyway.'

'The will's already complete. All you have to do is drive to the hospital – you can take the firm's car – go up to ward seven, tell the duty nurse you're from Dufty Dufty Popple & Dunn and ask to see Mr Bentley. You may have to read the will to him as his eyesight's not too good – I've drafted the attestation clause accordingly. Then ask him if he understands it and, if, in your professional opinion, he does, then get hold of a couple of nurses, get him to sign it in their presence and the nurses then sign as witnesses. Simple as that.'

'What if he doesn't understand it?'

'He will. He's as sharp as a knife. It's his heart that's the problem, not his brain. I wouldn't suggest you take this on if I was worried about that. You'll be providing a service that's of immense importance to him. That's real work, Bernard.'

Bernard drew a deep breath and nodded. 'OK, I'll do it.'

'Good man. I'll put the will in an envelope. Three o'clock this afternoon at Walchester Hospital, ward seven, Mr Bentley. Any problems, give me a call.'

Walchester Hospital had a depressing effect on Bernard ever since he suffered the removal of his tonsils there against his will at the age of six. As he stood now in a sterile corridor, clutching his briefcase and peering anxiously at a signboard which appeared to give directions to every ward except number seven, he remembered the lonely, confused feeling of waking alone at night in a strange place which smelt of disinfectant. And his throat hurt like hell.

'Where are you trying to find?'

A tall man was standing at his side, his white coat contrasting with his dark skin, his features kindly and understanding.

Bernard collected himself. 'Er . . . ward seven. It doesn't seem to be mentioned on the board there.'

'That's because you're in the wrong block.' The man's voice was deep and reassuring. 'You want C Block. If you go out of the door there and . . . Well, I'm going that way so I'll take you.'

Bernard followed the man through the door indicated, across a courtyard, through another door and along another maze of identical corridors, through a deserted refreshment area, up some stairs and into ward seven. 'You're there!' smiled his guide, patting him on the back and disappearing back into the maze.

On his right was a small office with a glass partition through which Bernard could see two nurses loading a trolley with unidentifiable medical equipment. The older woman caught sight of Bernard and came out to him with an enquiring glance.

'I'm from Dufty Dufty Popple & Dunn, the solicitors,' he explained, 'and I've come to see . . .'

'Mr Bentley,' said the nurse. 'Yes, we knew you were coming. He's going to sign his will, I believe?'

'That's right,' he nodded as the nurse began to lead the way. He hung back as they neared the public ward. 'Er . . . how is he?' he asked.

The nurse came back to him and spoke quietly, her voice sympathetic but matter of fact. 'He's not very well. If you'd left it until tomorrow, it might have been too late.'

Bernard swallowed hard and followed her along the ward between beds occupied by patients in a variety of conditions, some sitting on their beds and chatting with their neighbours, others lying comatose with drip tubes taped to their arms. Towards the end of the ward, Bernard could see a middle-aged man lying on his back and staring at the ceiling and, beyond him, an old man sitting up in his bed, hands clasped behind his large, domed, shiny bald head.

'Mr Bentley, this is the gentleman from the solicitors,' called the nurse as they approached.

The shiny bald head turned in their direction and nodded. Bernard walked to the bedside and held out a hand. 'I'm Bernard Summers, Mr Bentley. I'm very pleased to meet you.'

The old man took the proffered hand and peered into Bernard's face. 'What's your name?' he asked in a surprisingly resonant tone.

'Bernard . . . Bernard Summers. I've brought your will for you to sign.'

The nurse whispered to Bernard: 'You might have to speak up, he's a bit deaf.'

Bernard nodded to her and she turned to go. 'Just give me a call if you need anything . . . you know, witnesses or anything. Sorry I can't draw the curtains round the bed but Mr Bentley just won't have it.'

Bernard watched her retreating figure and, with an effort, turned back to his client on whose face was an amused expression. 'Good name for a solicitor!' he boomed.

Bernard looked confused. 'Er . . . pardon?'

'Summons,' said Mr Bentley. 'Good name for a solicitor, Bernard Summons.'

'No, it's Summers,' explained Bernard.

'Yes,' said Mr Bentley. 'That's what I mean. Good name for a solicitor.'

Not wishing to pursue this, Bernard smiled, nodded, sat on the chair next to the bed and opened his briefcase.

'Now, Mr Bentley, I have here your will. I suggest I read it out to you and, if there's anything you don't understand, just stop me and I'll explain it. I want to be quite sure that the will is in accordance with your wishes before you sign it. Is that clear?'

The old man nodded with an expression of complete understanding. 'Have you brought my will?' he asked.

Bernard cleared his throat and, leaning forward to bring his face closer to Mr Bentley's ear, adjusted his voice to a moderate shout: 'Yes, Mr Bentley, I've got your will here. I'll read it to you.'

A rustle of paper behind him signified that the man in the next bed had put down his newspaper.

'You'll have to speak up,' said Mr Bentley, patiently, 'I'm afraid the acoustics in here are a bit muffled.'

Deciding to omit the explanation, Bernard took up the will and began to read in as dignified a bellow as possible. 'THIS IS THE LAST WILL AND TESTAMENT OF ME, AUGUSTUS BERTRAM BENTLEY. I REVOKE ALL FORMER WILLS AND TESTAMENTARY . . .'

The old man nodded his head as the reading continued, indicating that his attention was fully secured – as was that of the entire population of ward seven with the exception of those whose condition precluded them from taking an interest.

'I GIVE THE FOLLOWING PECUNIARY AND SPECIFIC LEGACIES,' went on Bernard. 'TO MY GOOD FRIEND THOMAS BRIGGS THE SUM OF FIVE HUNDRED POUNDS.'

This produced a murmur of interest from the adjoining beds. Bernard looked round and flushed but carried on: 'TO SUCH OF MY GRANDCHILDREN WHO SHALL BE ALIVE AT MY DEATH THE SUM OF TWO HUNDRED AND FIFTY POUNDS EACH.'

Gentle applause from the audience, many of whom were now sitting up and putting aside their books and audio equipment.

'TO MY FORMER BUSINESS PARTNER JACK PATTERSON MY WOODWORKING TOOLS.'

By this time, ambulatory patients were drifting in from the adjoining dayroom and perching on the beds of their ward mates.

'TO MY DEAR FRIEND GLADYS ALTHROPP, IN RECOGNITION OF HER LOVING CARE AND ATTENTION TOWARDS ME SINCE THE DEATH OF MY DEAR WIFE, MY MOST PRIZED POSSESSION, THE GRANDFATHER CLOCK WHICH STANDS IN THE HALLWAY OF MY COTTAGE.'

Enthusiastic applause followed by a call of 'Good on yer, Gladys!' from a bed further down the ward which provoked more applause and a general murmur of approval.

'THE RESIDUE OF MY ESTATE AFTER PAYMENT OF ALL DEBTS TAXES AND TESTAMENTARY EXPENSES I LEAVE TO . . .' Here, Bernard left a theatrical pause, hearing a rustle of anticipation from the assembled company. He went on: 'TO . . . THE SECRETARY AND COMMITTEE OF HOCKAM WORKING MEN'S CLUB TO BE USED TO PURCHASE A NEW MINIBUS TO FACILITATE THE MEMBERS' ANNUAL OUTINGS.'

This produced a standing ovation from those sufficiently agile to achieve it and, for a fleeting instant, Bernard wondered whether to turn round and take a bow but, seeing the duty nurse's head peer round the door of her office, made hurried preparations for the signing of the will, first establishing that Mr Bentley understood and approved of the contents. During the ensuing formalities, the ward returned to normal and, when all was complete, he took Mr Bentley's hand and said goodbye. The old man held on to his hand for a moment with a surprisingly firm grip and murmured: 'Thank you, Mr Summons. You'll do well.' He then lay back on his pillows and Bernard returned to the firm's car, the signed will secure in his briefcase.

The Pig and Whistle was usually quiet on a Wednesday evening but tonight it seemed somehow livelier as Bernard made his way back from the bar to the table where Joanna sat. He put down their drinks and sat down. 'How's your grandfather?' he asked.

'Still very poorly,' she replied. 'Mum's coming in this evening so I'll find out if there's any news. It'll also be an opportunity for you to meet her. How are things in the legal world?'

Bernard's expression brightened. 'Well, not too bad. Since Mark Dunn's come back to the firm I'm getting some proper work to do. For instance, only yesterday, I had an opportunity to get some real experience under my belt – matter of life and death, as a matter of fact.'

As he expected, Joanna looked at him with renewed interest, waiting for him to go on. 'Well? What did you have to do?'

He scratched his cheek, giving every appearance of reluctance. 'Well, I can't go into details – client confidentiality, you know. But it involved visiting an old client of the firm in Walchester Hosp—'

Joanna was waving towards the door of the saloon bar where a middle-aged woman had entered and was making her way past a group of men who were clustered around the bar, talking loudly and excitedly. She reached their table and sat down. 'What's that all about?' she asked as the group at the bar cheered noisily.

'Oh, I don't know,' said Joanna. 'It's been a bit silly in here this evening. Mum, this is Bernard.'

He stood and shook her hand. 'Mrs Dickinson, it's nice to meet you at last. Can I get you a drink?'

'That'd be nice, Bernard. A gin and Dubonnet would be lovely.'

He crossed to the bar and, at last catching the barman's eye, ordered the drink. 'Something special on tonight, then?' he asked, gesturing at the slightly rowdy group.

'Oh, they're all from the Working Men's Club – just had a bit of good news or something, I don't really know. Good for custom, though.'

Returning to the table, he noticed that Joanna was looking brighter than when she had first arrived. Mrs Dickinson was talking to her as he sat down. 'In fact when I saw him this afternoon, he was positively perky. The nurse was saying the doctors think he's rallied remarkably over the past twenty-four hours and could be going home in a day or two.'

'Is this your grandfather?' Bernard asked Joanna who nodded, smiling. 'He'll be so glad to go home,' she said. 'He hates hospitals.'

'I don't blame him,' said Bernard. 'As a matter of fact I had to visit Walchester Hospital only yesterday to see an old client of the firm who was . . .'

Two of the men from the noisy group at the bar had just sat down at the table next to them and were laughing loudly. 'What, old Gladys Althropp?' said one. 'Old Gus Bentley loves that grandfather clock. Mind you, he and Gladys were pretty close.'

Joanna and her mother were now listening open-mouthed as the man went on: 'So how do you know all this? Old man Bentley's not dead is he?'

'No,' replied the other man. 'Well, at least, he wasn't yesterday. I was in his ward at Walchester Hospital yesterday for some tests about me stomach, see, and this bloke comes in – young trainee solicitor or something – and he reads old Bentley's will out to him at the top of his voice. You know how deaf the old boy is. Anyway, we was all listening, obviously, and he comes to the bit about the grandfather clock and everybody . . .'

Joanna and her mother were staring at each other. 'Is that . . .

the grandfather clock that Granddad always said would be yours one day?' asked Joanna.

Mrs Dickinson had paled noticeably. 'That bloody Gladys Althropp,' she murmured, the colour returning to her cheeks. Turning to the two men, she called: 'What else did he say in his will?'

'Ah, well . . .' he replied. 'You'll never guess who's been left the rest of his estate and whatnot . . . do you know old man Bentley, by the way?'

Joanna's mother stood up, knocking over her gin and Dubonnet in the process. 'Old . . . man . . . Bentley, as you call him, happens to be my father and I want to know what else is being bandied about concerning his private affairs!'

Joanna was now also standing, as were the two men at the table. 'Whoah, Missus. We didn't know old . . . er, Mr Bentley was your dad.'

'What do you mean *was*,' shouted Joanna. 'He still is. Look, you've upset my mum with all this.'

The barman, hearing the developing rumpus, came over to clear the fragments of Mrs Dickinson's glass and Joanna, her arm round the shoulder of her weeping mother, turned to enlist Bernard's assistance.

But Bernard had gone.

∾

Henry laughed, a pained expression on his face. 'The young fool allowed himself to be swept along by events at the hospital. Should have taken control and insisted on a private room to see his client. We can see that because we've got the experience to see it.'

Charles took a pull from his newly charged glass. 'So has Bernard now,' he pointed out.

In Trust for Life

Charles Dufty moved his bishop two squares, took up his glass and leant back in his chair.

Henry Middleton stared at the board for some minutes before slowly and deliberately taking up his king and placing it on its side. 'Game's up,' he said, quietly.

Charles regarded him silently for a while, sipping his whisky. 'You could get out of that,' he said.

The other shook his head. 'Not this time, old boy.'

Silence again descended on the two occupants of the corner table in the lounge bar of the Dog and Tadpole.

'So, how did you get on at the quack's yesterday?' asked Charles at length.

Henry shrugged. 'Nothing unexpected,' he replied. 'By the way, I shan't be able to make our fishing expedition with young James on Sunday – got to go up to London for a while. Make my apologies to him, would you?'

'Are they going to operate?' asked Charles.

'Bloody waste of time, of course,' said Henry. 'But you have to go through the motions, don't you?'

Charles nodded. 'Time for another?'

Henry drew himself up. 'Why not?' he said.

The two old friends regarded one another across the table.

'Why not, indeed?' said Charles.

The sun emerged from behind a fluffy white summer cloud and shone on a group of three small children building sandcastles, patting and smoothing with intense concentration, each trying to outdo their siblings in the design and execution of their creations while their parents lay prone on a beach towel, Mum with her face turned towards the sun with one eye on the children, Dad asleep with a paperback novel spread face down on his chest.

'I used to be pretty good at sandcastles,' remarked Bernard, looking down at the little family from his vantage point on the sand dunes above the beach. Joanna put on the sunglasses she had been cleaning on a corner of the car rug on which they sat and peered at the children.

'I bet you used to trample on your sister's castle so that yours was the only one in the contest,' she said.

Bernard was silent for a while, watching the children, the youngest of which was now getting bored and turning his attention to burying his father's legs with sand from his little bucket.

'You realise,' he said, quietly, partly to himself, 'that could be us in a few years' time.'

She looked at him with raised eyebrows. 'Bernard Summers! You're jumping the gun a bit, aren't you? Firstly, who said I wanted to start a family? Secondly, if I did, who said I'd want it to be with you? And thirdly, you haven't even finished your articles yet!'

He smiled wryly, colouring slightly and picking up a handful of sand, which he allowed to trickle through his fingers. 'I was just daydreaming,' he said. 'And anyway, I'll have finished my articles in about eighteen months. I'll be a qualified solicitor – I'll have you know I've got prospects, Miss Dickinson.'

She leant back on her elbows. 'Just being a qualified solicitor doesn't mean anything. You've still got to find a position some-where before you can start earning some money.'

'There'll be a job for me at Dufty's,' he protested. 'There's a . . . well . . . a tacit agreement that I'll carry on there as an assistant solicitor and then, in a year or two, who knows . . . maybe a partnership.'

The girl regarded him, her eyes hidden behind the sun-glasses. 'You were next in line before and then Mark Dunn came back and jumped the queue. It could happen again.'

He looked back at her, his eyes screwed up in bafflement. 'What do you mean, "it could happen again"? Yes, Mark came back but he can't come back again, can he? He's already there.'

'What about Popple?' she asked.

'Popple?' his puzzled frown deepening. 'What about him?'

'Well, the firm's called Dufty Dufty Popple & Dunn. Dunn left and came back. Why shouldn't Popple do the same – and then you'd be further still down the pecking order.'

He smiled patiently. 'Give me some credit, Joanna. Popple left years ago – there was some sort of trouble, I gather. For crying out loud, you can't even mention his name in the office without somebody coughing loudly and changing the subject. There's no way the Duftys would allow him back in the building – he's gone. *Persona non grata.*'

She took off her sunglasses as the sun passed behind a cloud. 'Well, Mark Dunn wasn't exactly the blue-eyed boy after he left, was he? But he is now. What sort of trouble, anyway – why did Popple leave – or was he pushed?' She was now sitting up, her interest increasing.

'I don't know,' protested Bernard. 'I told you, we're not allowed to talk about it.'

'Well, if you're hoping to be a partner in the firm, don't you think you should be in on the secret?' she asked. 'Don't you know anything at all about Popple? What was he like? What's he doing now?'

Irritated now, Bernard got up, brushed the sand from his trousers and glanced at his watch. 'Look, we'd better be getting back, I'm supposed to put the firm's car back in the car park by four o'clock and put the keys through the letterbox. Mark needs it to visit a client this evening.'

She shrugged, got to her feet and shook out the rug. 'Just seems a bit strange to me, that's all,' she said.

They walked back to the car in silence.

The air in the little cellar room was sour from the presence of mouldering documents detailing the intricate circumstances of human affairs once important but now long forgotten. As Bernard pulled out yet another packet from the cobwebbed shelves, dust rose and swirled in the dim light of the bare forty-watt bulb suspended from the timbered ceiling. He drew out the contents of the packet, spread them on the trestle table in the corner and began to read.

After a while, tiring of the task, he began to replace the flimsy, slightly damp documents in their envelope when the door opened to reveal Mark, his figure silhouetted against the light from the stairs leading up to the reception area. 'Hello, hello! Trawling the archives, are we?' His brisk, matter-of-fact tone contrasted oddly with the stagnant, lifeless atmosphere of the room. 'Thought I saw a chink of light around the door. Anything I can help you with?'

He crossed to the table and peered at the papers the trainee had been studying. Picking up a draft conveyance, he whistled softly. 'This is twenty years old,' he said, holding it delicately between thumb and forefinger and handing it back to Bernard with an expression of distaste. 'You won't learn much from this stuff, old son. Things have moved on a bit since then.'

Slightly embarrassed, Bernard shoved the document back into the envelope with the other papers. 'I was just getting the flavour of what the firm was like then,' he said, lamely.

Mark regarded him for a few moments, the silence becoming oppressive. 'Fair enough,' he said, brushing dust from his sleeve. 'It's past six o'clock, you know. Fancy a pint?'

Bernard sat back in the armchair and sighed comfortably. This was the first time he had visited Hockam Valley Golf Club and he gazed appreciatively around the thickly carpeted club room, its walls hung with heavy-framed paintings of golfing scenes and plaques listing the names of trophy holders and past team captains. There was a pervading scent of leather, furniture polish and new-mown grass.

The room was deserted save for Mark who walked across from the bar, bearing two pint glasses which he placed on the coffee table before sitting down in the armchair opposite Bernard who was looking at a set of ancient golf clubs arranged on the wall adjacent to his chair. 'Niblick,' he muttered, peering at the labels. 'Mashie . . . brassie. It's a different language.'

Mark grinned. 'Relics of the past, old son. No use to us now. The game's still the same but the equipment we use is light years ahead of the stuff they used then. A bit like those musty old files you were shuffling through in the cellar compared with today's legal practice. What were you looking for, by the way?'

'I told you,' said Bernard, defensively. 'I was just trying to get an idea of the history of the firm. I might be only a trainee but I am a member of the firm and I think I've got the right to . . . well, to know about things. After all, if there's anything in the firm's history which . . .' He broke off, flushing slightly.

Mark regarded him thoughtfully for several moments and then leant towards him, confidentially.

'I joined Dufty's not long after Robert Popple left and, like you, I was interested in finding out why there was so much secrecy about his departure. Like you, I poked about in the archives and talked to various people who knew the firm and eventually managed to piece together some kind of fragmented picture, though some essential pieces of the jigsaw are still missing – and I suspect always will be.'

Bernard was now himself leaning forward, intrigued. 'Well . . . ?' he prompted. 'Spill the beans.'

Mark smiled, wryly. 'Very few beans to spill, I'm afraid; certainly nothing about the reasons for Popple's apparently abrupt departure. But I did find out that Robert Popple and Hugo were at university together, studying law. Then, when they graduated, Popple went off to a large firm in London and Hugo joined his father at Dufty & Co., as it was then.'

'Did they keep in touch?' asked Bernard.

'Oh, yes. I gather Hugo would travel up to London occasionally to visit Popple in his swish office and no doubt they'd go out on the town and Popple would introduce Hugo to the bright lights of the city – a very different way of life from the one he was used to in Hockam.'

Bernard spluttered as he took a swig of his pint. 'Hard to imagine Hugo going out on the pull,' he grimaced.

'Oh, I don't imagine he was ever much of a "man about town" – he was married to Helen by then, remember – but I suspect he felt rather stifled by the traditional ways of his father at Dufty's and admired Popple's drive and sophistication. Even now, he has ideas about "streamlining" the firm and bringing it into line with what he sees as "the modern world". He's just not very good at it – and, deep down, he accepts that his father knows best when it comes to practising law in a community like Hockam.'

'So how did Popple come to be a partner in Dufty's?' asked Bernard, opening a packet of crisps.

'Hugo insisted on it,' explained Mark. 'You see, when Charles decided it was time to make Hugo a partner, Hugo dug his heels in and said he was thinking of joining a big firm in Walchester – Pollock's, in fact – where he could stretch himself and be in the mainstream of the profession. Charles, being Charles, said "no problem", and suggested that, instead of Hugo going off to be in the "mainstream", they'd bring the "mainstream" to Dufty's by taking on a young, go-getting solicitor to work with Hugo. Hugo straight away said he knew the very man – Robert Popple.'

Bernard considered this. 'But why the heck would Popple leave a fancy, high-powered firm in London to come to a small-town practice like Dufty's?'

Mark stroked his chin. 'I've wondered about that myself,' he said. 'Maybe he was just tired of the pressures in London. Or perhaps the London firm offered little in the way of a partnership. But whatever his reason, join Dufty's he did and he and Hugo were made partners at the same time. All seemed to be well until eleven years ago when Popple just . . . disappeared. End of story.'

Bernard frowned. 'But it's his disappearance I'm interested in. Why did he go and where is he now? And why aren't we allowed even to mention his name in the office? Everybody seems to be "in on the secret" but nobody wants to talk about it.'

The other man shook his head. 'No, I don't think anyone at the office is "in on the secret", as you put it. I think they've just been told that the subject is banned.'

'Told by whom?'

Mark took a deep pull from his glass before answering. 'Charles,' he said.

'So you're saying Charles Dufty knows why Popple . . . disappeared, but wants to keep it a secret? But surely Hugo knows? He and Popple were long-term buddies, not to mention partners in the firm.'

'I tried broaching the subject with Hugo once,' said Mark. 'To be honest, I got the impression that he just didn't want to know anything about it. He said his father had told him that Popple had written a letter to him and, as his father was content to draw a line under the matter, so was he.'

'So Charles could be the only one who knows? What happened to the letter?'

'If you ask me, I don't think there was any letter. I think when
Charles realised Popple wasn't coming back, he thought it best
simply to accept it and move on. And, at the end of the day, he's
probably right. It's not as though Popple had done a runner with
the firm's money. His reasons for staging a disappearance must
have been personal and, as such, nothing to do with anyone
else. I think Charles accepted that and wanted the firm to keep
moving and just get on with it. That's why he doesn't allow any
of us to waste time tittle-tattling about something which doesn't
concern us. And I can accept that. I suggest you do the same.'

Bernard nodded slowly. 'So Charles made up the letter just to
satisfy Hugo?'

'That's what I believe.'

'So, for once, Charles knows no more than any of us?'

'Charles Dufty's a wise old bird,' said Mark. 'But even he
doesn't know everything. I find that quite reassuring. Time for
another? Or are you meeting Joanna tonight?'

Bernard shook himself, looked at his watch and got up. 'Yes,
we're supposed to be going to the cinema in Walchester. In fact,
I'd better get a move on. Thanks for the drink.'

'Mustn't keep the lady waiting,' said Mark. 'Enjoy your evening – and, if I were you, I'd forget about Robert Popple. None of
us know why he left but it doesn't matter now. It's all in the
past.'

'How was the film last night, Bernard?' called Trish as he passed
the reception desk where she was opening the post.

'Boring,' said Bernard. 'Typical chick-flick – all about feelings
and emotions and stuff; not a lot in the way of action. Joanna
liked it, though – well, she cried all through it so I suppose she
enjoyed it.'

He continued on his way along the corridor but turned back

and put his head round the half-open door of Bill's office. 'Morning, Bill. How's your father? I heard he's in hospital at the moment.'

The office manager looked up. 'Oh, 'morning Bernard. Yes, he's due to have an operation tomorrow.' He put his pen down on the desk. 'Not looking very good, I'm afraid. But you never know.'

'Must be a worry for you,' said Bernard. 'Surprised you're in today.'

Bill sighed deeply. 'Yes, it is a worry. But at least if the worst happens, I'm on hand. Dad's a tough old codger, bless him. Carries on, no matter what. It certainly wouldn't help him if I started cracking up and giving way to emotion and so forth. Life goes on – until it doesn't. Not that there's anything wrong with cracking up, you understand. Look at poor old Hugo back in . . . what, eleven years ago now, isn't it? He had his bit of a break-down. But he got over it and look at him now.'

Bernard hesitated a moment and then came in and closed the door.

'Eleven years ago? Wasn't that about when Robert Popple pushed off?'

Bill pursed his lips and tutted. 'Shouldn't really talk about that, should we? I gather the name Popple is banned on the premises.'

Bernard sat down. 'I'm just interested in why he disappeared so suddenly, that's all.'

Bill took out his handkerchief and sneezed. 'No use asking me,' he said. 'I'm still a new boy here. All I know is what I heard from my father.' He paused thoughtfully. 'It appears Popple had to leave his London firm – under a cloud, as it turned out later – some sort of scam involving clients' money. Anyway, Hugo seized on the opportunity to get him here. Hugo knew nothing about his previous misdemeanours and, so far as he was concerned, Robert Popple was the very man to bring Dufty's into the twentieth century – as it was then. I think they must have known each other before and Hugo was rather in awe of the man.'

'They were at university together,' explained Bernard.

'Ah!' said Bill. 'That could explain their friendship. Anyway, I don't know whether Popple had been up to his old tricks again or what, but he left Dufty's very suddenly and it was at that time that Hugo suffered a mild breakdown of sorts – which may not have been connected with Popple's disappearance, of course, but he was out of action for a while. His father was worried sick, which, in turn, worried my father – they've been life-long friends, you know. But after a month or two, everything seemed to return to normal and life went on as before.'

Bernard nodded. 'Where's Popple now?'

'No idea,' Bill replied. 'I heard his family came originally from Northumberland or some such place. Maybe he went back there. Or maybe he emigrated to South America or somewhere. I don't know. Anyway, it doesn't matter now, does it? It's all in the past. Best leave it there, eh?'

It was some weeks later that the subject of Robert Popple came up again.

The engagement of Mark Dunn and Caroline Adams, the estate agent from the offices next door, had just been announced and the staff of Dufty Dufty Popple & Dunn gathered in the reception area where Charles Dufty was in the process of opening a bottle of champagne to toast the couple.

Hugo's wife, Helen, arrived with eleven-year-old James in tow just as the cork popped and those nearest were forced to duck as spray rained down around them. 'Helen!' called Charles above the hubbub. 'Nice timing. Glad you could make it. Have one of these.' He placed a glass in her hand and motioned to Miss Metcalfe to bring a soft drink for James.

'Wouldn't have missed it for the world,' she said, raising her glass towards Mark who made his way over and kissed her on the cheek.

'Nice of you to come,' he grinned. 'Caroline and I didn't expect all this . . .' He waved a hand at the festivities. 'Rowdy lot, aren't they?'

'Well,' smiled Helen. 'There hasn't been a cause for celebration in the firm for quite some time – and this is certainly a reason to celebrate. If ever there was a perfectly matched couple, they're standing in front of me now.'

Caroline had joined them, her blonde hair, slightly damp from champagne spray, falling prettily over her left eye. 'That's nice of you to say so, Helen. I feel I'm becoming part of a large . . .' she raised her voice over laughter as Bernard spilt the contents of his glass over Hugo's shoes as he stumbled over Miss Spiers's shopping bag on the floor . . . 'a large and very noisy family!' continued Caroline.

Three loud knocks captured everyone's attention as Charles rapped on the reception desk with the base of another champagne bottle. His quietly modulated voice produced a rapt silence. 'This old building has stood here in the High Street for almost three hundred years. And for the last fifty of those years we've enjoyed the privilege of its shelter – and, by *we*, I mean the little association of close colleagues we call Dufty Dufty Popple & Dunn – and that includes not just those who labour within these walls but also their nearest and dearest. We're all, in the broadest sense of the word, family – from the youngest of young shrimps . . .' he raised his glass towards James who grinned back at him . . . 'to the oldest of old codgers . . .' here he squinted around the room as everyone chuckled and raised their glasses towards him.

'Well, today we're delighted to welcome the latest addition to the family. Shall we first ensure that our glasses are fully charged with the finest champagne Dawson's off-licence could provide – personally delivered, I may say, by Don Dawson himself only half an hour ago . . . many thanks, Don.' Here everyone turned to the plump, fresh-faced off-licence proprietor who stood at the back, beaming at the celebrations.

There followed further popping of corks and clinking of glasses as Charles continued: 'Congratulations to Mark and welcome to Caroline!'

'Actually,' said Charles, returning, as an afterthought, to his position behind the reception desk, 'I should have said welcome *back* because, of course, both Mark and Caroline have been members of the family previously – Caroline as Hugo's secretary and Mark as . . . well, Mark. However, I'm delighted that, after a brief absence, they've seen the error of their ways and returned to the fold in one way or another. Welcome back to you both!'

As the applause died away, Don Dawson's voice could be heard over the general hubbub: 'It only needs Popple to return to the fold and your family would really be complete!' His broad smile faded as a silence fell over the room. 'You know . . . Popple,' he explained, lamely. 'I thought . . . you know . . . Dufty Dufty *Popple* & Dunn.' As a murmur of general conversation resumed, Bill caught Dawson's eye and shook his head almost imperceptibly. Seeing the man's puzzled embarrassment, he made his way through the crowd to him.

'I say . . . look, I'm sorry,' murmured Dawson. 'I seem to have . . .'

'It's all right, you weren't to know. We just don't mention that man's name – all in the past, you know the sort of thing. Have another glass of your rather good champagne.'

Dawson accepted gratefully. 'It's just that . . . you know . . . I assumed in view of the name of the firm there must have been a Popple involved at some stage and I just thought . . .'

As the man continued to apologise, Bill caught sight of the street door closing and, through the leaded light window, saw Hugo, pale-faced, walking past the window. A moment later, Helen too slipped away unnoticed, trotting after her husband with James in tow and the three got into her car which was parked in the street and drove off.

The little party was now getting back into its stride, the cheerful sounds of spirited conversation and chinking glasses amplified by the cramped confines of the reception area. Mark, perched on a coffee table in the corner, was holding forth to Conchita on the subject of the firm's history while Trish was giggling at an outrageous joke with which Bernard had regaled the assembled company, much to the disgust of Miss Spiers, whose glass was being replenished by Don Dawson against her better judgement. Caroline chatted vivaciously to Don Dawson and Miss Metcalfe who was nodding understandingly and glancing from time to time out of the window with an abstracted air.

Bill's gaze was diverted from Caroline's animated profile to the coffee table corner, where Charles stood, thoughtfully, glass in hand. Catching Bill's eye, he glanced meaningfully at his watch. Bill, understanding the unspoken request, rapped on the table and, to everyone's enthusiastic agreement, suggested they all adjourn to the King's Arms to continue the celebrations in more appropriate surroundings.

Some ten minutes later, a little procession led by Bill was making its way convivially along the High Street towards the nominated hostelry, leaving only Charles and Miss Metcalfe to clear up the empty glasses and other debris.

'I do hope Hugo's all right,' said Miss Metcalfe as she busied herself with a brush and pan. 'He looked so pale when he left. Such a pity Don Dawson brought up . . . well, you know.'

'Dawson wasn't to know,' said Charles.

The pair went on with their tasks for some minutes before Miss Metcalfe laid down her brush and pan and asked quietly: 'Do you think, after all this time, Hugo still blames himself for . . .'

Charles carried on wiping the reception desk with a damp

cloth. 'Hugo'll be all right,' he said, without looking up. 'Why don't you toddle off now, Miss Metcalfe? It's been a long day and that cat of yours, Judge Jeffries, will be waiting for his supper. I'll finish off here and lock up.'

'No, I couldn't leave you to do all this,' she protested. 'It's not right.'

'Nonsense,' he returned. 'There's only a couple of glasses to put in the kitchen – and, besides, what I don't do now Trish will do in the morning. You run along – and thanks for all your help this evening. There are one or two bits and pieces I need to finish off at my desk and then I'll be heading off home, too.'

'Well . . . if you're sure,' she said, taking her coat from the stand. She turned as she opened the door into the High Street. 'Thank you. Goodnight, Mr Dufty.'

'Goodnight, Joan,' he smiled, waving cheerily. 'Give my regards to the Judge!'

The little gathering at the King's Arms had now been augmented by several of Mark's friends from the golf club and the occasion was developing into a fully-fledged revel. A slightly flushed Caroline was, of course, the centre of attention; Trish was dancing in an abandoned manner with a young man who everyone assumed (wrongly) was there as a friend of Mark, and Bernard, who had been persuaded to take up golf the very next weekend, was proposing an immediate session on the driving range by torchlight.

Halfway down the High Street, a glimmer of light was visible through the window of the half-timbered home of Dufty Dufty Popple & Dunn. This light proceeded from the shaded lamp on Charles Dufty's desk where its occupant sat, deep in thought. His elbows rested on the desk and his hands slowly ruffled his shaggy white eyebrows. The only sound was the ticking of the clock on the mantelpiece.

At length, he rose stiffly and crossed to a corner of the room where, between a bookcase and a built-in cupboard, the barely noticeable metal door of a small wall safe nestled. He placed a hand on the combination knob and made several turns, squinting short-sightedly at the dial. With a tug on the lever, the door opened and Charles reached in to withdraw an envelope, which he carried back to his desk and sat down.

The envelope was dusty, slightly yellowed and its postmark was indistinct except for the date which had been imprinted eleven years ago. The words *private and confidential* were written on the front in a neat hand and the address was: Charles Dufty Esq., Messrs Dufty Dufty Popple & Dunn, High Street, Hockam.

The old solicitor drew from the envelope a single sheet of paper which he placed on the desk before him. The handwriting was identical to that on the envelope, though larger and firmer:

Dear Charles,

I need you to know that Hugo played no part in my (thankfully unsuccessful) plan to defraud our clients other than as a wholly unwitting pawn in my game. Neither, in fact, was he responsible for my joining your firm in the first place. My reasons for accepting your generous offer of a partnership went far beyond my friendship with him – a friendship, incidentally, which I valued greatly. I only wish his influence on me had been greater than mine on him.

Hugo is, and always has been, an honourable man – as, indeed, are you, Charles. Perhaps, if things had been otherwise, I could have aspired to . . .

But it's too late for that.

By the time you read this, I shall be gone. My life began among lonely, barren, godforsaken moors, where I'm on my way back to end it. The world would have been a better place had I stayed there.

There's nothing else I can say.

Robert.

Charles's gaze rested in turn upon the photographs on his desk, each in its gilt frame catching the dim light from the desk lamp. His late wife gazed back at him, her eyes gentle and understanding. And there was Hugo as a boy, looking awkward in his new school uniform and clutching the model sailing ship, which he and Charles had spent hours constructing.

On the other side of the desk, Hugo and his bride, Helen, smiled happily outside the church door and there, between the telephone and the desk calendar, was Helen in the maternity ward, her expression radiant as she looked lovingly into the tightly squeezed eyes of baby James.

And lastly, in the centre of the desk, a larger photograph of James taken earlier in the year. He, too, was proudly holding up a model galleon over which he and Hugo had laboured long and lovingly.

The clock continued to tick.

Then, as though making up his mind, he reinserted the letter in the envelope, rose and placed it, carefully, deep within the safe in the wall. With a soft thud, the door of the safe closed and, with a firm hand, Charles turned the locking lever until it gave a final, conclusive *click*.

~

The warm August sunshine, beating its way through the overhanging trees, was making dappled patterns on the rippling waters of the river. As he sat on his folding stool, watching his float bobbing on the current, Charles caught a flash of white out of the corner of his eye and glanced up to see a heron, standing motionless some yards downstream. He nudged James and pointed. The boy's clear blue eyes widened as he saw the creature and they watched in silence for some minutes before the beak flashed and the bird flapped off with his prize.

'He's doing considerably better than we are,' remarked Charles.

James nodded glumly. 'We've been here for almost an hour,' he said. 'Maybe the fish don't like our maggots.'

'Good point,' agreed Charles. 'Tell you what, let's ditch the maggots and try something else.'

'What . . . you mean go back to Dennis Wilson's fishing shop and buy some different bait?'

'No need for that,' said Charles. 'People were fishing very successfully long before the fishing shop was a twinkle in Dennis Wilson's eye, you know. They took their bait from what was available around them.'

His grandson looked about, at the trees overhead, the rough grasses of the riverbank and the tangled undergrowth beyond, his brow wrinkling beneath his fringe of fair hair. After a few moments, his expression brightened. 'Worms!' he said. 'Maybe the fish like worms.'

Charles beamed. 'Brilliant thinking for one so short.' He rummaged in his fishing bag and drew out a pointed trowel which he handed to James. 'See if you can find some while I get these maggots off the hooks.'

The boy began to dig in a patch of rough turf while the old man remained on his stool, busying himself with the rods and lines.

'Any luck yet, skipper?' he asked after a few minutes. The boy, having excavated a sizeable hole, was peering intently into it. 'No worms,' he said, 'but maybe I'll find some buried treasure – or maybe some dinosaur bones or something.'

'You never know,' nodded Charles. 'If you find any gold sovereigns, just give me a shout.'

The boy resumed his digging. 'Why couldn't Uncle Henry come with us today, Gramps?' he asked, panting from his exertions.

Charles shrugged. 'Like all grown-ups, he sometimes has stuff to do. He had to go to London, I believe. I'm sure he'd rather be here with us but . . . there you are . . . what was that?'

James looked up, his face now grimy from spattered soil. 'What was what?' he asked.

'That noise,' said Charles. 'Sounded as though your trowel struck

246

something solid.' He rose stiffly from his stool and came over to peer into the hole. 'Dig around it and see if you can get it out.'

James reinserted his head and shoulders into the hole and laboured for some moments, at length pulling out the object which he turned over in his hands. 'Just an old stone,' he said and was about to throw it over his shoulder. Charles restrained him and, with an effort, lowered himself to sit on the ground beside his grandson. 'Brush off some of the soil,' he said. James did so to reveal a smooth, grey, irregularly shaped rock.

'Told you,' he said, 'it's just an old stone.'

The old man shook his head. 'That's not just any old stone, James. Just think for a moment. When do you think anyone last dug a hole in this spot – or, indeed, anywhere around here?'

James shrugged. 'Probably never,' he said, staring blankly at the stone in his hands.

'Exactly,' said Charles. 'So you're the first person ever to see that stone. It's lain here underground for thousands – possibly millions of years, never seeing daylight. And now, after all that time, you, of all the human race, have seen it and held it in your hands. It's an age-old secret shared between you and the stone.'

'And you, Gramps,' said the boy, running his hands gently over the stone's cool, smooth surface.

'And me,' agreed Charles. 'A secret between the three of us.'

James was silent for a while as he cradled the precious object. 'Dad says we shouldn't have secrets,' he said at length.

'And Dad's quite right,' said Charles. 'We shouldn't do things we have to keep hidden from others because we're ashamed – those sorts of secrets are bad secrets and the best thing to do is to get rid of them by telling someone about them. But there are some secrets that are not ours to give away. Who's your best friend at school?'

'Jason Pumphrey,' James replied.

'And if Jason told you, in secret – or, as we sometimes say, "in confidence" – that, say, he'd bought his mum a bunch of flowers as a surprise for Mother's Day, would you tell her?'

James shook his head.

'No, because the secret wouldn't be yours to give away. It's the same with this stone. It's been here, hidden from view for millions of years, living its little stone life, and it has now shared its secret with you. But the secret's not yours to give away.'

The boy nodded gravely, putting the stone carefully in his pocket.

'What are you doing?' said Charles.

'I'm going to take it home and put it by my bed so that I can see it always,' he said.

Charles shook his head.

'Why not?' said James. 'It's very precious.'

'Why not?' said Charles. 'Because if you take it home then everyone else would see it and it wouldn't be a secret any more.'

The boy considered. 'What should I do then?' he asked.

'That's up to you,' said Charles.

James took the stone from his pocket and gazed at it for a while. Then he placed it carefully in the hole where it had come from and, taking the trowel, scooped back the earth, smoothing it off and patting it down.

The old man and the boy sat looking at each other until Charles raised his shaggy white eyebrows and smiled. 'The secret's safe with us?' he said.

The boy smiled back and nodded.